More praise for

MILLEN
PEOP

Library Journal Best

"Ballard has depicted a future—and now a present—with disturbing prescience and clarity. *Millennium People* arrives at a time when the foundations that support our own middle classes feel more unsettled than ever, and the specters of apocalyptic obsession and the nihilism of consumer culture all bear an increasing resemblance to the world Ballard has been creating in one fiction after another—or perhaps warning us about."
—Will Menaker, *Salon*

"Vintage Ballard, smartly observed and tartly written. Let's hope there's more in the vault."   —*Kirkus Reviews*, starred review

"As intriguing as it is perplexing. . . . [Ballard is] one of the great virtuosos of 20th-century fiction."   —*Library Journal*,
starred review

"Ballard volleys back and forth from absurdity to drum-tight tension to evocative commentary in a sparsely-plotted novel . . . [with] passages of diamond perfection."   —Chris Barsanti,
PopMatters

"[An] essential writer."   —Michael Upchurch, *Seattle Times*

"Brilliant, funny, disturbing, and quotable."   —Kier Graff,
Booklist, starred review

MILLENNIUM

PEOPLE

J.G. BALLARD

LIVERIGHT PUBLISHING CORPORATION
A DIVISION OF W. W. NORTON & COMPANY
NEW YORK · LONDON

For information about permissions to reproduce selections from this book,
write to Permissions, Liveright Publishing Corporation,
a division of W. W. Norton & Company, Inc.,
500 Fifth Avenue, New York, NY 10110

For information about special discounts for bulk purchases, please contact
W. W. Norton Special Sales at specialsales@wwnorton.com or 800-233-4830

Manufacturing by Courier Westford
Book design by Chris Welch
Production manager: Devon Zahn

Library of Congress Cataloging-in-Publication Data
Ballard, J. G., 1930–2009.
Millennium people / J.G. Ballard.
p. cm.
ISBN 978-0-87140-405-3 (pbk.)
1. Psychologists—Fiction. 2. Political activists—Fiction. 3. Political
violence—Fiction. 4. Middle class—England—Fiction. 5. Protest
movements—England—Fiction. 6. London (England)—Fiction. I. Title.
PR6052.A46M55 2012
823.'914—dc23

2011052774

ISBN 978-0-87140-405-3 pbk.

Liveright Publishing Corporation
500 Fifth Avenue, New York, N.Y. 10110
www.wwnorton.com

W. W. Norton & Company Ltd.
Castle House, 75/76 Wells Street, London W1T 3QT

1 2 3 4 5 6 7 8 9 0

CONTENTS

MILLENNIUM
PEOPLE

1

THE REBELLION AT CHELSEA MARINA

A SMALL REVOLUTION was taking place, so modest and well behaved that almost no one had noticed. Like a visitor to an abandoned film set, I stood by the entrance to Chelsea Marina and listened to the morning traffic in the King's Road, a reassuring medley of car stereos and ambulance sirens. Beyond the gatehouse were the streets of the deserted estate, an apocalyptic vision deprived of its soundtrack. Protest banners sagged from the balconies, and I counted a dozen overturned cars and at least two burnt-out houses.

Yet none of the shoppers walking past me showed the slightest concern. Another Chelsea party had run out of control, though the guests were too drunk to realize it. And, in a way, this was true. Most of the rebels, and even a few of the ringleaders, never grasped what was happening in this comfortable enclave. But then these likeable and over-educated revolutionaries were rebelling against themselves.

Even I, David Markham, a trained psychologist infiltrated into Chelsea Marina as a police spy—a deception I was the last to discover—failed to see what was going on. But I was distracted by my unusual friendship with Richard Gould, the hard-working paediatrician who was the leader of the revolt—

the Doctor Moreau of the Chelsea set, as our shared lover, Kay
Churchill, christened him. Soon after our first meeting, Richard
lost interest in Chelsea Marina and moved on to a far more radical revolution, which he knew was closer to my heart.

I APPROACHED the crime-scene tapes that closed the King's
Road entrance to the estate, and showed my pass to the two
policemen waiting for the Home Secretary's arrival. The driver
of a florist's delivery van was arguing with them, pointing to a
large display of arum lilies on the seat beside him. I guessed that
a local resident, some happily married solicitor or account executive, had been too busy with the revolution to cancel his wife's
birthday bouquet.

The constables were unmoved, refusing to let the driver into
the estate. They sensed that something deeply suspect had taken
place in this once law-abiding community, an event that required
the presence of a cabinet minister and his retinue of worthies.
The visitors—Home Office advisers, concerned churchmen, senior social workers and pyschologists, including myself—would
begin their tour at noon, in an hour's time. No armed police
would guard us, on the safe assumption that a rebellious middle
class was too well mannered to pose a physical threat. But, as I
knew all too well, that was the threat.

Appearances proved nothing and everything. The policemen
waved me through, barely glancing at my pass. Having been
harangued for weeks by articulate mothers in the scruffiest
jeans, they knew that my fashionable haircut, courtesy of BBC
make-up, dove-grey suit and sunbed tan ruled me out as a native
of Chelsea Marina. The residents would die rather than resemble
a minor television guru, a renegade intellectual from the dubious
world of video-conferencing and airport seminars.

But the suit was a disguise, which I had put on for the first
time in six months, after stuffing my torn leather jacket and den-
ims into the dustbin. I sprang lightly over the crime-scene tapes,

far fitter than the policemen guessed. The 'terrorist actions', as
the Home Secretary termed them, had soon toughened up a lazy
physique softened by years of boarding lounges and hotel atri-
ums. Even my wife Sally, forever tolerant and never surprised,
was impressed by my muscular arms as she counted the bruises
left by scuffles with police and security guards.

But a disguise could go too far. Catching sight of myself in
the broken windows of the gatehouse, I loosened the knot of my
tie. I was still unsure what role I was playing. Richard Gould
and I had been seen together so often, and the constables should
have recognized me as the chief accomplice of this hunted terrorist. When I waved to them they turned away, scanning the
King's Road for the Home Secretary's limousine. I felt a pang of
disappointment. For a few seconds I had wanted them to challenge me.

IN FRONT OF ME lay Chelsea Marina, its streets empty as never
before in its twenty-year existence. The entire population had
vanished, leaving a zone of silence like an urban nature reserve.
Eight hundred families had fled, abandoning their comfortable
kitchens, herb gardens and book-lined living rooms. Without the
slightest regret, they had turned their backs on themselves and
all they had once believed in.

Beyond the rooftops I could hear the west London traffic, but it
faded as I walked down Beaufort Avenue, the estate's main thoroughfare. The vast metropolis that surrounded Chelsea Marina
was still holding its breath. Here the revolution of the middle
class had begun, not the uprising of a desperate proletariat, but
the rebellion of the educated professional class who were society's
keel and anchor. In these quiet roads, the scene of uncountable
dinner parties, surgeons and insurance brokers, architects and
health service managers, had built their barricades and overturned their cars to block the fire engines and rescue teams who
were trying to save them. They rejected all offers of help, refus-

ing to air their real grievances or to say whether any grievances existed at all.

The siege negotiators sent in by Kensington and Chelsea Council were met first by silence, then by mockery, and finally by petrol bombs. For reasons no one understood, the inhabitants of Chelsea Marina had set about dismantling their middle-class world. They lit bonfires of books and paintings, educational toys and videos. The television news showed families arm in arm, surrounded by overturned cars, their faces proudly lit by the flames.

I passed a fire-gutted BMW, lying wheels uppermost beside the kerb, and stared at its ruptured fuel tank. An airliner cruised over central London, and hundreds of broken windows trembled under the droning engines, as if releasing their last anger. Curiously, the residents who destroyed Chelsea Marina had shown no anger at all. They had quietly discarded their world as if putting out their rubbish for collection.

This uncanny calm and, more worryingly, the residents' indifference to the huge financial penalties they would pay, had prompted the Home Secretary's visit. Henry Kendall, a colleague at the Institute with close Home Office contacts, told me that other sites of middle-class unrest were coming to light, in well-to-do suburbs of Guildford, Leeds and Manchester. All over England an entire professional caste was rejecting everything it had worked so hard to secure.

I watched the airliner cross the Fulham skyline, then lost it among the exposed roof-beams of a burnt-out house at the end of Beaufort Avenue. Its owners, a local headmistress and her doctor husband, had left Chelsea Marina with their three children, after holding out to the last minutes before the police riot teams overwhelmed them. They had been in the forefront of the rebellion, determined to expose the blatant injustice that ruled their lives. I imagined them endlessly circling the M25 in their muddy Land Rover, locked in a deep trance.

Where had they gone? Many of the residents had retreated

to their country cottages, or were staying with friends who supported the struggle with food parcels and cheerful e-mails. Others had set off on indefinite tours of the Lake District and the Scottish Highlands. Towing their trailers, they were the vanguard of an itinerant middle class, a new tribe of university-trained gypsies who knew their law and would raise hell with local councils.

Kay Churchill, the film studies lecturer at South Bank University who became my landlady, was arrested by the police and released on bail. Still proclaiming the revolution, she held forth on an afternoon cable channel. Her cramped but comfortable home, with its shabby sofas and film stills, had been drowned by the powerful hoses of the Chelsea Fire Service.

I missed Kay and her shaky crown of ash-grey hair, her erratic opinions and ever-flowing wine, but her abandoned house was my reason for arriving an hour before the Home Secretary. I hoped that my laptop was still on the coffee table in Kay's living room, where we had laid out our maps and planned the arson attacks on the National Film Theatre and the Albert Hall. During the final moments of the revolt, as the police helicopters hovered overhead, Kay was so determined to convert the handsome fire chief to her cause that his men had ample time to shatter her windows with their water jets. A neighbour had pulled Kay from the house, but the laptop was still there for the police forensic teams to find.

I reached the end of Beaufort Avenue, at the silent centre of Chelsea Marina. A seven-storey block of flats stood beside Cadogan Circle, banners hanging limply from the balconies and offering their slogans to the unlistening air. I crossed the road to Grosvenor Place, Kay's raffish cul-de-sac and a reminder of another, older Chelsea. The short road had been home to a convicted antiques dealer, two lesbian marriages and an alcoholic Concorde pilot, and was a haven of bad company and good cheer.

I walked towards Kay's dishevelled house, listening to my

footsteps click behind me, echoes of guilt trying to flee the scene but managing only to approach itself. Distracted by the sight of so many empty houses, I tripped on the kerb and leaned against a builder's skip heaped with household possessions. The revolutionaries, as ever considerate of their neighbours, had ordered a dozen of these huge containers in the week before the uprising.

A burnt-out Volvo sat beside the road, but the proprieties still ruled, and it had been pushed into a parking bay. The rebels had tidied up after their revolution. Almost all the overturned cars had been righted, keys left in their ignitions, ready for the repossession men.

The skip was filled with books, tennis rackets, children's toys and a pair of charred skis. Beside a school blazer with scorched piping was an almost new worsted suit, the daytime uniform of a middle-ranking executive, lying among the debris like the discarded fatigues of a soldier who had thrown down his rifle and taken to the hills. The suit seemed strangely vulnerable, the abandoned flag of an entire civilization, and I hoped that one of the Home Secretary's aides would point it out to him. I tried to think of an answer if I was asked to comment. As a member of the Adler Institute, which specialized in industrial relations and the psychology of the workplace, I was nominally an expert on the emotional life of the office and the mental problems of middle managers. But the suit was difficult to explain away.

Kay Churchill would have known what to reply. As I stepped through the pools of water outside her house I could hear her voice inside my head: bullying, pleading, sensible and utterly mad. The middle class was the new proletariat, the victims of a centuries-old conspiracy, at last throwing off the chains of duty and civic responsibility.

For once, the absurd answer was probably the right one.

THE FIREMEN had drenched the house, making sure that Kay would never set it alight. Water still dripped from the eaves, and a faint mist rose from the brickwork. The open-plan living room was a marine grotto, moisture seeping through the cracked ceiling, turning the walls into damp tapestries. I stood between the Ozu and Bresson posters, almost expecting Kay to emerge from the kitchen with two glasses and a bottle of some admirer's wine, insisting that the battle had been won.

Kay had left, but her cheerful and rackety world was still in place—the Post-it notes on the mirror above the fireplace, the lecture invitations from anarchist groups, and the cairn of white pebbles on the mantelpiece. Each stone, she told me, was a memento of a summer love affair on a Greek beach. Beads of moisture covered the framed photograph of her daughter, now a teenager in Australia, taken on a last holiday before custody was awarded to her husband. Kay had moved on, claiming that memory was a baited trap, last night's dregs in a lipstick-smeared glass, but sometimes I caught her wiping her tears from the photograph and pressing the frame to her breast.

The sofa where Kay and I had dozed together was a sodden hulk. But my laptop lay among the film scripts and magazines. The hard drive contained more than enough evidence to convict me as Richard Gould's co-conspirator. There were lists of video stores to be torched, travel agencies to be attacked, galleries and museums to be sabotaged, and the teams of residents assigned to each action. Trying to impress Kay, I had appended notes on the damage done, injuries to team members and likely insurance claims. Tapping out these unnecessary details, Kay's arm warmly around my shoulders, I sometimes felt that I was unrolling a carpet that ran straight to my prison cell.

Thinking fondly about Kay, I reached out to straighten the portrait of her daughter. A shard of glass slipped from the frame and cut my palm, lightly severing the life-line. As I stared at the bright smear and searched for my handkerchief, I realized that this was the only blood I had shed in Chelsea Marina during the entire rebellion.

LAPTOP UNDER my arm, I closed the front door behind me. I stared for a last time at the wooden panelling, and in the smooth enamel saw a window move and catch the sun. An open casement swung on the top floor of the apartment building beside Cadogan Circle. Bizarrely, a hand reached out and cleaned the panes, shook a duster and then withdrew.

I stepped into the street and walked towards the apartments, passing a burnt-out Saab sitting in its long-term bay. Were squatters moving into Chelsea Marina, giving up their soft drugs and hard mattresses? Were they ready to try a new lifestyle, to face the problems of school fees and Brazilian daily helps, ballet classes and BUPA subscriptions? Our modest revolution would become part of the folkloric calendar, to be celebrated along with the last night of the Proms and the Wimbledon tennis fortnight.

PRESSING THE handkerchief to my palm, I pumped the elevator buttons in the hall of the apartment building. Frustratingly, all electric power to Chelsea Marina had been disconnected. I climbed the stairs, resting on each landing, surrounded by the open doors of abandoned apartments, an actor searching for the right stage set. I was light-headed when I reached the top floor. Without thinking, I pushed back the unlocked door and stared across the empty living room at the window that had swung in the sunlight.

A third-floor tenant of the same apartment house, Vera Blackburn, was a former government scientist and a close friend of Kay Churchill's. I remembered that the top-floor flat was owned by a young optician and her husband. The living-room windows had the clearest views in Chelsea Marina, looking down Beaufort Avenue along the route that the Home Secretary would take on his inspection tour.

I stepped over a discarded suitcase and entered the room. A

blue canvas bag lay on the desk, its side embossed with the seal of the Metropolitan Police, part of the equipment carried by riot-control teams. Inside would be stun guns, canisters of tear gas and the cattle prods with which the police defended themselves against their ever-present enemies.

The laptop had grown more heavy in my hand, a half-conscious warning signal. I could hear two people speaking in the nearby bedroom, a man's curt but low tones and a woman's sharper replies. I assumed that a police constable and a woman colleague were keeping watch on the Home Secretary's approach. Methodical to a fault, they had wiped the windows to give themselves the clearest view possible of the Cabinet Minister and his sagely nodding advisers. Finding me in their observation post, they would assume the worst, and soon decide that a psychologist's laptop was a potentially offensive weapon.

Trying not to trip over the suitcase, I edged towards the door, aware for the first time of the optician's diagrams pinned to the wall above the desk, target-like circles and rows of meaningless letters that resembled coded messages.

The bedroom door opened and a distracted man in a shabby suit stepped into the living room. The sun was behind him, but I could see his undernourished face, and the light flaring off his high temples. He noticed me, but seemed preoccupied with a problem of his own, as if I were a patient who had called at his surgery without an appointment. He stared through the window at the empty streets and fire-damaged houses with the tired gaze of an overworked doctor trying to carry out his medical work in a wartorn Middle East suburb.

At last he turned to me, smiling with a sudden show of warmth.

'David? Come in. We've all been waiting for you.'

Despite myself, I knew that I was eager to see him.

2

THE HEATHROW BOMB

MY SEDUCTION by Dr Richard Gould, and the revolution he launched at Chelsea Marina, began only four months earlier, though I often felt that I had known this disgraced children's doctor since my student years. He was the maverick who attended no lectures and sat no exams, a solitary with an unpressed suit and a syllabus of his own, but who managed to move on to a postgraduate degree and a successful professional career. He came into our lives like a figure from one of tomorrow's dreams, a stranger who took for granted that we would become his most devoted disciples.

A telephone call was our first warning of Gould's arrival. My mobile rang as we were leaving for Heathrow Airport and a three-day conference of industrial psychologists in Florida. I was steering Sally down the staircase and assumed the call was one of those last-minute messages from the Institute designed to unsettle my flight across the Atlantic—the resignation of a valued secretary, the news that a much-liked colleague had gone into rehab, an urgent e-mail from a company chairman who had discovered Jung's theory of archetypes and was convinced that it outlined the future of kitchenware design.

I left Sally to answer the phone while I took our suitcases into the hall. A natural mender and healer, she had the knack of making everyone feel better. Within minutes the check-in queues at Heathrow would melt away, and the Atlantic would smooth itself into a dance floor. I stood outside the front door and scanned the crescent for our hire car. A few taxis penetrated into this quiet turning off the Abbey Road, but were soon commandeered by Beatles fans making their pilgrimage to the recording studios, or by well-lunched MCC members swaying from Lord's cricket ground into the unsettling world beyond pad and crease. I had booked the car to arrive two hours before our Miami flight from Terminal 3, but the usually reliable Mr Prashar was already twenty minutes late.

Sally was still on the phone when I returned to the sitting room. She leaned against the mantelpiece, smoothing her shoulder-length hair with a casual hand, as handsome as an actress in a thirties Hollywood film. Mirrors held their breath around Sally.

'So . . .' She switched off the phone. 'We wait and hope.'

'Sally? Who was that? Not Professor Arnold, please . . .'

Gripping a walking stick in each hand, Sally swayed from the mantelpiece. I stepped back, as always humouring her little fantasy that she was handicapped. Only the previous afternoon she had played ping-pong with a colleague's wife, sticks forgotten on the table as she batted the ball to and fro. She had not needed the sticks for months, but still reached for them at moments of stress.

'Your friend Mr Prashar.' She leaned against me, scented scalp pressed to my cheek. 'There's a problem at Heathrow. Tailbacks as far as Kew. He thinks there's no point in leaving until they clear.'

'What about the flight?'

'Delayed. Nothing's taking off. The whole airport is down.'

'So what do we do?'

'Have a large drink.' Sally pushed me towards the liquor cabinet. 'Prashar will ring in fifteen minutes. At least he cares.'

'Right.' As I poured two Scotch and sodas I glanced through

the window at Sally's car, with its fading disability sticker on the windscreen, wheelchair folded in the rear seat. 'Sally, I can drive us there. We'll take your car.'

'Mine? You can't cope with the controls.'

'Dear, I designed them. I'll use the hard shoulder, headlights, plenty of horn. We'll leave it in the short-term car park. It's better than sitting here.'

'Here we can get drunk.'

Lying back on the sofa, Sally raised her glass, trying to revive me. The war of succession at the Adler, the struggle to replace Professor Arnold, had left me tired and scratchy, and she was keen to get me to the other side of the Atlantic. The conference at Celebration, Disney's model community in Florida, was a useful chance to park an exhausted husband by a hotel swimming pool. Travelling abroad was an effort for her—the knee-jarring geometry of taxis and bathrooms, and the American psychologists who saw a glamorous woman swaying on her sticks as a special kind of erotic challenge. But Sally was always game, even if for much of the time her only company would be the minibar.

I lay beside her on the sofa, our glasses tapping, and listened to the traffic. It was noisier than usual, the Heathrow tailback feeding its frustration into inner London.

'Ten minutes.' I finished my Scotch, already thinking not of the next drink, but of the one after that. 'I have a feeling we're not going to make it.'

'Relax . . .' Sally poured her whisky into my glass. 'You didn't want to go in the first place.'

'Yes and no. It's having to shake hands with Mickey Mouse that drives me up the wall. Americans love these Disney hotels.'

'Don't be mean. They remind them of their childhoods.'

'Childhoods they didn't actually have. What about the rest of us—why do we have to be reminded of American childhoods?'

'That's the modern world in a nutshell.' Sally sniffed her empty

glass, nostrils flaring like the gills of an exotic and delicate fish.
'At least it gets you away.'

'All these trips? Let's face it, they're just a delusion. Air travel,
the whole Heathrow thing, it's a collective flight from reality.
People walk up to the check-ins and for once in their lives they
know where they're going. Poor sods, it's printed on their tickets.
Look at me, Sally. I'm just as bad. Flying off to Florida isn't what
I really want to do. It's a substitute for resigning from the Adler. I
haven't the courage to do that.'

'You have.'

'Not yet. It's a safe haven, a glorified university department
packed with ambitious neurotics. Think of it—there are thirty
senior psychologists cooped up together, and every one of them
hated his father.'

'Didn't you?'

'I never met him. It was the one good thing my mother did for
me. Now, where's Prashar?'

I stood up and went to the telephone. Sally picked up the TV
remote from the carpet and switched on the lunchtime news.
The picture swam into view, and I recognized a familiar airport
concourse.

'David . . . look.' Sally sat forward, gripping the sticks beside
her feet. 'Something awful . . .'

I listened to Prashar's voice, but my eyes were held by the
news bulletin. The reporter's commentary was drowned by
the wailing of police sirens. He stepped back from the camera
as an ambulance team pushed a trolley through the mêlée of
passengers and airline personnel. A barely conscious woman lay
on the trolley, rags of clothing across her chest, blood speckling
her arms. Dust swirled in the air, billowing above the boutiques
and bureaux de change, a frantic microclimate trying to escape
through the ventilator ducts.

Behind the trolley was the main arrivals gate of Terminal
2, guarded by police armed with sub-machine guns. A harried

group of hire-car drivers waited at the barrier, the names flagged
on their cardboard signs already at half-mast. A man carrying
an executive briefcase stepped from the arrivals gate, the sleeve-
less jacket of his double-breasted suit exposing a bloodied arm.
He stared at the signs raised towards him, as if trying to remember his own name. Two paramedics and an Aer Lingus hostess
knelt on the floor, treating an exhausted passenger who clutched
an empty suitcase that had lost its lid.

'Mr Markham?' A voice sounded faintly in my ear. 'This is
Prashar speaking . . .'

Without thinking, I switched off the phone. I stood beside the
sofa, my hands steadying Sally's shoulders. She was shivering
like a child, her fingers wiping her nose, as if the violent images
on the screen reminded her of her own near-fatal accident.

'Sally, you're safe here. You're with me.'

'I'm fine.' She calmed herself and pointed to the set. 'There
was a bomb on a baggage carousel. David, we might have been
there. Was anyone killed?'

'"Three dead, twenty-six injured . . ."' I read the caption on
the screen. 'Let's hope there are no children.'

Sally fumbled with the remote control, turning up the sound.
'Don't they issue a warning? Codewords the police recognize?
Why bomb the arrivals lounge?'

'Some people are mad. Sally, we're all right.'

'No one is all right.'

She held my arm and made me sit beside her. Together we
stared at the pictures from the concourse. Police, first-aid crews
and duty-free staff were helping injured passengers to the waiting ambulances. Then the picture changed, and we were watching an amateur video taken by a passenger who had entered the
baggage-reclaim area soon after the explosion. The film-maker
stood with his back to the customs checkpoints, evidently too
shocked by the violence that had torn through the crowded hall
to put down his camera and offer help to the victims.

Dust seethed below the ceiling, swirling around the torn sections of strip lighting that hung from the roof. Overturned trollies lay on the floor, buckled by the blast. Stunned passengers sat beside their suitcases, clothes stripped from their backs, covered with blood and fragments of leather and glass.

The video camera lingered on the stationary carousel, its panels splayed like rubber fans. The baggage chute was still discharging suitcases, and a set of golf clubs and a child's pushchair tumbled together among the heaped luggage.

Ten feet away, two injured passengers sat on the floor, watching the suitcases emerge from the chute. One was a man in his twenties, wearing jeans and the rags of a plastic windcheater. When the first rescuers reached him, a policeman and an airport security guard, the young man began to comfort a middle-aged African lying beside him.

The other passenger gazing at the baggage chute was a woman in her late thirties, with a sharp forehead and a bony but attractive face, dark hair knotted behind her. She wore a tailored black suit pitted with glass, like the sequinned tuxedo of a nightclub hostess. A piece of flying debris had drawn blood from her lower lip, but she seemed almost untouched by the explosion. She brushed the dust from her sleeve and stared sombrely at the confusion around her, a busy professional late for her next appointment.

'David . . . ?' Sally reached for her sticks. 'What is it?'

'I'm not sure.' I left the sofa and knelt in front of the screen, nearly certain that I recognized the woman. But the amateur cameraman turned to survey the ceiling, where a fluorescent tube was discharging a cascade of sparks, fireworks in a madhouse. 'I think that's someone I know.'

'The woman in the dark suit?'

'It's hard to tell. Her face reminded me of . . .' I looked at my watch, and noticed our luggage in the hall. 'We've missed our flight to Miami.'

'Never mind. This woman you saw—was it Laura?'

'I think so.' I took Sally's hands, noticing how steady they felt.
'It did look like her.'

'It can't be.' Sally left me and sat on the sofa, searching for
her whisky. The news bulletin had returned to the concourse,
where the hire-car drivers were walking away, placards lowered.
'There's a contact number for relatives. I'll dial it for you.'

'Sally, I'm not a relative.'

'You were married for eight years.' Sally spoke matter-of-
factly, as if describing my membership of a disbanded lunching
club. 'They'll tell you how she is.'

'She looked all right. It might have been Laura. That expression of hers, always impatient . . .'

'Call Henry Kendall at the Institute. He'll know.'

'Henry? Why?'

'He's living with Laura.'

'True. Still, I don't want to panic the poor man. What if I'm
wrong?'

'I don't think you are.' Sally spoke in her quietest voice, a sensible teenager talking to a rattled parent. 'You need to find out.
Laura meant a lot to you.'

'That was a long time ago.' Aware of her faintly threatening
tone, I said: 'Sally, I met you.'

'Call him.'

I walked across the room, turning my back to the television
screen. Holding the mobile, I drummed my fingers on the mantelpiece, and tried to smile at the photograph of Sally sitting in
her wheelchair between her parents, taken at St Mary's Hospital
on the day of our engagement. Standing behind her in my white
lab coat, I seemed remarkably confident, as if I knew for the first
time in my life that I was going to be happy.

The mobile rang before I could dial the Institute's number.
Through the hubbub of background noise, the wailing of ambu-
lance sirens and the shouts of emergency personnel, I heard
Henry Kendall's raised voice.

He was calling from Ashford Hospital, close to Heathrow. Laura had been caught by the bomb blast in Terminal 2. Among the first to be evacuated, she had collapsed in Emergency, and now lay in the intensive-care unit. Henry managed to control himself, but his voice burst into a torrent of confused anger, and he admitted that he had asked Laura to take a later flight from Zurich so that he could keep an Institute appointment and meet her at the airport.

'The Publications Committee . . . Arnold asked me to chair it. For God's sake, he was refereeing his own bloody paper! If I'd refused, Laura would still be . . .'

'Henry, we've all done it. You can't blame yourself . . .' I tried to reassure him, thinking of the stream of blood from Laura's mouth. For some reason, I felt closely involved in the crime, as if I had placed the bomb on the carousel.

THE DIALLING TONE sounded against my ear, a fading signal from another world. For a few minutes all the lines to reality had been severed. I looked at myself in the mirror, puzzled by the travel clothes I was wearing, the lightweight jacket and sports shirt, the tactless costume of a beach tourist who had strayed into a funeral. There was already a shadow on my cheeks, as if the shock of the Heathrow bomb had forced my beard to grow. My face looked harassed and shifty in a peculiarly English way, the wary glower of a deviant master at a minor prep school.

'David . . .' Sally stood up, the sticks forgotten. Her face seemed smaller and more pointed, mouth pursed above a childlike chin. She took the mobile from me and gripped my hands. 'You're all right. Bad luck for Laura.'

'I know.' I embraced her, thinking of the bomb. If the terrorist had chosen Terminal 3, an hour or two later, Sally and I might have been lying together in intensive care. 'God knows why, but I feel responsible.'

'Of course you do. She was important to you.' She stared at me, calmly nodding to herself, almost convinced that she had caught me in a minor but telling gaffe. 'David, you must go.'

'Where? The Institute?'

'Ashford Hospital. Take my car. You'll get through faster.'

'Why? Henry will be with her. Laura isn't part of my life. Sally . . . ?'

'Not for her sake. For yours.' Sally turned her back to me. 'You don't love her, I know that. But you still hate her. That's why you have to go.'

3

'WHY ME?'

WE REACHED Ashford Hospital an hour later, a short journey into a very distant past. Sally drove with verve and flourish, her right hand gripping the accelerator control mounted beside the steering wheel, working the throttle like a fighter pilot, left hand releasing the brake lever next to the gate of the automatic transmission. I had designed the controls, helped by an ergonomics specialist at the Institute, who had taken Sally's measurements with the painstaking care of a Savile Row tailor. By now she had recovered all the strength in her legs, and I suggested that we ask the Saab garage to reconvert the car. But Sally liked the adapted controls, the special skills unique to herself. When I gave in, she teased me that I secretly enjoyed the perverse thrill of having a handicapped wife.

Whatever my motives, I watched her with husbandly pride. She steered the Saab through the dense midday traffic, flashing the headlights at the overworked police on the motorway, fiercely tapping the handicapped driver's sticker on the windscreen. Seeing the wheelchair on the rear seat, they waved us onto the hard shoulder, a high-speed alley that only a glamorous woman could make her own.

As we sped along, hazard lights flashing, I almost believed

that Sally was eager to meet her one-time rival, now lying in the intensive-care unit. In a sense, a kind of justice had been done. Sally had always seen her accident as a random event, a cruel deficit in the moral order of existence that placed it firmly in her debt.

Sightseeing with her mother in the Bairro Alto district of Lisbon, a maze of steeply climbing streets, Sally had crossed the road behind a stationary tram. The fleet of ancient vehicles with their wooden panelling and cast-iron frames had been installed by British engineers almost a century earlier. But charm and industrial archaeology both came at a price. The tram's brakes failed for a few seconds, and it rolled backwards before the safety clutch locked the wheels, knocking Sally to the ground and trapping her legs under the massive chassis.

I met Sally in the orthopaedic wing at St Mary's, at first sight a plucky young woman determined to get well but inexplicably not responding to treatment. The months of physiotherapy had produced a grumpy temper, and even a few foul-mouthed tantrums. I overheard one of these tirades, an ugly storm in a private suite, and put her down as the spoilt daughter of a Birmingham industrialist who flew to see her in the company helicopter and indulged every whim

I visited St Mary's once a week, supervising a new diagnostic system developed in collaboration with the Adler. Instead of facing a tired consultant eager for a large gin and a hot bath, the patient sat at a screen, pressing buttons in reply to prerecorded questions from a fresh-faced and smiling doctor, played by a sympathetic actor. To the consultants' surprise, and relief, the patients preferred the computerized image to a real physician. Desperate to get Sally onto her feet, and well aware that her handicaps were 'elective', in the tactful jargon, her surgeon suggested that we sit Sally in front of the prototype machine.

I distrusted the project, which treated patients like children in a video arcade, but it brought Sally and me together. I rewrote the dialogue of a peptic ulcer programme, adapting the questions to Sally's case, put on a white coat in front of the camera and played the caring doctor.

Sally happily pressed the response buttons, revealing all her anger over the injustice of her accident. But a few days later she swerved past me in the corridor, almost running me down. Pausing to apologize, she was amazed to find that I existed. Over the next days her good humour returned, and she enjoyed mimicking my wooden acting. As I sat on her bed she teased me that I was not completely real. We talked to each other in our recorded voices, a courtship of imbeciles that I was careful not to take seriously.

But a deeper, unspoken dialogue drew us together. I called in every day, and the nursing staff told me that when I was late Sally climbed from her bed and searched for me, dispensing with her wheelchair. As I soon learned, she was a more subtle psychologist than I was. Gripping her volume of Frida Kahlo paintings, she asked me if I could track down the make of tram that had injured Kahlo in Mexico City. Was the manufacturer by any chance an English firm?

I could grasp the anger that linked the two women, but Kahlo had been grievously wounded by a steel rail that pierced her uterus and gave her a lifetime of pain. Sally had crossed a foreign street without looking to left or right, and lost nothing of her beauty. It was her curious obsession with the random nature of the accident that prevented her from walking. Unable to resolve the conundrum, she insisted that she was a cripple in a wheelchair, sharing her plight with other victims of meaningless accidents.

'So you're on strike,' I told her. 'You're conducting your own sit-in against the universe.'

'I'm waiting for an answer, Mr Markham.' She played with her hair as she lay back against three huge pillows. 'It's the most important question there is.'

'Go on.'

'"Why me?" Answer it. You can't.'

'Sally . . . does it matter? It's a fluke we're alive at all. The chances of our parents meeting were millions to one against. We're tickets in a lottery.'

'But a lottery isn't meaningless. Someone has to win.' She paused to get my attention. 'Like our meeting here. That wasn't meaningless . . .'

HEATHROW APPROACHED, a beached sky-city, half space station and half shanty town. We left the motorway and moved along the Great West Road, entering a zone of two-storey factories, car-rental offices and giant reservoirs. We were part of an invisible marine world that managed to combine mystery and boredom. In a way it seemed fitting that my former wife was lying in a hospital here, within call of life and death, in an area that hovered between waking and the dream.

Sally drove with more than her usual zest, overtaking on the inside, jumping the red lights, even hooting a police car out of her way. The Heathrow bomb had recharged her. This vicious and deranged attack confirmed her suspicions of the despotism of fate. For all her wifely concern, she was eager to visit Ashford Hospital, not only to free me from my memories of an unhappy marriage, but to convince herself that there was no meaning or purpose in the terrorist bomb. Already I was hoping that Laura had made a sudden recovery and was on her way back to London with Henry Kendall.

I switched on the radio and tuned in to the reports of rescue work at Terminal 2. The airport was closed indefinitely, as police searched for explosives in the other three terminals. Scarcely noticed by the newspapers, several small bombs had detonated in London during the summer, mostly smoke and incendiary devices unclaimed by any terrorist group, part of the strange metropolitan weather. Bombs were left in a Shepherd's Bush shopping mall and a cineplex in Chelsea. There were no warnings and, luckily, no casualties. A quiet fever burned in the mind of some brooding solitary, a candle of disaffection that threw ever-longer shadows. Yet I only heard about the incendiary device that destroyed a McDonald's in the Finchley Road, a mile from our house, when I glanced through the local free-sheet left by Sally's manicurist. London was under siege from a shy, invisible enemy.

'We're here,' Sally told me. 'Now, take it easy.'

We had reached Ashford Hospital. Outside the Accident and Emergency entrance the ambulance lights rotated ceaselessly, hungry radars eager to suck any news of pain and injury from the sky. Paramedics sipped their mugs of tea, ready to be recalled to Heathrow.

'Sally, you must be tired.' I smoothed her hair as we waited to enter the car park. 'Do you want to stay outside?'

'I'll come in.'

'It could be nasty.'

'It's nasty out here. This is for me, too, David.'

She released the brake lever, pulled sharply onto the pavement and overtook a Jaguar driven by an elderly nun. A security man leaned through Sally's window, noticed the adapted controls and beckoned us into the car park of a nearby supermarket, where the police had set up a command post.

The Jaguar pulled in beside us, and the nun stepped out and opened the door for a grey-haired priest, some monsignor ready to give the last rites. I was helping Sally from the car when I noticed a bearded figure in a white raincoat outside the Accident and Emergency entrance. He was staring over the heads of the police and ambulance drivers, eyes fixed on the silent sky, as if expecting a long-awaited aircraft to fly over the hospital and break the spell. He carried a woman's handbag, holding it against his chest, a life-support package that might work its desperate miracle.

Distractedly, he offered the bag to a concerned paramedic who spoke to him. His eyes were hidden by the ambulance lights, but I could see his mouth opening and closing, a subvocal speech addressed to no one around him. Despite all our years at the Adler, the tiresome clients and their impossible secretaries, this was the first time I had seen Henry Kendall completely at a loss.

'David?' Sally waited for me to lift her from the driving seat. When I hesitated, she moved her legs out of the car, seized the door pillar in both hands and stood up. Around her were endless rows of parked cars, a silent congregation that worshipped death. 'Has something happened?'

'It looks like it. Henry's over there.'

'Grim . . .' Sally followed my raised hand. 'He's waiting for you.'

'Poor man, he's not waiting for anything.'

'Laura? She can't be . . .'

'Stay here. I'll talk to him. If he can hear anything I say . . .'

FIVE MINUTES LATER, after trying to comfort Henry, I walked back to Sally. She stood by the car, a stick in each hand, blonde hair falling across her shoulders. Carrying Laura's handbag, I stepped around the monsignor's Jaguar, sorry that our aggressive driving had delayed his arrival by even a few seconds.

I embraced Sally tightly, aware that I was trembling. I held the handbag under my arm, realizing that Laura's death had driven a small space between us.

4

THE LAST RIVAL

AS I LEFT the chapel and joined the mourning party in the sunlight, a passenger jet was making its descent towards Heathrow. I watched it ease its way over the Deer Park at Richmond, above the disused observatory where the Astronomer Royal had once scanned the imperial heaven. Perhaps the airliner was bringing back to London the last delegates to the Celebration conference, skins toned by the Florida air, minds numbed by the babble of podium-speak.

In my secretary's office that morning I had scanned the e-mail summaries of the papers. The confident claims for the new corporate psychology seemed to float above the world like a regatta of hot-air balloons, detached from the reality of modern death that the mourners at the west London crematorium had gathered to respect. The psychologists at the Adler were trying to defuse the conflicts of the workplace, but the threats from beyond the curtain-walling were ever more real and urgent. No one was safe from the motiveless psychopath who roamed the car parks and baggage carousels of our everyday lives. A vicious boredom ruled the world, for the first time in human history, interrupted by meaningless acts of violence.

The airliner soared over Twickenham, undercarriage lowered,

confident that firm ground waited for it at Heathrow. Still unsettled by Laura's death, I imagined a bomb exploding in the cargohold, scattering the scorched lectures on the psychology of the new century across the rooftops of west London. The fragments would rain down on blameless video shops and Chinese takeaways, to be read by bemused housewives, the fading blossom of the disinformation age.

My colleagues at the Adler, uncomfortable in their dark suits, stood in small groups as the organ voluntary sounded from the chapel's loudspeakers. Henry Kendall was talking to the funeral director, a suave figure in morning dress with the air of a senior concierge who could always supply tickets to the most sought-after shows, in this world or the next.

Henry, I was glad to see, had recovered from his moments of despair outside Ashford Hospital. He had shaved off his beard, clearing away the past now that he faced a future without Laura. He had grown the beard soon after the start of their affair, and I always suspected that this was an ill omen. He had aged rapidly during his time with Laura, and already he looked younger, with the keen edge to his eye that he had first brought to the Adler.

I nodded to Professor Arnold, the Institute's director, an affable but shrewd man with the mind of a small-claims lawyer, well aware that he was surrounded by rivals eager to take his job. Laura's death had unsettled them all, reminding them how much she had once despised them. She would have been amazed by the presence of her former colleagues—'grey men with hangups they cling to like comfort blankets,' she once remarked—and would have laughed the lid off her coffin if she had heard the straight-faced tributes to her. For years she had nagged me to leave the Adler and set up in practice on my own, claiming that my loyalty to the Institute concealed a refusal to grow up. During our last years together, I needed the security that the Adler offered, and when she resigned to set up a consultancy of her own I knew that our marriage was over.

But then security was not something that Laura ever pretended to offer. I remembered her sharp humour and the depressions that showed a warmer and more interesting side, and the sudden enthusiasms that made everything seem possible. Sadly, I was far too stable and cautious for her. Once she deliberately provoked me into slamming a door in her face. A torrent of blood sprang from her strong nose, about which she had always been sensitive. Strangely, it was the blood on the face of the injured woman by the baggage carousel that had first made me think of Laura.

Leaving the mourners, I strolled along the display of flowers, each a burst of colour that reminded me of another explosion. The bomb in Terminal 2 had detonated as the baggage on a BA flight from Zurich was reaching the carousel. There had been no warning, and no organization claimed responsibility for all the deaths and injuries. Nothing explained why these passengers had been targeted, a group of bank couriers, holidaymakers and Swiss wives visiting their London-based husbands. Laura had been speaking to an urban-studies seminar run by Nestlé. She died in the intensive-care unit at Ashford Hospital, half an hour before our arrival, her heart torn by a shard of the timing mechanism that had set off the bomb.

I strolled back to the chapel, leaving the flowers to shine their last at the afternoon sun. The mourners were returning to their cars, ready for the consoling Montrachet that Professor Arnold would offer in lieu of a wake. Henry Kendall stood on the chapel steps, talking to a thickset man with pale ginger hair who wore a sheepskin coat over his suit. I had seen him in the back row when I entered the chapel, scanning the mourners as if familiarizing himself with the men in Laura's life. He left when I approached, and walked briskly to his car.

'David . . .' Henry held my arm. He seemed affable and confident, relieved that more than the funeral was over. 'I'm glad you came.'

'It went well.' I gestured at the departing mourners. 'Short, but . . .'

'Laura would have hated it. All those bogus last words. I'm amazed everyone turned up.'

'They couldn't keep away. She'd frightened the wits out of all of them. You look . . .'

'Fine, fine . . .' Henry turned from me, a hand feeling his cheek. He was searching for his beard, aware that his handsome face and all its insecurities were open to the air. Not for the first time, I suspected that it was nothing more than his looks, and a certain passivity, that Laura found attractive. In his eyes we had always been rivals, and he was puzzled whenever I failed to follow up a chance of weakening his position. His affair with Laura was in part an attempt to flush me out. I liked him, but I could afford to, knowing that he would never become director of the Adler.

I pointed to the man in the sheepskin coat, now sitting alone in the car park, large hands resting on the steering wheel. 'Who is he? Some old flame of Laura's?'

'I hope not. Major Tulloch, ex-Gibraltar Police. A bit of a bruiser. He's attached to the Home Office, in some kind of anti-terrorist unit.'

'He's looking into the Heathrow bomb? Any news?'

'Hard to make out. Intelligence people always know less than you think. He wanted to talk to you before the service, but you looked a little preoccupied.'

'Weren't you?'

'Yes and no.' Henry smiled shiftily, still testing me out. 'According to Tulloch they've found a suspicious poster near the baggage reclaim in Terminal 2.'

'Connected with the bomb?'

'It's possible. Someone crammed a bag into an air shaft behind a lavatory cubicle. Only fifty feet from the bomb.'

'It might have been there for months. Or years.'

Henry gazed at me patiently, nodding to himself as if confirming something that Laura had once said about me. 'Yes, but one can be too sceptical. Some things we have to take at face value. There was a tape protesting against holiday flights to the Third World. You know, sexual tourism, concreting over native habitats. The marina culture.'

'In Switzerland?'

'Who knows?' Aware that he had unsettled me, Henry lowered his voice. 'Do you want to talk to Tulloch? The Home Office values our expertise.'

'On violent death? I don't think I have any.'

'They're worried about new terrorist groups. Thrill-seekers with a taste for random violence. There's been a spate of bombings recently, mostly hushed up. In fact, Tulloch asked if I'd like to work for them. Unofficially, that is. Join demos, stand back and observe, map the emerging psychology.'

'Go undercover?'

'Semi-undercover.'

'Will you?' I waited for him to reply. 'Henry?'

'Hard to say. In a way I owe it to Laura.'

'You owe her nothing. There are hundreds of these groups. "Defend the Killer Whale." "Save the Smallpox Virus."'

'Exactly, where would you start? Tulloch admits there's an element of danger.'

'Really? Keep clear, Henry.'

'Sound advice. Perhaps too sound.' As we shook hands, he said: 'Tell me, David—why did you drive to the hospital? Ashford is a long way from St John's Wood.'

'We were worried about Laura. And about you.'

'Good. By the way, Laura's handbag . . . ?'

'It's in my car. I'll give it to you.'

'Fair enough. Did you open it?'

'No.'

'I know the feeling. There are some secrets that none of us can face.'

I WATCHED HIM drive off, leaving me alone with Tulloch. Wisps of smoke rose from the crematorium chimney while the combustion chamber warmed to its fiercest temperature. There was a puff of darker smoke, as if part of Laura had freed itself from the drag-anchor of her body—perhaps a hand that had once caressed me, or the soft foot that would touch mine while she slept. I watched the smoke rising, a series of bursts as if this dead woman was signalling to me. Under my dark suit my shirt was drenched with sweat. Her death had freed me from all resentments, all pain of memory. I remembered the quirky young woman I had met in the bar at the National Film Theatre, and invited to a late-night screening of Antonioni's *Passenger.*

Major Tulloch was watching me from his car, while the smoke rose rapidly into the sky. I resented the presence of this thuggish policeman, sitting in his slaughterman's coat as my wife's body dispersed into the sky. But he knew that I needed to find her killer, hunting down the secret love of Laura's life, and my last rival.

5

CONFRONTATION AT OLYMPIA

AROUND ME everyone was calm, a sure sign that the moment
of crisis had come. Cheered by the arrival of a television camera
crew, the demonstrators were resolute, their confidence boosted
by the sense that a larger audience was sharing their indignation. They waved their hand-lettered placards and jeered good-
humouredly at the visitors entering the Olympia exhibition.
But the police seemed bored, usually an omen of violent action.
Already they were tired of this pointless protest, one group of cat
lovers ranged against another.

Locking arms with two middle-aged women from Wimbledon, I stood in the front row of demonstrators in Hammersmith
Road. As the traffic cleared, we surged across the eastbound lane
towards the watching police, like an advancing chorus in an agit-
prop musical. Behind me, a young woman held aloft a banner.

'a cat in hell's chance? stop breeding now!'

Leaning back, I tried to restrain my Wimbledon partners
from colliding into the nearest group of constables. By now, two
months after Laura's funeral, I was a veteran of a dozen demos.
I knew that however difficult it was to read the shifts in crowd
psychology, the mood of the police was impossible to predict. In
a few seconds, with the departure of a radio van or the arrival

of a senior officer, friendly banter could turn into outright hostility. After a flurry of concealed blows, we would be forced to
withdraw, leaving some grey-haired man on the pavement with
a broken placard and a bloody nose.

'*Moggie, moggie, moggie . . . out, out, out!*'

We surged across the road again, fists drumming on the roof
of a taxi bringing more visitors to the cat show. As we reached
the line of surly constables I noticed once again how huge the
police seemed when one stepped up to them, and how they con-
strued almost any behaviour as threatening. Pushed forward by
the scrum of demonstrators, I brushed against a small policewoman dwarfed by her male colleagues. She was looking over
my shoulder, quite unfrightened by the noisy crowd. Barely
changing her stance, she kicked me twice in the right shin.

'MR MARKHAM? Are you all right? Lean on me . . .'

The young woman with the 'cat in hell's chance' banner
gripped me around the waist. Bent double in the scrum of police
and protesters, I joined the retreat across Hammersmith Road,
limping and hopping on one leg.

'That was vicious. Totally unprovoked. Mr Markham, can you
breathe?'

Likeable and intense, Angela was a computer programmer in
Kingston with a husband and two children. We had teamed up
soon after our arrival at Olympia, bought tickets and carried out a
reconnaissance of the vast cat show, with its five hundred exhibi-
tors and its population of the world's most pampered pets.

I gripped her hand and sat on the entrance steps of a block of
mansion flats. Rolling up my trousers, I touched the huge blood-
bruises already forming.

'I'll walk again. I think . . .' I pointed to the policewoman,
now efficiently on traffic duty, moving the lines of waiting cars
towards Kensington and Hammersmith Broadway. 'She was
nasty. I hate to imagine what's she's like in bed.'

'Unspeakable. Don't even think about it.' Angela stared across
the road with narrowed eyes and all a suburbanite's unlimited
capacity for moral outrage. Walking around the exhibition two
hours earlier, I was impressed by her unswerving commitment
to the welfare of these luxurious pets. The protest rallies I had
recently attended against globalization, nuclear power and the
World Bank were violent but well thought out. By contrast, this
demonstration against the Olympia cat show seemed endearingly
Quixotic in its detachment from reality. I tried to point this out
to Angela as we strolled along the lines of cages.

'Angela, they look so happy . . .' I gestured at the exquisite
creatures—Persians, Korats and Russian blues, Burmese and col-
ourpoint short-hairs, drowsing on their immaculate straw, coats
puffed and gleaming after their shampoos and sets. 'They're
wonderfully cared for. We're trying to rescue them from heaven.'

Angela never varied her step. 'How do you know?'

'Just watch them.' We stopped in front of a row of Abyssinians
so deeply immersed in the luxury of being themselves that they
barely noticed the admiring crowds. 'They're not exactly unhappy.
They'd be prowling around, trying to get out of the cages.'

'They're drugged.' Angela's brows knotted. 'Mr Markham, no
living creature should be caged. This isn't a cat show, it's a con-
centration camp.'

'Still, they are rather gorgeous.'

'They're bred for death, not life. The rest of the litter are
drowned at birth. It's a vicious eugenic experiment, the sort of
thing Dr Mengele got up to. Think about that, Mr Markham.'

'I do, Angela . . .'

We completed our circuit of the upper gallery. Angela noted
the exits, the ancient elevators and stairs, the fire escapes and
surveillance cameras. The ground floor was dominated by man-
ufacturers' stands, displays of health tonics for cats, toys and
climbing frames, cosmetics and grooming kits. Every worldly
pleasure a cat could experience was lavishly provided.

But logic was not the strongest suit of the protest movements, as I had found during the past two months. On the day after Laura's funeral I began to scan the listings magazines and internet sites for details of the more extreme protest rallies, searching for fringe groups with a taste for violence. One of these fanatical sects, frustrated by its failure to puncture the soft underbelly of bourgeois life, might have set off the Heathrow bomb.

I decided not to contact Major Tulloch and the Home Office, who would have an agenda of their own and write off the Heathrow atrocity when it no longer served their purpose. The police, Henry Kendall told me, were making little progress in their investigation. They now discounted the holdall with its audiocassette stuffed into the lavatory air vent near the Terminal 2 carousel. The muddled threats about Third-World tourism belonged to the deluded mind-set of some backpacker returning from Goa or Kathmandu, head clouded by pot and amphetamines.

The forensic teams had combed through every fragment of glass, metal and plastic. Curiously, they found no trace of a barometric device designed to set off a mid-air explosion. The bomb had been furnished with an acid-capsule trigger, probably primed no more than five minutes before the explosion. Not only had Laura's death been meaningless, but the killer was almost certainly among the fleeing crowd we had watched on television.

Protest movements, sane and insane, sensible and absurd, touched almost every aspect of life in London, a vast web of demonstrations that tapped a desperate need for a more meaningful world. There was scarcely a human activity that was not the target of a concerned group ready to spend its weekends picketing laboratories, merchant banks and nuclear-fuel depots, trudging up muddy lanes to defend a badger sett, lying across a motorway to halt the reviled race enemy of all demonstrators, the internal combustion engine.

Far from being on the fringe, these groups were now part of the country's civic traditions, along with the Lord Mayor's

parade, Ascot week and Henley Regatta. At times, as I joined
a demonstration against animal experiments or Third-World
debt, I sensed that a primitive religion was being born, a faith
in search of a god to worship. Congregations roamed the streets,
hungry for a charismatic figure who would emerge sooner or
later from the wilderness of a suburban shopping mall and scent
a promising wind of passion and credulity.

Sally was my field researcher, scanning the net for advance
news of obscure protest rallies, and only too keen to help. Both of
us had been shaken by Laura's death, Sally more than I expected.
Using her sticks again, she moved around the house with the
same wristy determination she had shown in the physiotherapy
unit at St Mary's where I had first courted her. She was returning to the period of wounded time when she was obsessed with
Frida Kahlo and their shared tram accidents. If only for Sally's
sake, I needed to crack the conundrum of Laura's death.

From the backs of halls, and behind the barricades at protest
meetings, I searched the rows of determined faces for a genuinely
disturbed mind, some deranged loner eager to live out a dream
of violence. But in fact almost all the demonstrators were good-
humoured members of the middle class—level-headed students
and health-care professionals, doctors' widows and grandmothers
working on Open University degree courses. Some prick of conscience, some long-dormant commitment to principle, brought
them out into the cold and rain.

The only frightening people I met were the police and television crews. The police were morose and unpredictable, paranoid
about any challenge to their authority. The television reporters
were little more than agents provocateurs, forever trying to pro-
pel the peaceful protests into violent action. Neutrality was the
most confrontational stance of all, while the nearest I came to an
exponent of political violence was Angela, the Kingston housewife and cat lover.

———

AS I SAT on the steps of the mansion block, she produced antiseptic spray and surgical lint from her jacket. She cleaned my
wounds and sprayed the stinging vapour over the weals. All the
while she kept a baleful eye on the policewoman, now threatening to arrest two cyclists who had stopped to observe the demo.

'Feel better?' Angela flexed my knee. 'I'd visit your doctor
pronto.'

'I'm fine. I ought to bring a complaint, but I didn't see her
move.'

'You never do.'

I pointed to the medical kit. 'You were expecting trouble?'

'Of course. People feel very strongly.'

'For the cats?'

'They're political prisoners. Start experimenting on animals
and human beings will be next.' She smiled with surprising
sweetness and kissed my forehead, a field decoration for a valiant
trooper. With a wave, she left me to look after myself.

Touched by her warmth, I watched the protesters regroup and
make a second attempt to block the exhibition hall's entrance
foyer and ticket office. Placards rose into the air, and a pole carried a small cage occupied by a stuffed marmalade cat, paws
handcuffed through the bars. A stream of yellow plastic confetti
struck the policewoman, dribbling across her uniform jacket.
Brushing the sticky threads from her chin, she stepped into the
group of demonstrators and tried to seize the aerosol can from a
young man in a tiger mask.

An ugly struggle broke out, blocking the traffic in Hammersmith Road, a series of running scuffles that left half a dozen
middle-aged protesters sitting stunned beside the wheels of
stalled taxis. But I was watching Angela as she crossed the road,
hands deep in the pockets of her jacket. She ignored the demonstrators wrestling with the police, and held the arm of a ponytailed man who stepped from the pavement to join her.

I stood up and made my way towards the exhibition hall, walking through the startled tourists and curious passers-by who were milling about in the centre of the road. Angela and her pony-tailed companion moved through the entrance foyer, arms around each other's waists, like lovers immersed in their own world.

I was following them past the ticket office when I heard a thunderflash explode in the exhibition hall. Startled by the harsh air burst, and the re-echo of slammed doors, the visitors around me flinched and ducked behind each other. A second thunder-flash detonated in the overhead gallery, lighting up the mirrors in the antique lifts. An elderly couple in front of me stumbled into a pyramid of jewelled flea collars, throwing it to the floor in a gaudy sprawl.

A violent struggle was taking place among the cages on the main floor. Angela and the ponytailed man forced their way through the confused breeders and wrenched the doors off the display hutches. I guessed that a group of infiltrators had been waiting for the police to be distracted by the commotion in Hammersmith Road, giving them time to carry out their action.

I limped after Angela, aware that she would be no match for the outraged breeders. A police sergeant and two constables overtook me through the crowd, ducking their heads as a third thunderflash exploded inside a sales pavilion filled with quilted baskets.

A large cat, a sleekly groomed Maine Coon, streaked towards us, paused to get its bearings in the forest floor of human legs, and darted between the sergeant's boots. The sight of this liber-ated creature sent a spasm of rage through the onlookers. One of the constables blundered into me, pushed me aside and ran after Angela. Her ponytailed companion brandished a can of tear gas, holding back a circle of breeders while Angela snapped the cage locks with a pair of cutters.

The sergeant hurled Angela's colleague aside, struck the cut-ters from her hands and seized her shoulders from behind. He lifted her into the air like a child and threw her at his feet among

the sawdust and scattered rosettes. As he lifted her again, ready
to hurl this small and stunned woman to the cement floor, I ran
forward and gripped his arm.

Less than a minute later I was lying on the floor, my face
in the sawdust, hands cuffed behind me. I had been viciously
kicked by the angry breeders, shouting down my pleas that I was
defending a Kingston housewife, cat lover and mother of two.

I rolled onto my back, as the sirens sounded in Hammersmith
Road and the Olympia loudspeakers urged visitors to remain
calm. The protest had ended and the last cordite vapour from
the thunderflashes drifted under the ceiling lights. Breeders
straightened their cages and comforted their ruffled pets, and a
saleswoman rebuilt the pyramid of flea collars. Angela and the
ponytailed man had slipped away, but the police bundled several
handcuffed demonstrators towards the exit.

Two police officers lifted me to my feet. The younger, a black
constable baffled by the huge menagerie of cats and the attention
lavished on them, dusted the straw from my jacket. He waited as
I tried to breathe through my bruised ribs.

'You have something against cats?' he asked.

'Just against cages.'

'Too bad. You're going into one.'

I inhaled deeply, looking at the overhead lights. I realized that
a second odour had replaced the tang of cordite. As the thunderflashes exploded, a thousand terrified creatures had joined in a
collective act of panic, and the exhibition hall was filled with the
potent stench of feline urine.

6

RESCUE

A LESS BRACING SCENT, the odour of the guilty and unwashed, hung over the magistrates' court in Hammersmith Grove. I waited in the back row of the public seats, trying to hear the bench's verdict on a mother of three accused of soliciting outside Queen's Tennis Club. She was a depressed woman in her early forties, barely literate and in desperate need of remedial care. Her mumbled plea was drowned by the ceaseless activity in the court as solicitors, accused, police officers, ushers and witnesses roamed up and down the aisles, a cast straight from the pages of Lewis Carroll. What was being dispensed was not justice but a series of tired compromises with the inevitable, the calls of a harassed referee at a chaotic football match.

I had been fined £100 and bound over to keep the peace. My solicitor's claim that I was an innocent visitor to Olympia who had tried to defend a woman demonstrator from unprovoked police violence was ignored by the magistrates. The guilt of everyone brought before the court—petty thieves, drunk drivers, animal rights protesters—was taken for granted. Only contrition carried the slightest weight. My solicitor rattled off my professional qualifications, lack of a criminal record and good standing in the community. But a police sergeant I had never seen before testified that I featured in numerous surveillance films and frequently attended violent street demonstrations.

The magistrates stared at me darkly, assuming that I was one of those middle-class professionals who was a traitor to the civil order and deserved the sharpest of short, sharp shocks. Before sentence I explained that I was searching for the murderers of my first wife, at which point the chief magistrate closed his eyes.

'At a cat show?'

Afterwards my solicitor offered me a lift to central London, but to his relief I declined. I needed to find somewhere to rest, even in the bedlam of the magistrates' court. The vicious kicks that the cat lovers had aimed at my chest and genitals three days earlier, and rough handling in the police van, had left me with badly bruised arms and ribs, and a swollen testicle that startled Sally. Standing in the dock was deeply embarrassing, but I was too exhausted to sense any real shame. Many of the patients treated at the Adler felt a vast sourceless guilt, but none of those convicted by the magistrates showed the slightest remorse. Justice achieved nothing, wasted police time and trivialized itself.

I rested on the punitive wooden pew, as the court heard a plea that the next case be referred to a jury trial. A confident woman in a tailored suit stood before the bench, gesturing in a theatrical way with a sheaf of documents in her hand. Behind her, standing at the altar table that served as a dock, were the accused, a young Chinese woman with black bangs and a combative expression, and an uneasy clergyman in dog collar and motorcycle jacket, eyes lowered over unshaven cheeks. Together they were charged with a breach of the peace in a Shepherd's Bush shopping mall, causing damage estimated at £27.

I had seen the group on the steps of the courthouse when I arrived, and assumed that the well-dressed woman was their lawyer. She strode up and down before the magistrates, now and then pausing to give these three worthies time to catch up with her. She swung on a high heel, ash-grey hair swirling around her shoulders, showing off her hips to the attentive court, and confident enough of her good looks to wear her glasses on the tip of her nose.

Intrigued by her command of the stage, I wished I had asked her to represent me. People in the public benches were already laughing at her sallies, and she played up to the applause like a skilled actress. When the chief magistrate dismissed her plea for a jury trial she threw aside her papers and strode to the bench in an almost threatening way. A policeman restrained her and led her back to the dock, where she stood defiantly with the Chinese girl and the downcast clergyman.

So this spirited advocate was not a solicitor but one of the accused. She stared defiantly at the magistrates, aware that her moment was over. She took off her glasses in a petulant way, like a child separated from her toy. I guessed that she and her fellow-accused were part of some evangelical group, a cranky New Age cult trying to perform a stone-age solstice ritual in the atrium of a shopping mall.

I made my way out of the courtroom, keen to get back to sanity, Sally and my work at the Institute. Sally had agreed not to attend the hearing, saving me any further embarrassment. The search for Laura's killers would have to take some other course, or be left to the police and the antiterrorist units.

I eased myself through the crowd of relatives and witnesses in the lobby, conscious of the unpleasant scent that rose from my shirt, a medley of sweat and guilt. In front of me was a uniformed chauffeur who had testified against his boss, a local businessman convicted of kerb-crawling. He turned suddenly and collided into me, his elbow catching my chest, then gripped my arms in apology and plunged away through the crowd.

A rush of pain tore at my breastbone, as if my bruised ribs had been opened to the air. Barely able to breathe, I stepped into the daylight of Hammersmith Grove, and tried to flag down a passing taxi, but the effort of raising my arm left me winded. I

leaned against the stone lion on the balustrade, and the policeman on duty waved me away from the courthouse steps as if I
were a tottering wino.

I stepped into the crowded lunch hour, filled with office staff
heading for the sandwich bars. All the air in the street had vanished. I was about to faint, and had the desperate notion that if I
lay on the pavement someone would think that I was dying and
call an ambulance.

Hands on my knees, I rested against a parked car, and managed to draw a little air into my lungs. Then a woman's arm
gripped me around the waist. Resting against her hip, I could
smell a heady blend of perfume and woollen suiting, overlaid by
perspiration brought on by sheer indignation, an unsettling aura
that made me look up at her.

'Mr Markham? I think you could use some help. You're not
drunk?'

'Not yet. I can't breathe . . .'

I stared into the strong face of the woman who had harangued
the magistrates. She was watching me with genuine concern,
but also an element of calculation, one hand on the mobile phone
in her bag, as if I were a possible recruit to her evangelical cell.

'Now, try to stand.' She propped me against the car, and waved
cheerily to the watching constable. 'I'm parked somewhere here,
if the car hasn't been stolen. Police courts create their own crime
waves. You look awful—what happened to you?'

'I bruised a rib,' I explained. 'Someone kicked me.'

'At Olympia? A police boot, I bet.'

'Cat lovers. They're very violent.'

'Really? What were you doing to the poor mogs?' Almost carrying me, she searched the lines of parked cars. 'Let's get you
somewhere safe. I know a doctor who can look at you. Believe me,
nothing brings out violence like a peaceful demonstration.'

7

ODD MAN OUT

STRONG HANDS steered my head from the car and helped
me towards a front door beside a bay window covered with protest stickers. Kay Churchill, the woman who had come to my aid,
put her shoulder to the door and forced it open, as if leading a
police raid. I assumed that we were breaking into an unoccupied
house somewhere in Chelsea, but she strode confidently into the
hall and tossed her car keys onto the coat stand. She sniffed the
air, clearly unsure whether she liked her own body scent, and
beckoned me to follow her.

Framed film posters hung in the living room, scowling samurai from a Kurosawa epic, a screaming woman from *Battleship
Potemkin*. Kay lifted a pile of scripts from a leather armchair
and eased me among the cushions, waiting with an encouraging
smile until I started to breathe. Eager to care for a fellow demonstrator who had been brutalized by the police, she found a small
bottle of whisky among the scripts and produced a tumbler from
her desk drawer. She nodded approvingly as I inhaled the heady
vapour.

'Poor man—you needed that. Those bastards really had a go.'

'It's kind of you . . .' I leaned back, trying not to breathe. 'If you
ring my wife, she'll come and collect me.'

'Let's get the doctor here first. I'm not sure your wife ought to see you now.' She leaned forward. 'Mr Markham? Still there?'

'Right. You know my name?'

'I heard the clerk call you.' She sat on the arm of the settee, tight skirt exposing her thighs. She was generous and likeable, if overly self-conscious, and used to being the centre of attention. For all her friendliness, she was curious about me, as if I failed somehow to convince her. During the journey from the magistrates' court she drove with one hand on the wheel of her Polo, the other reaching between the front seats to hold my shoulder, checking that I was still alive. After introducing herself, she kept a close eye on the rear-view mirror.

'The clerk?' I sipped the sharp whisky. 'The court was a madhouse. Whatever they dish out there, it isn't justice.'

'You didn't do too badly. Criminal damage, setting off explosives, assaulting the police? Even for a first offence, a fine was pretty lenient.'

'I can't explain it. Believe me, I don't work for the security services.'

'I didn't think so.' She nodded to herself, giving me the benefit of the doubt. 'Still, we can't be too careful. Our ancient democracy has its eyes and ears everywhere—cameras in teapots, microphones behind the chintz. Every time you take a pee some security man at MI5 is making a note of your manhood. We all do it. Those old togs you're wearing—I take it they're your disguise?'

'In a way.' I tried to straighten the lapels of the shiny herringbone suit. 'I bought it from our gardener. I didn't want to look too . . .'

'Middle class?'

'We're supposed to know better. Anyway, we're deeply unfashionable now. People think we need a good kicking.'

'We do.' She spoke matter-of-factly, as if confirming a change in the weather. 'Your solicitor gave the game away. David Markham, consultant psychologist to Unilever and BP. Now

you're fighting with the police and trying to change the world.
You're lucky you weren't locked up.'

'And what about you? The Chinese girl and the clergyman?'

'Sounds like a Bartok opera.' She searched for her mobile. 'I'll
call my doctor friend again. He should be in the theatre by now.'

'Operating?'

'Putting on a play written by his patients. *Queen Diana*.'

'That sounds rather touching.'

'No, sadly. They're Down's children. It's sweet, but a total bore.
Snow White rewritten by Harold Pinter.'

'Interesting . . . It might make more sense.' I tried to stand up.
'I'll see my GP on the way home.'

'No.' She placed a firm hand on my forehead. 'Your wife doesn't
want you dying in the back of a cab. Besides, I need you to help
us with our next project . . .'

I WATCHED HER stride away on a stylish heel. She had brought
me home out of genuine concern for me, but already I felt that
I was becoming a prisoner. I lay back in the armchair, scanning what I could see of this scruffily attractive house, so different from our formal pile in St John's Wood, furnished by a
rich man's daughter endowed with too much good taste. I liked
the faint smell of pot, garlic and outrageous perfumes. Children's
drawings were pinned to the mantelpiece, stained with wine
tossed into the fireplace, but it was clear that Kay Churchill lived
alone. Dust lay on the coffee table and writing desk, a nimbus
that seemed like an ectoplasmic presence, a parallel world with
its own memories and regrets.

A school bus moved past the window, filled with small girls
in felt hats and purple blazers, the uniform of an exclusive private primary, whose fees would educate an entire East End ban-
tustan. I was sitting somewhere in Chelsea Marina, an estate of
executive housing to the south of the King's Road and, to my
mind, the heart of another kind of darkness.

Built on the site of a former gasworks, Chelsea Marina was designed for a salaried professional class keen to preserve its tribal totems—private education, a dinner-party culture, and a never-to-be-admitted distaste for the 'lower' orders, which included City dealers, financial consultants, record industry producers and the lumpen-intelligentsia of newspaper columnists and ad-men. All these were blackballed by the admissions committee, though most would have found Chelsea Marina too modest and well bred for their rangier tastes.

As Kay paced the hall, speaking into her phone, I wondered how she fitted into this enclave of middle-class decorum. She was telling off a luckless hospital receptionist, raising her voice to a fishwife shriek as she described my chest injuries and likely brain damage. All the while, she was watching herself admiringly in the coat-stand mirror. When she poured a tumbler of Scotch I noticed the deeply bitten nails, and the strong nose she had picked since childhood.

'Dr Gould's on his way.' She sat on the arm of my chair and checked my eyes, bringing her body close to me. 'Actually, you look better.'

'Good. Anything to get away from that court.' I pointed to the quiet street beyond the bay window. 'So this is Chelsea Marina. It feels more like . . .'

'Fulham? It is Fulham. "Chelsea Marina" is an estate agent's con. Affordable housing for all those middle managers and civil servants just scraping by.'

'And the marina?'

'The size of a toilet and smells like it.' She raised her head, as if catching a whiff of this noxious aroma. 'The whole place was purpose-built for the responsible middle class, but it's turning into a high-priced slum. No City bonuses here, no share options or company credit cards. A lot of us are really stretched. That's why we're waking up and doing something about it. We're holding a series of street demos.'

'The problem is the streets all lead to the nearest police court.'

'We can cope with that. Remember, the police are neutral—they hate everybody. Being law-abiding has nothing to do with being a good citizen. It means not bothering the police.'

'Sound advice.' I caught myself breathing too deeply, and eased the air from my lungs. 'Learn the rules, and you can get away with anything.'

'That's always a shock to the middle classes.' She ran a finger through the dust on the coffee table, like a bacteriologist surprised by a new growth in a Petri dish. 'What was going on at Olympia?'

'Nothing . . .' I waited as Kay settled herself on the settee, ready to listen to me, and realized that this strong-willed and attractive woman was lonely. I was tempted to describe my search for the Heathrow bomber, but she was a little too watchful. She had heard my statement to the magistrates, and probably assumed that I was involved in the protest movements at a more serious level. Defensively, I added: 'A cat show—sounds trivial, but it reaches the headlines. It's unexpected, and makes people think.'

'Spot on.' She nodded vigorously. 'We need to unsettle them. It's not enough to be sincere—they assume you're a whining Trot or some dotty old dear. You have to stick your neck out. I've tried, and God knows I've paid the price.'

I pointed with my glass to the wall posters. 'You're a movie critic?'

'I teach film studies at South Bank University. Or did.'

'Kurosawa, Klimov, Bresson . . . ?'

'The last gasp. After that came entertainment.'

'Fair enough.' It was time to leave, but I found it difficult to rise from the chair. The whisky sealed in the pain, as long as I sat still. I scanned the titles printed on the hundreds of videos packed into the shelves behind the desk. 'No American films?'

'I don't like comic strips.'

'Film noir?'

'Black is a very sentimental colour. You can hide any rubbish behind it. Hollywood flicks are fun, if your idea of a good time is a hamburger and a milk shake. America invented the movies so it would never need to grow up. We have angst, depression and middle-aged regret. They have Hollywood.'

'Good for them.' I pointed to the folders on the coffee table. 'Script submissions?'

'From my class. I thought they needed a day trip to reality. There's too much jargon around——"voyeurism and the male gaze", "castration anxieties". Marxist theory-speak swallowing its own tail.'

'But you cured that?'

'I told them to take their cameras into the bedroom and make a porn film. Fucking is what they do in their spare time, so why not look at it through a camera lens? They wouldn't learn much about sex, but they'd learn a lot about film.'

'And that went down a treat?'

'They loved it, but the dean of studies wasn't impressed. I'm on suspension until they work out how to handle me.'

'Quite a challenge.'

'I thought so too. So, with all this time on my hands, I decided to start a revolution.'

'A revolution?' I tried to seem impressed. She appeared edgy and frustrated, staring at the frayed carpet like an actress deprived of her audience. The revolution, when it arrived, would at least provide a good script and some valuable parts.

'You put on a great show this morning,' I told her. 'In fact, I'm surprised they found you guilty. Fining someone in holy orders . . .'

'Stephen Dexter? Chelsea Marina's resident vicar. I'm not sure if that qualifies as a holy office.'

'So the Shepherd's Bush protest was religious?'

'Not for Stephen. Poor boy, he's one of those priests who feels obliged to doubt his God. Still, it makes him useful to have around, especially on a demo.'

'Twenty-seven pounds worth of damage? What did you do— upset a litter bin?'

'We tore down some posters.' She shuddered with genuine revulsion. 'Corrupting stuff.'

'Ungodly?'

'In a way. Deeply seductive.'

'At a shopping mall? What was this? A pro-vivisection reading room?'

'A travel agency.' She turned to face me, chin raised. 'As it happens, we're against the whole concept of travel.'

'Why?'

'Tourism is the great soporific. It's a huge confidence trick, and gives people the dangerous idea that there's something interesting in their lives. It's musical chairs in reverse. Every time the muzak stops people stand up and dance around the world, and more chairs are added to the circle, more marinas and Marriott hotels, so everyone thinks they're winning.'

'But it's another con?'

'Complete. Today's tourist goes nowhere.' She spoke confidently, with the self-assurance of a lecturer never interrupted by her audience, holding forth in this shabby living room in her passionate way. 'All the upgrades in existence lead to the same airports and resort hotels, the same pina colada bullshit. The tourists smile at their tans and their shiny teeth and think they're happy. But the suntans hide who they really are—salary slaves, with heads full of American rubbish. Travel is the last fantasy the 20th Century left us, the delusion that going somewhere helps you reinvent yourself.'

'And that can't be done?'

'There's nowhere to go. The planet is full. You might as well stay at home and spend the money on chocolate fudge.'

'The Third World gains something . . .'

'The Third World!' Her voice rose to a derisive hoot. 'Gangs of coolies who mix the cement and lay the runways. A select few get to mix the cocktails and lay the tourists.'

'Hard grind, but a living.'

'They're the real victims. God, I'd like to let off a bomb in every travel agency in the country.'

I held my ribs, no longer thinking of whether I could walk as far as the King's Road. Kay Churchill was launched into a well-rehearsed rant, counting off the chipped beads in her catechism of obsessions. According to Henry Kendall, the tape found in the Heathrow air vent had contained a similar tirade. I remembered the amateur video of Laura lying among the glass and suitcases, and listened to Kay addressing her real audience, the weary magistrates who would finally consign her to a cell in Holloway. It was hard to believe that this intriguing but erratic woman had the self-control to plant a bomb. But had she heard on the protest grapevine of the carousel attack, and fed the Heathrow tragedy into her inflamed world-view?

'David?' She sat beside me, a motherly hand on my forehead. 'I enjoyed our chat. I'm sure we see things the same way. We need more recruits, especially someone at the Adler. When you're better we'll talk about it. We're moving into a more serious phase.'

'Violence isn't for me, Kay.'

'Please, I don't want violence.' From her lips a soft scent breathed over me. 'Not yet. But the time may come sooner than people think.'

I looked up at her wary but determined face, at her uneven teeth and steady eyes. I guessed that for years she had been detaching herself from the real world, and in her mind rode a ghost train through a fairground she had built herself.

'There was a bomb at Heathrow,' I reminded her. 'Two months ago. People were killed.'

'That was dreadful.' She gripped my hands in sympathy.

'Meaningless, though. People who use violence have to be responsible. It's such a special key. Everyone dreams about violence, and when so many people dream the same dream it means something terrible is on the way . . .'

A MOTORCYCLE'S throat-clearing rumble disturbed the road, drumming against the windows. After a coda of obligatory throttle work, a Harley-Davidson approached the kerb and stopped beside Kay's Polo. The rider, in full biker's gear, switched off the engine and sat back to savour the last tang of the exhaust. Behind him on the pillion was a small Chinese woman in a Puffa jacket, helmet hiding her face. I had seen them both at the magistrates' court, but now they seemed less demure.

They sat together, black astronauts of the road, in no hurry to dismount, preparing themselves for re-entry into the non-biker world. Kay waved to them from the window, but neither acknowledged her, immersed in the arcane formalities of unbuckling the clips and press studs that held their costumes together.

'I need to get home.' With a huge effort I managed to stand, propped upright by the ballast of alcohol. 'The local vicar? He was at Hammersmith Grove this morning. I need a doctor, not the last rites.'

'I'm not sure Stephen would pronounce them. He's grounded himself.'

'Grounded? He's a pilot?'

'As it happens, he was. Though that isn't what I meant. He was a flying vicar in the Philippines, island-hopping with the word of God. Then he crash-landed on the wrong island.'

'He can't fly?'

'Spiritually. Like you, he's unsure about everything.'

'And the Chinese girl?'

'Joan Chang. She's his navigator, steering him through the dark wood of the world.'

———

I LISTENED to the sound of heavy boots on the stone path. My head was clearing, as the anaesthetic effects of the whisky rapidly faded. Somewhere inside my chest a Rottweiler had woken from its sleep and was eyeing the world.

'David, try to rest. Doctor's coming . . .'

Smiling at me in the kindest way, Kay took my hands and steered me towards the settee. Behind the living-room door was a poster of *The Third Man*, a still showing Alida Valli, a haunted European beauty who expressed all the melancholy of post-war Europe. But the poster reminded me of another Carol Reed film, about a wounded gunman on the run, manipulated and betrayed by the strangers with whom he sought refuge.

Trying to steady myself as Kay went to the door, I realized that I was a prisoner in this modest house, trapped among the dreams of melodramas I had seen years earlier with Laura at the National Film Theatre. I could hear leather jackets unzipped in the hall, velcro strips torn back, and voices that talked of police heavy-handedness, an unnamed doctor and then, very distinctly, Heathrow. The doorbell rang again as I tried to calm the Rottweiler inside my chest and slumped to my knees on the dusty carpet.

8

THE SLEEPWALKERS

WOMEN MOVED gently around me, easing off my shoes and loosening my belt. The Chinese girl leaned over the settee and unbuttoned my shirt. A faint but expensive scent floated between us, the tang of an unusual toothpaste, hints of the first-class lavatories on long-haul Cathay Pacific flights, a dream of sable coats and Hong Kong boarding lounges.

Then a harsher odour intervened, the coarse petroleum reek of lubricating oil. The biker-clergyman, Stephen Dexter, lifted my head onto a corded cushion handed to him by Kay. His heavy thumbs touched my forehead, the clasp of a priest summoning a soul into the light.

There was another figure in the room, a slim man in a black suit whose face I never saw. I guessed this was the doctor, Richard Gould, whom Kay had called. He sat behind me, listening to my lungs through his stethoscope. When he gave me an injection I noticed his bloodless hands and chipped nails, moving in the furtive manner of a Philippine faith-healer.

Waiting for the painkiller to take effect, he rested a hand on my shoulder, and I sensed a fleshless body anchored to me like an incubus, the drained physique of a doctor in his thirties, some exhausted houseman roused by Kay from his afternoon sleep.

A less agreeable odour than engine oil or Cathay Pacific tooth-paste hung around the stained sleeves of his suit, a hint of the unwashed bodies of Down's children.

Seeing that I was almost asleep, he finished with me and withdrew to the kitchen. The others deferred to him as he spoke, but I caught only my own surname. A refrigerator door closed and feet moved down the hall to the front steps. Chairs scraped around the kitchen table, and there were the sounds of the television news as I fell into a blurred half-sleep, the report of a fire in the bookshop at the British Museum.

WHEN I WOKE, Joan Chang was sitting on the chair beside me, smiling amiably under her bangs. The news broadcast was still playing in the kitchen, and I guessed that I had only been asleep for a few minutes. But I felt surprisingly better, and the pain in my chest and diaphragm was a faint echo of itself. I remembered the clear reference to Heathrow I had overheard before falling asleep, but decided not to follow this up for the time being.

'Mr Markham? You've come back to us.' Joan nodded with relief, as if expecting someone else to emerge from my sleep. 'Kay was really worried.'

'God, I'm breathing again. That pain . . .'

'Richard gave you a shot.' She wiped something from my chin. 'Rest for half an hour and then go home. See your doctor tomor-row. No ribs broken, but maybe your spleen is bruised. Those police boots, I guess.'

'Green wellingtons—much more dangerous.'

'The cat lovers? Kay told me.' She winced in sympathy as I sat up and gripped her small hands. 'It looks like they really hurt you.'

'One species is sacred—cats.' I glanced around the room, which seemed smaller and more domestic. Even the scowling samurai was less threatening. 'Your doctor friend has a special touch.'

'Richard Gould. He's a great doctor, especially with children.

Kay's driving him back to his flat.' She lowered her voice, smiling slyly. 'He doesn't like the Adler Institute. In fact, he said everyone there should be hanged. I think he made an exception for you.'

'Thanks for warning me.'

'I always tell the truth.' She beamed winsomely. 'It's a new way of lying. If you tell the truth people don't know whether to believe you. It helps me in my work.'

'Where? The Foreign Office? The Bank of England?'

'I'm a fund-raiser for the Royal Academy. It's an easy job. All those CEOs think art is good for their souls.'

'Not so?'

'It rots their brains. Tate Modern, the Royal Academy, the Hayward . . . they're Walt Disney for the middle classes.'

'But you swallow your doubts?'

'I'm going to resign. The work here is more important. We have to set people free from all this culture and education. Richard says they're just ways of trapping the middle class and making them docile.'

'So it's a war of liberation? I'd like to meet Dr Gould.'

'You will, David.' Stephen Dexter entered the room, beer can in hand. 'We need new recruits, even a psychologist . . .'

THE CLERGYMAN had changed out of his leathers, and wore jeans and a Timberland shirt, at first sight the very picture of a fashionable Chelsea vicar with a passion for line dancing, weekend flying, and his parishioners' wives. He was a tall, thin-cheeked man in his late thirties, with a professionally steady gaze and a strong head that was almost handsome in the right lighting. Hundreds of hours in an open cockpit had seared his face, and a horizontal scar marked his forehead, perhaps a memento of some unexpectedly short runway in the Philippines.

But the scar was a little too fresh, and I suspected that he kept it deliberately inflamed. When he smiled at me I noticed that one of his canines was missing, a gap he made no attempt to hide, as if advertising an innate flaw in his own make-up. I remembered Kay hinting that he had lost his faith, but this was almost an obligation in the contemporary priesthood. He placed his hand on Joan Chang's shoulder, a schoolmaster with a favourite pupil. His affection was clear, but somehow lacked confidence, part of a larger failure of nerve.

'Let's have a look.' Sipping his beer, like an actor with a stage prop, he stood by the settee. 'Kay says the cat lovers gave you a kicking. You'll feel better by tomorrow. We need you with us, David.'

'I'll do what I can.' Unsure what I was committing myself to, I added: 'If I ever walk again.'

'Walk? You'll run.' Dexter moved his chair, so that the desk light shone into his face. He was playing both interrogator and suspect, testing himself in either role. 'I watched you in court this morning. The magistrates were faced with something they hate above anything else—a responsible citizen ready to sacrifice himself for his principles.'

'I hope I am. Aren't we all?'

'Alas, no. Protest is one thing, action another. That's why we need you on the project.'

'I'm with you. What exactly is the project? Picketing travel agencies? Banning tourism?'

'Much more than that. We aren't defined by Kay's obsessions.' Aware that this might sound harsh, he took Joan's hand. Sitting forward, he massaged his cheeks, trying to bring colour into the gaunt bones. 'Look at the world around you, David. What do you see? An endless theme park, with everything turned into entertainment. Science, politics, education—they're so many fairground rides. Sadly, people are happy to buy their tickets and climb aboard.'

'It's comfortable, Stephen.' Joan traced a Chinese character on the back of his hand, a familiar symbol at which the clergyman smiled. 'There's no effort involved, no surprise.'

'Human beings aren't meant to be comfortable. We need tension, stress, uncertainty.' Dexter gestured at the film posters. 'The kind of challenge that comes from flying a Tiger Moth through zero visibility, or talking a suicide bomber out of a school bus.'

Joan frowned at this, her eyes losing their focus. 'Stephen, you tried that in Mindanao. You nearly got killed.'

'I know. I lost my nerve.' Dexter raised his head and stared bleakly at the grimacing samurai. 'When it came to it, I didn't . . .'

'You didn't have the balls?' Joan shook his shoulder, irritated by him. 'So what? Nobody does. Any idiot can get killed.'

'I had the balls . . .' Dexter calmed her with his quirky smile. 'What I didn't have was hope, or trust. I was relying on myself. For me, those children were already dead. I should have remembered who I was trying to be. Then I would have climbed on the bus and been with them when the end came.'

'At least you're here.' I waited for Dexter to reflate himself, jaw flexing as it re-engaged with his scarred face. 'The travel agency you tried to attack. I take it there's a larger target—Chelsea Marina?'

'Far larger.' Relaxed again, Dexter raised his hands. 'One of the biggest of all. The 20th Century.'

'I thought it was over.'

'It lingers on. It shapes everything we do, the way we think. There's scarcely a good thing you can say for it. Genocidal wars, half the world destitute, the other half sleepwalking through its own brain-death. We bought its trashy dreams and now we can't wake up. All these hypermarkets and gated communities. Once the doors close you can never get out. You know all this, David. It keeps you in corporate clients.'

'Right. But there's one problem about this trash society. The middle classes like it.'

'Of course they do,' Joan chipped in. 'They're enslaved by it. They're the new proletariat, like factory workers a hundred years ago.'

'So how do we free them? Bomb a few theme parks?'

'Bombs?' Dexter raised a hand to interrupt Joan. 'How exactly?'

'Violent action. A direct attack.'

'No.' The clergyman stared at the stained carpet. 'No bombs, I think . . .'

Silence had fallen across the room, and I could hear the refrigerator in the kitchen working away, a metallic groaning at the ice face. Dexter released Joan's hand, and turned to switch off the desk light, his performance over. Something had subdued him, and he fingered the scar on his forehead, trying to rub it away and at the same time make it more prominent, an oblique caution to himself. His Chinese girlfriend was watching him with a mixture of irritation and concern, aware that he had led himself onto dangerous ground that could never bear his weight. I wondered if he had allowed the Philippine military to use him in their aerial attacks on the guerrilla forces. Sitting beside me in the shabby room, he had a certain bleak dignity, but I almost suspected that he was an imposter.

I STOOD UNSTEADILY by the window as they took their seats astride the Harley-Davidson. Kay had returned in her Polo and waved them goodbye from the gate. In their black helmets, sitting on this fat American machine, they seemed worldly in the extreme, the fashionably agnostic priest and his hyper-observant girlfriend, outriders challenging the placid streets around them.

In fact, they were completely detached from reality, with their naive talk of overturning an entire century. In pursuit of a new millennium, they had torn down a travel poster in a shopping mall, and society had assessed the cost to itself at £27.

Despite my injuries, I felt nearer to my goal. Most of the protesters I had met, like Angela at the Olympia cat show, were sane and self-disciplined, but there was a wilder fringe of animal rights fanatics who planted bombs under scientists' cars and were prepared to kill. Had one of these madmen, focused on tourism and the Third World, strayed across the path of Kay, Stephen Dexter and Joan Chang? I needed to unpack their obsessions, and unroll them in the daylight like a cheap carpet.

I SAT BESIDE Kay as she drove me to a taxi rank in the King's Road. She seemed content with the day's activities, and I was grateful for her kindness to a fellow demonstrator. I admired her for the way she openly wore her insecurities like a collection of favourite costume jewellery.

As we were leaving Chelsea Marina a group of residents had gathered by the estate offices. Strong-willed and confident, they shouted down the young manager who tried to address them. Their voices, honed at a hundred school open days and business conferences, drowned the manager's efforts to make himself heard.

'What is it?' I asked Kay, as she edged the car through the throng. 'It looks serious.'

'It is serious.'

'Some paedophile on the prowl?'

'Parking charges.' Kay stared sternly at the luckless manager, who had taken refuge behind his glass door. 'Believe me, the next revolution is going to be about parking.'

At the time, I thought she was joking.

9

THE UPHOLSTERED
APOCALYPSE

'THEY'RE ALL a little mad,' I told Sally, pointing to the swirl
of excited bubbles in the jacuzzi. 'A strange fringe group. Huge
obsessions floating around a cozy living room. It's useful to see
just how odd apparently sane people can be.'

'So they're harmless cranks?'

'I'm not sure they're harmless. They're in the grip of some
bizarre ideas. Abolish the 20th Century. Ban tourism. Politics,
commerce, education—all corrupt.'

'It's a point of view. They are a bit.'

'Sally . . .' I smiled down at her, lying comfortably in the whirl-
bath with a stack of fashion magazines, the picture of comfort
and security. 'See it in context. This is Kropotkin with pink gins
and wall-to-wall Axminster. These people want to change the
world, use violence if they need to, but they've never had the central heating turned off in their lives.'

'They've got you going, though. You haven't been so fired up
for years.'

'That's true. I wonder why . . . ?' I stared at myself in the
bathroom mirror, hair springing from my forehead, face as
tense as the Reverend Dexter's. I seemed twenty years younger,
the newly graduated man of science with an askew tie knot and

a glowing desire to straighten out the world. 'I might write a paper about the phenomenon. "The Upholstered Apocalypse." The middle classes have moved from charity work and civic responsibility to fantasies of cataclysmic change. Whisky sours and Armageddon . . .'

'At least they cared for you. This doctor, Richard Gould—I looked him up on the net. He helped to invent a new kind of shunt for babies with hydrocephalus.'

'Good for him. I mean it. He never let me see his face—why, I don't know.'

'Perhaps they were having you on.' Sally caught my hand as I prowled the bathroom. 'Let's face it, dear. You're just waiting to be shocked.'

'I've thought about that.' I sat on the edge of the bath, inhaling the heady scents of Sally's body. 'I'd been pushed around by the police, and they knew I was an amateur. Hard-core demonstrators never get knocked to the ground—far too dangerous. They do their thing and skip off before the rough stuff begins. Like Angela, the Kingston housewife at Olympia. Really quick on her feet, and happy to leave me to face the music.'

'This film lecturer helped you. She sounds sweet.'

'Kay Churchill. She was great. Completely scatty, but she saved me outside the court. I was in a bad way.'

I waited for Sally to sympathize, but she lay passively in the bath, playing with the bubbles on her breasts. The X-rays at the Royal Free Hospital had shown no rib fractures, but the cat fanciers' boots had bruised my spleen, as Joan Chang predicted. Collecting me from the hospital, Sally glanced at the plates with a perfunctory nod. She was immersed in her own perpetual recovery, and had no wish to share her monopoly of doubt and discomfort with anyone, even her husband. In her mind, my bruises were self-inflicted, far removed from the meaningless injuries that presided over her life like an insoluble mystery.

'David, towel . . . When are you going back to Chelsea Marina?'

'I'll give them a miss. They're not the kind of people who set off bombs.'

'But they mentioned Heathrow. You overheard them when they thought you were asleep. That was the first thing you said when the cab driver helped you up the steps.'

'They were trying to impress me. Or impress themselves. They feed on conspiracy. This biker priest—he's frightened of violence. Something happened in the Philippines, long before Heathrow.'

'What about Dr Gould? When he was fourteen he was hauled before a juvenile court, charged with an arson attack on a Kilburn department store.'

'Sally, I'm impressed.' I watched her fasten the bath towel under her arms. 'You should be working for the Antiterrorist Squad.'

'It's all on the net. Dr Gould has his own website. He's uploaded his testimony to the juvenile court—he's obviously proud of it.'

'Being arrested by the police is part of the thrill. The teacher catches you out, and you feel loved.'

'The department store in Kilburn was built by Gould's father.' Sally examined her teeth in the mirror. 'He was a commercial architect and builder. When he died the firm was bought up by McAlpine's.'

'Sally . . . take it easy.'

She stood with her back to the mirror, body and hair swathed in white towels, staring at me through the drifting steam like a priestess at an archaic marine shrine. Looking into her eyes, I sensed that I could see my whole future.

'David, listen to me.'

'For God's sake . . .' I opened the window, letting the steam float away. 'Sally, you're obsessed by this.'

'Yes, I am.' She held my shoulders and made me sit on the edge of the bidet. 'We have to find the truth about the Heathrow bomb. Or Laura's death is going to hang over you for ever. You might as well have her mummy sitting in your chair at the office.'

'I agree. I'm trying to pick up the scent.'

'Good. Don't give up. I want to lock the past away and turn the key.'

Sally broke off when her mobile rang. She greeted a friend and strolled into the bedroom, listening intently. She cupped the phone and said to me: 'David, there's a picture of you in the *Kensington News.*' She sat on the bed and huddled happily over a pillow. 'He was fined. A hundred pounds. Yes, I'm married to a criminal . . .'

I WAS GLAD to see Sally enjoying my new-found fame. I had taken a week's sick leave from the Institute, but Henry Kendall rang to confide that Professor Arnold was unhappy with my conviction. Corporate clients might prefer not to be advised by a psychologist with a criminal record. Clearly my status had slipped, along with my claims on the director's chair.

Luckily there was a long tradition of maverick psychologists with a taste for oddball behaviour. My mother had been a psychoanalyst in the 1960s, a friend of R.D. Laing and a familiar figure on CND marches, joining Bertrand Russell at anti-nuclear sit-ins and being glamorously dragged away by the police. Latenight discussion programmes on television were as much her natural home as the consulting room.

As a child I watched her on my grandmother's TV set, deeply impressed by the caftans, waist-length black hair and fiercely articulate passion. Free love and legalized drugs meant little to me, though I guessed they were in some way connected to the friendly but unfamiliar men who appeared on her weekend visits, and to the home-made cigarettes she taught me to roll for her and which she smoked despite the protests of my wearily tolerant grandmother.

For all her acclaim, her magazine profiles and pronouncements on Piaget and Melanie Klein, her knowledge of motherhood was almost entirely theoretical. Until the age of three, I was brought up by a series of au pairs, recruited from the waiting room of her once-a-week free clinic—moody escapees from provincial French universities, neurotic American graduates unwilling to grasp the concept of childhood, Japanese deep-therapy freaks who locked me into my bedroom and insisted that I slept for twenty-four hours a day. Eventually I was rescued by my grandmother and her second husband, a retired judge. It was some years before I noticed that the other boys at school enjoyed a social phenomenon known as fathers.

By the time I joined University College London my mother's hippy phase was long over, and she had become a quiet and serious-minded analyst at the Tavistock Clinic. I hoped that her maternal instinct, suppressed through most of my childhood, might find a late flowering. But we never became more than friends, and she failed to attend my graduation ceremony.

'She sounds a bitch,' Laura had commiserated, inviting me to join her family at the lunch after the ceremony. I replied truthfully: 'She's a free spirit. She loved me deeply—for ten minutes. Then it was over.'

At the Adler, dealing with dysfunctional families, I found that all too many parents were indifferent to their children. Popular myth assumed that child–parent relationships were rich and fulfilling, but in some families they were absent altogether. Laura stepped into a waiting vacuum; with her aggressive emotions, fiercely for or against me, she was the opposite of my mother. After my gentle grandmother, treating the smallest tantrum with the wisdom of Solomon, Laura had been a typhoon of cleansing passion.

Now my mother was an elderly patient in a Highgate hospice, dying of inoperable ovarian cancer. Her huge and still swelling abdomen made her look pregnant, a seventy-year-old woman still unaware that she was with child. Sitting beside the bed of this barely responsive being, I realized rather sadly that I was no longer very interested in her.

———

'DAVID . . .' Sally switched off her phone. 'You're a celebrity. Dinner invitations are pouring in . . .'

'Heaven forbid. I'll have to think up a party turn.'

'Don't mock yourself—you do that too often.' Sally stared at me with real respect. 'You've fought with police. How many people can say that?'

'How many want to? They're on our side.'

'Almost. What about Heathrow? It's the one real lead we've had. David, you've got to change your mind.'

'All right, then. I'll go back to Chelsea Marina and ask around. This clergyman, and the people close to Kay Churchill. I'll see if I can contact Dr Gould.'

'Good. We need to know what happened to Laura. A lot hangs on it, David . . .'

There was more than a faint threat in her voice. She still wore the bath towel around her body, and was waiting for me to leave the room before tossing it onto the bed, a sure sign of a slight estrangement between us. She had decided that Laura's pointless death carried some kind of defiant message that would at last bring closure to my first marriage.

But already I knew that my quest for Laura's murderer was really about my second marriage. Avoiding Sally's stare, I remembered the furious knotting of her eyebrows when she took her first unaided steps in the orthopaedic ward at St Mary's. Damp with sweat, her nightdress clung to her skin, and I could see the muscles coming alive in her thighs, diagrams of an ambivalent will to walk. We had exchanged confidences during my visits, friendly teasing with only the slightest hint of flirtation. But at that moment, as she hobbled towards me on her sticks, wrists white with pain and anger at herself, I had known that we would become lovers.

As always, a perverse calculus refreshed and redefined the world.

10

APPOINTMENT WITH
A REVOLUTION

LIKE EVERY obedient professional, I arrived punctually for my appointment with a revolution. At noon three Saturdays later, bruises faded and spleen settled, I parked my Range Rover in a side street off the King's Road. I had called Kay Churchill soon after breakfast, watched by a mildly curious Sally. Against a background of angry middle-class voices, Kay answered in a shriek, and said she would meet me by the entrance to Chelsea Marina.

'We'll go on a field trip. You'll be the David Attenborough of the suburbs . . .'

Pleased that she remembered me, I walked along the King's Road and turned left into a small riot. A police car was drawn up by the gatehouse, light flashing and radio squawking to itself. A crowd of more than a hundred residents were packed around the estate office. Most were women in weekend wear, freed from the tailored suits they wore in their surgeries and executive corridors. Their children were with them, faces lit by the sight of their mothers angry with someone other than themselves. A few cautious husbands hung around the fringes, warily joining in the din.

Two policemen pushed through the crowd, trying to calm the

protesters, and called to the speaker who was haranguing her neighbours. But their voices were lost in the boos and jeers, and a five-year-old boy sitting on his father's shoulders tried to knock the peaked cap from a constable's head.

Ash-grey hair in furious disarray, the bones in her face displayed at their television best, cleavage deep enough to daunt every male gaze within a mile radius, Kay Churchill was in her element. She stood on a swivel chair taken from the estate office, thighs shown off as she teetered deliberately, heedless of anything but her fierce commitment. It was a pleasure to see her in full spate. The students watching her lectures on Godard and the New Wave had probably scripted their pornographic films long before she came up with the project.

'What's happening?' I asked a young woman beside me, pushchair and child forgotten at her feet. 'Parking meters? Speed humps?'

'Maintenance charges. They're going sky high.' She nodded approvingly. 'Kay's locked the manager in his office. The poor man had to call the police.'

An anxious male face peered through the glass door. He was clearly appalled by the hostile women jeering at him, a fearsome sight that struck at all the certainties of estate management. Kay produced a set of keys, which she waved at him and then dangled in front of the policemen. When they moved in, threatening to arrest her, she flung the keys over their heads. Hands on hips, she laughed good-naturedly as they were snatched from the air and tossed around the crowd.

I joined in the applause and turned to leave, accepting that Kay would be too busy with her pocket revolution to bother with me. A second police car had arrived, and a harder-faced sergeant in the passenger seat was speaking into his radio. Within minutes this middle-class playgroup would be sent back to its toy cupboard.

'Mr Markham! Wait . . . !'

A slim woman wearing a white linen jacket, severe hair swept back from a high forehead, stopped me before I reached the entrance. Somehow she managed to smile and scowl at the same time, and reminded me of the official guides at scientific conferences in Eastern Europe. She looked me up and down, unconvinced by my tweedy appearance.

'Mr Markham? I'm Vera Blackburn, a friend of Kay's. She said you were joining us.'

'I'm not sure.' I watched the crowd hooting the police. The sergeant had stepped from his car and was coldly surveying the scene, like an abattoir director at a foot-and-mouth cull. 'This isn't my thing . . .'

'Too childish?' She stopped me from moving on, a firm hand on my lapel. She was thin but strong, with a muscular body honed on exercise machines. Her lips moved, as if she were forever biting back a cutting remark. 'Or too bourgeois?'

'Something like that.' I pointed to the King's Road. 'I have my own problems with parking meters . . .'

'It looks childish, and probably is.' She stared at her fellow residents with half-closed eyes. 'We really need your input, Mr Markham. Things are getting complicated.'

'Are they? I'm not sure I can help.'

I turned from her as more police entered the estate, larger men like the constables at Olympia. One of them stared at me, as if he recognized my face from an earlier demo.

'Mr Markham, time to go. Unless you want to be beaten up again. We'll wait for Kay at my flat.'

Vera took my arm and steered me through the crowd, her bony hand as hard as a tiller. Kay Churchill stepped from her swivel chair into the shelter of her admirers. The two constables by the estate office had custody of the keys, and released the unhappy manager hiding behind his glass door. Sensibly, the demonstrators were dispersing.

We walked along Beaufort Avenue to the centre of the estate.

The herb gardens, the cheerful children's rooms filled with sensible toys, the sounds of teenagers at violin practice, were given an odd spin by the notion of an imminent revolt. Most revolutionaries in the last century had aspired to exactly this level of affluence and leisure, and it occurred to me that I was seeing the emergence of a higher kind of boredom.

We reached Cadogan Circle, where an apartment block stood beside the roundabout. Vera strode ahead of me in a brisk bobbing walk, like a whore with a soon-to-be-fleeced client, or a moody prefect at a girls' school on some sly mission of her own. Waving her swipe card at a watching sparrow, she led the way into the foyer.

'Kay'll be along when she's changed. All that indignation tends to make you steam . . .'

'Half an hour—then I have to leave, revolution or no revolution.'

'No problem. We'll postpone it for you.' She treated me to a quick grin. 'Think of this as your Finland Station, Mr Markham.'

We rode a small lift to the third floor. From her shoulder bag she took out a set of keys, and worked the triple locks of her front door like the entrance to a crypt. Her flat was sparsely furnished, with armless black chairs, a glass-topped writing desk that resembled an autopsy table, and low-wattage lamps that barely lit the gloom. This was a nightclub at noon. There were no books, and I sensed that this hard-minded young woman came here to erase the world. A chromium-framed photograph hung above the mantelpiece, a blow-up of herself in full Helmut Newton mode, all emotion eliminated from her face. But the room was a shrine to a desperate narcissism.

She walked to the window and rolled up the blind onto a clear view of Beaufort Avenue. The protest had broken up, and families were strolling back to their houses.

'It's over. At least we gave the manager something to think about.'

'Locking him in his office?'

'Sixth-formish? I know. But people have to work with the conventions they're used to. Feasts in the dorm, fags behind the cricket pavilion, debaggings . . .'

'You make it sound like a new kind of deprivation.'

'In a way, it is.' Vera sat down in a replica Eames chair that gave her an uninterrupted view of her portrait photograph. Leaving me to stand, she said: 'It may not be obvious, but people at Chelsea Marina are very unsettled. There's something stirring here.'

'Really? It's hard to believe.' I sat on a black leather sofa. 'It all looks very pleased with itself. No sign of rickets, scurvy or leaking roofs.'

'Only on the surface.' Vera glanced at her compact mirror. 'My neighbours are the new poor. These aren't City high-flyers, or surgeons with their own clinics and rich Arab patients flying in from the Gulf. Very few are self-employed. They're middle managers, journalists, lecturers like Kay, architects working for big practices. The poor bloody foot soldiers in the professional army.'

'Prosperous enough?'

'They're not. Salaries have plateaued. There's the threat of early retirement. Once you're forty it's cheaper to hire some bright-eyed graduate clutching her little diploma.'

'So there's a backlash. But why here, at Chelsea Marina? It's a fashionable area, close to the King's Road . . .'

Vera turned to stare at me. 'Are you an estate agent? This place is a dump. Maintenance is almost nil but the charges keep going up. This flat cost me more than my father earned in his lifetime.'

'There's a wonderful view. Aren't you happy here?'

'I've thought about it.' She sniffed her black nail polish. 'Happiness? I like the idea, but it doesn't seem worth the effort. Also . . .'

'It's not intellectually respectable?'

'Exactly.' She nodded approvingly. 'We need some principles.

Anyway, one of the lifts has been out of order for months. For two hours a day the taps don't run. You have to plan when you need a shit.'

'Talk to the management company. Your lease should guarantee prompt repairs.'

'We do. They don't want to listen. They're in cahoots with a property developer who'd like us all out of here. They want to run the place down, buy us out and raze it to the ground. Then they'll bring in Foster and Richard Rogers to design huge blocks of luxury flats.'

'As long as you stay you're safe. Why worry about what may never happen?'

'It is happening. We're being squeezed, and there's nothing subtle about a hand grabbing your balls. The council have just painted double yellow lines everywhere.'

'Can they do that?'

'They can do anything. These are public streets. So they've graciously provided us with meters. Kay pays to park outside her own house.'

'Why not move?'

'We can't.' Her temper rising, Vera raised her fists and stared for sympathy at the ceiling. 'For God's sake, we've sunk everything into Chelsea Marina. We're all locked into huge mortgages. People have sky-high school fees, and the banks breathing down their necks. Besides, where do we move to? Darkest Surrey? Some two-hour commute to Reading or Guildford?'

'Heaven forbid. So you're trapped?'

'Right. Like the old working class in their back-to-backs. Knowledge-based professions are just another extractive industry. When the seams run out we're left high and dry with a lot of out-of-date software. Believe me, I know why the miners went on strike.'

'I'm impressed.' With a straight face, I said: 'Chelsea Marina, shoulder to shoulder with the old working class . . .'

'It isn't a bloody joke.' Vera stared darkly at me, the bones in her forehead pressing through her pale skin. 'We're getting restless. The middle classes are meant to be the great social anchor, all that duty and responsibility. But the cables are dragging. Professional qualifications are worth nothing—an arts degree is like a diploma in origami. As for security, it's nonexistent. Some computer at the Treasury decides interest rates should go up a point and I owe the bank manager another year's hard work.'

'I'm sorry.' Concerned for her, I watched her fingers fretting with her compact, brows knitted fiercely. Though she made me uneasy with her quiet anger, I found myself almost liking her. 'And where is this work? The TUC? Labour Party Headquarters?'

'I'm . . . a kind of consultant.' She waved airily, but her face was blank. 'I used to be at the Ministry of Defence—senior scientific officer. I analysed depleted uranium residues scraped from Kosovan hillsides.'

'Interesting work. And important.'

'Not interesting, and not important. Now, I have another job. Far more valuable.'

'And that is?'

'I'm Richard Gould's bomb-maker.'

I waited for her to go on, aware that she was both teasing me and trying to tell me something. But she sat silently, eyebrows lifting as she savoured a favourite phrase. I said: 'Dangerous, for you as well as everyone else. What sort of bombs do you make?'

'Smoke bombs, percussion devices, slow-release incendiaries. No one gets hurt.'

'Good. Nothing like the bomb at Heathrow?'

'Heathrow?' Surprised, she remembered to close her mouth, and then said quickly: 'Definitely not. That was designed to kill. Heaven knows why. Richard says that people who find the world meaningless find meaning in pointless violence.'

'Richard? Dr Richard Gould?'

'You'll meet him again, when he's ready. He's the leader of our middle-class rebellion. His mind is amazingly clear, like those brain-damaged children he looks after. In a way, he's one of them.'

She smiled to herself, as if thinking about a lover, but I could see the clear sweat that had formed on her upper lip, glistening like the ghost of a second presence, a secret self. She had been unsettled by my mention of the Heathrow atrocity.

'These bombs,' I asked. 'What are the targets?'

'It's early days. Shopping malls, cineplexes, DIY centres. All that C20 trash. The regurgitated vomit people call the consumer society.' Almost pedantically, she added: 'They're not really bombs—they're acoustic provocations. Like the thunderflashes your friends let off at Olympia. Though once I did make a real bomb. Years ago . . .'

'What happened?'

'It killed someone. The intended target.'

'For the Ministry of Defence? SAS? Special Branch?'

'Defence, in a way. I was defending my father. After my mother died he met this awful woman. He hated her, but he was under her thumb. A real alcoholic, who wanted me to just fade away. I was twelve, but I was clever.'

'You put together a home-made bomb?'

'Using household ingredients, off the supermarket shelves. She and my father went to the pub on Sunday lunchtimes; she'd come back thick with drink, huge bladder ready to burst. While they were out I took the cover off the lavatory cistern, jammed the float and flushed away the water. Then I filled the cistern with household bleach, released the float and put back the cover. Next, I poured caustic soda crystals into the toilet bowl, and stirred away until there was a concentrated solution. Then I went downstairs and waited.'

'The bomb was ready?'

'All set to go off. They came back from the pub, and she headed straight for the toilet. Locked the door and emptied her bladder. Then she pressed the flush handle.'

'And that triggered the bomb?'

'Sodium hydroxide and sodium hypochlorite form an explosive mix, especially when violently stirred together.' Vera smiled to herself, a steely little girl again. 'The reaction gives off huge quantities of chlorine gas. Lethal stuff for an alcoholic with a weakened heart. I went and put on my party dress. My father was asleep in front of the telly. It was two hours before he broke down the door.'

'She was dead?'

'Stone cold. By then all the gas had dispersed and the cistern had filled with water. My modest bomb had flushed itself away. Verdict: natural causes.'

'An impressive debut. It led you to . . . ?'

'A degree in chemistry, and the Ministry of Defence.' Vera's eyes narrowed at me. 'A sensible career choice, I think you'll agree.'

A satisfied smile played around her lips. The film of sweat had vanished, and I assumed that she had invented the story to give herself time to recover. But I realized that this lethal tale might just be true. The talk of bomb-making had been dangled in front of me, part of an extended tease that had begun as I lay half-drugged on Kay Churchill's settee. Another door had opened into a side corridor that might lead towards Terminal 2 at Heathrow.

The entryphone buzzed twice, and after a pause a third time. Vera stood up, spoke into the receiver and buttoned her jacket.

'David, are you coming? Kay's downstairs. We're going on a field trip . . .'

11

THE HEART OF DARKNESS

'DAVID, THINK OF Joseph Conrad and Mr Kurtz,' Kay told me when we crossed Richmond Bridge. 'You're entering an area of almost total deprivation.'

'Twickenham? The heart of darkness?'

'You'll be shocked.'

'Tennis clubs, bank managers, the Mecca of rugby?'

'Twickenham. A zone of intense spiritual poverty.'

'Right ... hard to believe.' As Kay drove her Polo at a cautious speed, both hands on the wheel, I pointed to the pavements. They were crowded with prosperous natives emerging from the delis and patisseries, or gazing through the windows of busy estate agents. 'No beggars rattling their tins, no malnutrition.'

'Physically, perhaps.' Kay nodded confidently. 'It's in their minds, in their customs and values. You agree, Vera?'

'Absolutely.' Vera Blackburn sat behind me, a large sports bag clasped in one hand. She was carefully examining her teeth, part of the continuous inspection of her body that took up most of her conscious moments. She glanced briefly at the cheerful forsythia and polished cars. 'Spiritually, it's a vast Potemkin Village ...'

We turned off the high street and entered a residential area of Twickenham, tree-lined roads of large detached houses, gar-

dens deep enough to hold a tennis court or a wedding marquee.
I noticed a Bentley in a drive, white-wall tyres set in the freshly
washed gravel.

'We could stop here,' I suggested. 'There's a distinct Third-
World feel in the air.'

'David, this isn't a joke.' Eyebrows knitted, Kay glanced at me
wearily. 'Just once, take off the blinkers . . .'

The morning's confrontation outside the estate office had given
her the appetite for another fight. I remembered how she had
dominated the magistrates' court in Hammersmith, using her
wayward personality like a skilled actress. I admired her spirit,
and the strong mind that had closed itself tightly around a single
obsession. Neither I nor the students in her film classes ever stood
a chance. At the same time, I thought of the childish drawings
pinned beside the Bresson and Kurosawa posters, and the photograph of her daughter, now on the other side of the world. Only
the deepest obsession could assuage that kind of sadness.

Vera Blackburn sat behind us, staring disapprovingly at the
drifting leaves. She reminded me of an experienced lady's companion, knowing her place and always ready to agree. But I
sensed that she had an agenda of her own, and would defer to
Kay only as long as it suited her. Whenever I glanced back at
her she closed her knees, a gesture that was both a long-distance
warning and an oblique come-on.

'David . . .' Kay pointed through the windscreen at the lines
of large, half-timbered houses. 'Take a good look. Twickenham
is the Maginot Line of the English class system. If we can break
through here everything will fall.'

'So class systems are the target. Aren't they universal—America, Russia . . . ?'

'Of course. But only here is the class system a means of political control. Its real job isn't to suppress the proles, but to keep the
middle classes down, make sure they're docile and subservient.'

'And Twickenham is one way of doing that?'

'Absolutely. The people here are gripped by a powerful illusion, the whole middle-class dream. It's all they live for—liberal educations, civic responsibility, respect for the law. They may think they're free, but they're trapped and impoverished.'

'Like the poor in a Glasgow tenement?'

'Exactly.' Kay nodded approvingly at me, and reached out to pat my wrist. 'Live here and you're surprisingly constrained. This isn't the good life, full of possibility. You soon come up against the barriers set out by the system. Try getting drunk at a school speech day, or making a mildly racist joke at a charity dinner. Try letting your lawn grow and not painting your house for a few years. Try living with a teenage girl or having sex with your stepson. Try saying you believe in God and the Holy Trinity, or giving a free room to a refugee family from black Africa. Try taking a holiday in Benidorm, or driving a brand-new Cadillac with zebra upholstery. Try bad taste.'

'And what's the alternative? What happens after the Maginot Line collapses?'

'We'll have to see.'

'We burn all the books and the croquet mallets and the charity donations? What takes their place?'

'We'll decide when the time comes. Now, here we are. This should do nicely.'

KAY TURNED into an avenue of three-storey houses with large gardens, labradors and Land Cruisers. The clump of tennis balls sounded, the fierce grunts of mothers determined to beat their fifteen-year-old daughters. Horses clip-clopped past us when we stopped by the kerb, ridden by teenagers secure in their middle-class sanctuary. As it happened, this was my grandmother's world, identical to the Guildford suburb where I spent my childhood. The disdain of metropolitan intellectuals was heaped on these bricky piles, but the lifestyle had been copied through-out the world. Not all Kay's indignation would disturb a single delphinium.

She stepped out, taking a clipboard from her briefcase. Leaving Vera to guard the car, she pinned a polling company's badge to her jacket. She fixed another, with a photograph of the Reverend Dexter, to my lapel.

'Right. Try to pass for Stephen. You're close enough. Haunted, a little lost. And not too pious . . .'

'That should be easy.'

We approached the first house, a comfortable Tudor-style mansion, and stepped over a child's bicycle that blocked the front door. A Mercedes estate car with a doctor's sticker was parked outside the garage.

A friendly woman in her forties greeted us, drying her hands on a kitchen towel. Kay beamed over her clipboard and introduced us.

'Could we have a moment of your time? We're carrying out a survey into social habits.'

'Fair enough. I'm afraid ours are pretty deplorable. I don't know if we fit in.'

'I'm sure you do. We're particularly interested in high-income families.'

'I'm flattered.' The woman folded her tea towel. 'I'll have to tell my husband. He'll be very surprised.'

Kay smiled tolerantly. 'You clearly have an immaculate home. Everything is so clean and polished. Could you estimate the number of hours a day you spend on housework?'

'None.' The woman pretended to bite her lip. 'We have a live-in housekeeper and a daily help. I'm a GP, far too busy at the health centre to flick a duster around. Sorry, that's not much use.'

'It is . . .' Certain that she had found a convert, Kay leaned forward, lowering her voice. 'Speaking as a doctor, do you think there's an overemphasis on domestic hygiene?'

'Yes and no. People are rather obsessed with germs. Most of them are harmless.' She paused as a teenage boy ambled past, berated by a sister somewhere in the kitchen. 'Look, there's a riot brewing.'

'A last question.' Kay scanned her clipboard, pencil poised. 'How often would you say your lavatories are cleaned?'

'I've no idea. Every day, I hope.'

'Would you consider having them cleaned every three days?'

'Three? Pretty risky around here.'

'Or once a week?'

'No.' The woman glanced at Kay's lapel badge. 'That doesn't sound like good idea.'

'You're sure? A less than snowy white bowl would worry you? How do you feel about the prevalence of toilet taboos among the professional middle class?'

'Toilet taboos? Are you working for a lavatory paper firm?'

'We're mapping social change.' Kay spoke soothingly. 'Personal grooming lies at the heart of people's sense of who they are. Would your family consider washing less often?'

'Less?' The doctor reached for the door handle, shaking her head. 'It's impossible to imagine. Look—'

'And you personally?' Kay pressed. 'Would you bathe less frequently? Natural body odours are an important means of communication, especially within families. You'd have time to relax, play with your children, adopt a freer lifestyle . . .'

THE DOOR CLOSED in our faces. Kay stared at the oak panelling, undaunted. As we walked down the drive, feet sinking in the deep gravel, she ticked the replies on her clipboard.

'That was useful.' She signalled to Vera, who started the Polo and followed us down the street. 'I call that a promising kick-off.'

'Perhaps. I don't think she grasped what you were getting at.'

'She'll think about it, when she tells her son to take a shower and change his socks. Believe me.'

'I do. Is this the first time you've been out here?'

'I've been coming for months.' Kay strode along the pavement, urging me to keep up with her. 'Remember, David, the middle class have to be kept under control. They understand that, and police themselves. Not with guns and gulags, but with social codes. The right way to have sex, treat your wife, flirt at tennis parties or start an affair. There are unspoken rules we all have to learn.'

'And you never bothered?'

'I'm unlearning them. Don't worry, I still shower every day . . .'

A HUNDRED YARDS along the avenue we approached another large house, a Georgian villa with a swimming pool in the rear garden. Light from its surface danced among the leaves of the tall oak that sheltered the drive. A six-year-old girl in a wet swimsuit answered the door, hanging on to the collar of an aire-dale delighted to find us on the step.

A smiling woman in her late thirties came to the door, ready for an evening out in her black satin dress and vampish make-up.

'Hello—you don't look like the babysitter.'

Kay explained our visit. 'We're carrying out a survey into lei-sure habits. How much time people spend on foreign travel, see-ing films, going to parties . . .'

'Not enough.'

'Really?' Kay busied herself with the clipboard. 'How many foreign holidays a year do you take?'

'Five or six. Plus a summer break. My husband's a BA pilot—he's in Cape Town this weekend.'

'So you have cheap flights? Do you feel that air travel is a bit of a con?'

'It's one of the perks.' The woman produced a gin and tonic from behind the door and sipped it reflectively, staring at the photograph of Stephen Dexter on my lapel. 'Wives get restless if husbands have all the fun.'

Kay sagely nodded. 'I meant travel generally. Is it a kind of confidence trick? The same hotels, the same marinas, car-rental firms. You might as well stay home and watch it on television.'

'People like going to airports.' The woman gazed at the sky, as if it had crossed her mind that her husband might make an early return. 'They like the long-term car parks, the check-ins, the duty-frees, showing their passports. They can pretend they're someone else.'

'You don't think it's a kind of brainwashing?'

'I want to be brainwashed.' The woman turned away as the sound of barking came from the pool. 'Must go. They're trying to drown the dog. Have a word with the people next door. He's in a wheelchair . . .'

'NOT SO GOOD,' Kay admitted as we stepped onto the pavement. She tapped the pencil against her teeth. 'Nobody can be that passive.'

'You have a problem,' I told her as we walked on. 'What happens if people like things as they are? Maybe they're happy being conned?'

'The prisoners polish their chains? I won't accept that.'

Followed by Vera and the Polo, we moved along the quiet road, ready to provoke the revolution. But the catalysts that had radicalized Chelsea Marina were missing. There were no redundancies, no impossible debt burdens or negative equity, no double yellow lines. Prosperous suburbia was one of the end-states of history. Once achieved, only plague, flood or nuclear war could threaten its grip. Nonetheless, Kay was undaunted, striding ahead of me down the Maginot emplacements of Arcadia Drive, searching for a trench in which to bury her mines.

AT THE THIRD HOUSE we were greeted by a slim, grey-haired woman with the clear eyes and thin mouth of a senior civil servant. She reminded me of the three worthies who had looked down at me in the magistrates' court. Beyond the hall I could see an elderly man seated in the living room, a whisky at his elbow as he squinted at a crossword.

Kay introduced us, omitting my clerical title. 'A few questions? We're carrying out a lifestyle survey.'

'I'm not sure we have a lifestyle. Or does everyone these days?' The woman listened to her husband's bellow, and called back: 'Lifestyles, dear.'

'Don't want one,' the husband shouted. 'Haven't had one for thirty years.'

'Well, there you are.' The woman's eyes were examining Kay's make-up, her chipped nails and the loose threads on her jacket. 'We don't seem to need a lifestyle.'

Kay pressed on with a game smile. A springer spaniel joined us and began sniffing her knees. 'Do you think there's too much emphasis on leisure these days? Foreign travel, dinner parties . . . ?'

'Yes, I do. There are far too many dinner parties. I don't know what people find to talk about.' Over her shoulder she replied to her husband: 'Dinner parties, dear.'

'Can't stand them. Judith?'

'That's what I said.'

'What?'

Kay tapped her clipboard. 'So would you favour legislation banning dinner parties?'

'Difficult to enact, and impossible to enforce. It's such a strange idea.'

'Tennis club dances?' Kay asked. 'Wife swapping? Should they be banned? Or are they the opiate that keeps the middle classes under control?'

'Judith?'

'Wife swapping, dear.' The woman glanced at me with skittish look in her eye. 'No, I'm not against wife swapping.'

Kay scribbled on her clipboard. 'You're a liberal in sexual matters?'

'Yes. I always have been, probably without realizing it. Now . . .'

Kay pushed away the spaniel. 'What's your position on consensual sex?'

'With one's husband? In theory, it's an excellent idea. Tell me, who is sponsoring this survey?'

'And animals?'

'I'm very fond of them, of course.'

'They need our affection?'

'Absolutely.'

'So you'd sign a petition to revoke laws against sexual intercourse with animals?'

'I beg your pardon?'

Kay smiled brightly at the spaniel. 'You could have sex with Bonzo . . .'

WE REACHED the safety of the street and returned to the Polo. Kay tossed away her clipboard and sat in the rear seat with me, taking my hand out of exhaustion. She waved at the house as we cruised past. The spaniel was barking, while husband and wife stood in the open door, staring at the unsettled gravel.

'Too bad,' Kay reflected. 'She doesn't want to fuck Bonzo. Still, the thought may cross her mind.'

'How did it go?' Vera asked. 'No problems?'

'It went well. David?'

'Surprisingly well. You certainly gave them food for thought.'

'That's the idea. Stir things up. Make them realize that they're the victims.' She sat forward and tapped Vera's shoulder. 'Stop here. I'll only be a moment.'

She had noticed a home-owner in his front drive, hosing away the weekend mud on his Rolls Royce. Seizing her clipboard, she dived from the car before it halted. I followed her as she straightened her skirt and approached the man, who wore a singlet and had the burly physique of a successful builder.

'Good evening, sir. All that mud on the Roller—looks like a

job for the wife. We're researching a new product for the dis-
criminating motorist.'

'You and the Reverend?' The man read my name-tag. 'You've
changed. All that kneeling must be hard work.'

'Reverend Dexter is a family friend. Tell me, sir, how would
you feel about Spray-on Mud?'

'Spray-on—?'

'Mud. A synthetic liquid mud, conveniently packed in an aerosol can.' Kay adopted the singsong voice of a department store
demonstrator. 'An effective way of impressing people in the office
car park on Monday mornings. A quick spray on the wheels and
your colleagues will think of rose pergolas and thatched cottages.'

'My colleagues will think I'm ready for the funny farm.' The
man turned back to his hose. 'Daft. Hasn't a prayer's chance.
You'll need more than the Reverend . . .'

'KAY, FOR HEAVEN'S SAKE . . .' I held her arm and bundled
her back to the car. As I pushed her into the rear seat she was
shaking with exhaustion and excitement. When we set off she
lay back with her head on my shoulder, roaring with laughter.

'"Spray-on Mud." Sorry, David, I couldn't resist that. Think
about it, though. We could make a million—it's the product for
our age . . .'

12

THE VIDEO STORE

WE DEBRIEFED ourselves over large gins in a pub near the Harlequins ground. Sitting on a stool by the bar, skirt hitched back, Kay combed out her hair, confident that she was the dominant presence in the room of rugby drinkers, middle-aged men eyeing her over their pints. Our expedition to the middle-class heartland had its absurd aspects, but these passed her by. She was engaging with the enemy—not the residents but the cultural prisons in which they languished.

I watched her with unfeigned admiration, aware that nothing at the Adler had prepared me for her. Psychiatry was at its best when dealing with failure, but had never coped with success. Kay was driven by the true fanatic's zeal, a belief system that was satisfied with only one convert, herself. In many ways she was right. The social conventions that tied people to their cautious and sensible lives had to be cleared away.

'Today Twickenham, tomorrow the world,' Kay announced, after telling me to order another round. 'Vera?'

'You were great.' Vera sniffed her gin, smoothing the hair off her high forehead and refusing to meet the eyes of the rugby crowd. 'Why do the women always come to the door? Where the hell are the men?'

'They're fading away. Sitting in soundproofed rooms, wondering what happened.' Kay patted my cheek. 'There are definitely fewer of you, David.'

'I'll tell my Green friends. We need a sanctuary.'

Vera finished her drink, exchanged a glance with Kay and went out to wait in the car. I watched her stride stony-faced through a door held open with mock gallantry by an amiable beer drinker with the shoulders of a prop forward.

'A moody soul,' I commented. 'She must miss the Defence Ministry. All those nasty weapons to play with.'

'I'm fond of her.' Kay tore the top sheet off her clipboard. 'She's very sweet. A fully house-trained sociopath. Did she tell you her murder story?'

'The wicked stepmother and the home chemistry kit? She dangled it in front of me.'

'Let's see how good a psychologist you are. Is she telling the truth?'

I hesitated, remembering Vera's knowing smirk. 'Yes.'

'Right . . . it made the papers for a day or two. They decided not to prosecute. Any child that dangerous is going to be very useful to society.' Relaxing at last, Kay took my hand. 'I'm glad you came back. We need people who aren't too wrapped up in some little hate of their own.'

'It was touch and go. But something's happened at Chelsea Marina. I want to be there.'

'Don't forget that. This afternoon was a bit of a farce; I know you disapproved. Still, you're more committed than you realize.' She eased herself from the stool, and pushed down her skirt, smiling at the beer drinkers. 'Right. One last call, then straight to a hot bath—you can scrub my back, David . . .'

WE SET OFF, Vera at the wheel, driving through the evening streets. Twickenham had become a TV suburb, where blue screens glowed in bungalow lounges and the bedrooms of teen-age girls readying themselves for their clubs. We passed a small supermarket that served a local residential area, and parked in a slip road thirty yards from a video store.

The supermarket had closed, and the last customers were leaving in their cars. Kay waited until we were alone in the slip road, unzipped the sports bag and pulled out three video-cassettes.

'David, be a love. I'm completely knackered. Drop these back for me.'

'No problem.' I opened the door, and glanced at the videos in the street lighting. '*Independence Day, Diva, Armageddon* . . . ? Not your kind of thing. Anyway, these are blanks.'

'I borrowed them last week—I'm writing a piece for *Sight and Sound* on cassette art. Just stick them back on the shelves.'

'The assistant—what if he sees me?'

'Say you found them in the supermarket.' Kay pushed me out of the car. 'Kids are always pinching them. Don't look at the security camera.'

The video store was quiet. A youth in his twenties sat behind the counter, engrossed in his computer screen. Keeping my back to the surveillance camera, I slipped the science-fiction movies onto the main shelves, and strolled to the modest display of for-eign language films, the cassette of *Diva* under my jacket.

I scanned the row of classics by Truffaut, Herzog and Fellini, and thought of the keen interest in film that brought Laura and me together. We hunted the programme guides of the National Film Theatre, searching for some obscure Portugese or Korean director. Tragically, Laura had lived out her last moments on an amateur videotape, and it occurred to me that I might try to track down the camcorder's owner.

'God, what . . . ?' A sharp stitch bit into the bruised ribs under my arm. A fierce heat was burning my chest, and smoke rose from my jacket, a choking hydrocarbon vapour. Ten feet away, a sooty cloud billowed from the shelf where I had left the *Armageddon* cassette. There was a flash of magnesium light, a blue-white glimmer of intense heat.

Smoke poured from the cassette under my jacket. I shook it onto the floor, and stepped back when it began to spit and ignite. As I tried to find the doorway there was a second explosion from the shelves. A harsh smoke filled the store and dimmed the overhead lights, faint glows in a blackout. The young assistant ran past me, hands cupped over his mouth, found the door and stumbled into the night.

A tall man in a motorcycle helmet swayed through the smoke, shielding his eyes from the spitting light. Seeing me, he seized my shoulders in his strong hands.

'Markham! Get out!'

I tried to mask my face, and felt the man bundle me to the door. In the clearer light I recognized the white notch of a dog collar. 'Dexter? Find the fire extinguisher . . . call 999.'

'Come on!'

The tarry smoke, a dense black cloud, billowed into the street. The clergyman released my jacket and ran out into the slip road, trapped smoke rising from his leathers. He waved his arms as Kay's Polo drove at speed towards him, Vera at the wheel. I waited for it to stop, but it accelerated away, throwing Dexter onto his knees.

I helped him to his feet, and followed him at a half-run. The tail lights of the Polo, two smudges of blood, swerved into the darkness, heading towards Richmond Bridge. The clergyman leaned against me, gasping through the phlegm that filled his mouth. He pushed back his visor and gulped at the night air. In the harsh magnesium light I could see his unsettled face, and the grimace of anger that exposed his missing tooth. He watched the Polo until it disappeared, and I realized that Kay Churchill had always intended to abandon me.

13

A NEUROSCIENTIST
LOOKS AT GOD

CHELSEA MARINA was quiet when we returned on Stephen Dexter's Harley. A police constable stood near the gatehouse, waving along the traffic in the King's Road and keeping careful watch on the residents strolling to the local restaurants. I expected to see a few stalwart pickets, a brazier of red-hot coke and a Christmas contributions tin. But the revolution had been rescheduled to a more convenient day. The middle-class rebels valued their leisure, and the assault on the barricades would be squeezed between concert and theatre visits and the pleasures of fresh seafood.

Dexter saluted the policeman, who beckoned us into the estate. He was about to caution me for not wearing a helmet, but let us pass, clearly assuming that I was a new recruit to the clergyman's flock, rescued from the street and conveyed to a more worthy life by the sacred despatch rider.

I slapped away the last of the sooty vapour, and realized that I was glad to see the constable. Kay's effort at cultural sabotage could easily have ended in disaster. Stephen Dexter and I had barely made our escape. The Harley was parked in a residential cul-de-sac a hundred yards from the video store. Retching into his leather gloves, Dexter started the soft American engine. We watched the fire engines arrive and play their hoses on the fierce magnesium blaze. Thousands of cassettes lay in the street, steaming in the arc lights, tapes uncoiling among the broken glass.

We set off for Richmond Bridge before the police could notice us. Leaning back in the pillion seat, I let the night air rush through me, sweeping away all anger and panic. I had never trusted Vera, but Kay had been far more ruthless than I expected. Rather than leave promptly, I had lingered in the video store, thinking of Laura and our evenings at the NFT. When I failed to return to the car, Kay had ordered Vera to drive off and leave me to my memories.

WE CROSSED Chelsea Marina and stopped in Nelson Lane, a row of houses overlooking the small tidal basin. Two yachts were moored together by the landing stage like sheltering lovers. Next to the last house in the terrace was a tiny chapel, its modest dimensions accurately reflecting the spiritual needs of Chelsea Marina.

A white Beetle was parked across the street, its sidelights glowing, and Joan Chang waved from the driver's window. She unclipped her Walkman and grinned at Dexter, glad to see him home, then started her engine and set off in an air-cooled clatter.

The clergyman watched her go, smiling bleakly through the exhaust, hands fretting at the controls of the Harley.

'Markham? Are you coming in?'

'Thanks. I'll take a drink off you.'

'A large one, right. I'd say you've earned it.'

He waited for me to dismount, but seemed less than eager to invite me into his rectory. While he shut down the Harley he left me to stare at the marina. I assumed that he had been the look-out posted by Kay at the video store, and that his job now was to point out my clumsy behaviour.

Carrying his helmet, he led the way into the house. In the narrow hallway I could smell the acrid smoke on my clothes.

'Fiendish stuff,' I commented. 'The kind of thing destroyers lay down.'

'It is. Vera Blackburn worked for the Ministry of Defence. If she'd had her way the whole street would have been depth-charged.'

The living room was a sparsely furnished cell. The desk and leather armchair had been pushed against the walls, and a camp bed took up the centre of the room, a low canvas tent erected around it. A primus stove stood on the carpet, along with a small selection of cans and cereal packets. A chasuble aired on a metal frame, and a folding wooden foot table carried a selection of hymn books and missals, a child's home-made advent calendar, and a copy of a BBC publication, *A Neuroscientist Looks at God*, the book of the television series to which I had contributed. Resting on the khaki pillow of the camp bed was a framed photograph of the Reverend Dexter in a black soutane and flying goggles, standing beside a Steerman biplane parked near a forest airstrip. With him were a village headman, his Filipina wife and four smiling daughters.

The rest of the house—the hall, the through dining room and what I could see of the kitchen—was untouched and apparently uninhabited. I realized that the clergyman was camping in his own house, as if the comforts of easy chairs, sprung mattresses and electric stoves were habits he had decided to forgo, in some partial resignation from the world. With his camp bed, primus and pup tent he was reminding himself of his temporary assignment to Chelsea Marina.

He waited as I adjusted myself to this odd scene. Dressed in his metal-trimmed boots and cycle leathers, at first sight he seemed handsomely confident. But his face was sallow and distracted, and he glanced at the street with the uneasy air of a fugitive expecting the police to appear at any moment and break down his door. I wondered how he had ever involved himself with Kay Churchill, a one-woman recipe for a nervous breakdown.

I was ready to confront him over the evening's action, and ask why we had destroyed the video store. Our mission to the middle class had ended in pointless vandalism. But he ducked into the tent, emerging with a bottle of Spanish wine and two glasses.

'There you are.' He filled my glass, watching the fluid climb towards the brim. 'I should have dropped you off at the gatehouse. You need to rest before you drive your car.'

'I'll take a cab. I still feel shaky.'

'Of course. Are you looking in on Kay?'

'Is she expecting me?'

'I imagine so. A little anger stimulates the glands. They say she's an interesting lover.'

'Then I'll miss a treat. One act of betrayal is enough for an evening.'

'Good for you.'

I tried to steady the glass in my hand. I was still trembling with tension and fear, a sense that I had stepped out of my own character and become an amateur terrorist.

'So . . .' Sipping the wine, I waited for my pulse to settle. 'Was that a successful mission?'

'I'm sure Kay thinks so.'

'I'm glad. I could get a year in prison. You, too.'

'Longer.' Dexter stared at the dust on the empty shelves. 'We all have previous convictions.'

'We did thousands of pounds' worth of damage.' I raised my voice, annoyed by the passivity of this muscular clergyman. 'The fire hoses must have destroyed the entire stock.'

'And the security cameras. At least no one will know you were there. The films aren't much of a loss, but I take your point.'

'Tell me, how do you explain all this to your bishop?'

'I don't. A parish priest has a great deal of discretion.'

'Discretion? A convenient concept. You can square everything with your . . . conscience?'

'Not a word your profession uses very often.' Dexter smiled for the first time. 'Have you noticed how vocabularies fluctuate in order to cope with our need to justify ourselves?'

'Dexter . . .' Irritated by this, I rammed my glass onto the mantelpiece. 'You used me to commit a crime.'

'Not quite . . .' Dexter tried to calm me, glancing at the window to see if my outburst had carried across the street. 'I assumed they were smoke devices, not incendiaries. Besides, I wasn't even sure you'd turn up.'

'Weren't you the lookout?'

'No. I was acting on my own. Kay still doesn't know I was there. She told me there was an action planned at the video shop. I guessed you'd be involved and might need a a little help.'

'I did.' Controlling myself, I said: 'I'm glad you were there. Still, why take a chance with me? I'm a complete amateur. I might have been arrested.'

'Kay wanted you arrested.' Dexter finished his wine, and eyed the bottle on the floor between us. 'She's still not sure who you are, or why you're here. Going to bed with you wouldn't reveal all that much. If you were sent down for a year that would prove where your real loyalties lie.'

'A little ruthless?'

'She'd have visited you in Wandsworth.' He raised a hand before I could reply. 'There are things happening here that have to be watched. On one level it's all rather absurd, but there's a darker side. Kay is a remarkable woman, but she's trapped on an escalator of self-expectation. Other people exploit that. Potentially dangerous people.'

'Like Vera Blackburn? And this Dr Gould? Those were magnesium fuses. They can melt steel. You'd have a real job explaining a blind child to yourself.'

'I couldn't. It was inexcusable.'

'I ought to go to the police. In fact, I'm seriously thinking about it.'

'You're right. I wouldn't stop you. I'd happily testify as a prosecution witness.'

'Then why take part? You're involved in some serious crimes.'

Dexter lowered his head and stared at the camp bed and pup tent, his refuge from this bleak rectory. 'Chelsea Marina is my parish. If I was a pastor in 18th-Century Cornwall, and found that everyone in the village took part in shipwrecking, it would be wrong to remain aloof. I'd have to join in.'

'You'd stand on the rocks and wave your lantern?'

'I hope not. But at least I could make sure that survivors weren't murdered or thrown back into the sea.'

'And that's what you're doing at Chelsea Marina? Locking the estate manager in his office? The poor man was deeply shocked.'

'Don't feel too sorry for him. People here may be middle class, but they're little more than an indentured coolie force.'

'The "new proletariat"? Furnished with private schools and BMWs?'

'There's genuine distress. Many families are at their wits' end. They listen to Kay and Richard Gould and start to question their lives. They see that private schools are brainwashing their children into a kind of social docility, turning them into a professional class who will run the show for consumer capitalism.'

'The sinister Mr Bigs?'

'There are no Mr Bigs. The system is self-regulating. It relies on our sense of civic responsibility. Without that, society would collapse. In fact, the collapse may even have begun.'

'Here, at Chelsea Marina?'

'No, it began years ago.' The clergyman stood by the window, watching a police helicopter patrol the river, its spotlight playing over the silent office buildings. 'All these protest movements—"Reclaim the Streets", "Save the Countryside", the demos against GM crops and the World Trade Organization. Worthy causes, but part of a revolt of the middle classes that started over forty years ago with the rise of CND. What's happening now is the beginning of the endgame—the abdication of civic responsibility. But you know that—it's why you're here.'

'Not entirely. I'm looking into the Heathrow bomb. My wife was killed.'

'Your wife? I know. A dreadful tragedy. Absolutely insane.'

'My first wife.' Annoyed with myself for the slip of the tongue, I said: 'I remarried, very happily. But I need to find out who placed the bomb on the carousel. I feel a debt of duty, a kind of moral involvement, as if part of me was there, in Terminal 2. Reverend . . . ?'

The clergyman had turned away from me, and was staring at the darkness over the marina, a well of nothingness. His face was pale and almost bloodless, eyes fixed like a mourner at a funeral, trying not to look down at the waiting grave between his feet. He fingered the scar on his forehead, as if hoping to switch off a warning light.

'I'm sorry.' He rallied himself, touching his dog collar. 'I was thinking about Heathrow. It's hard to grasp. I'm sure the police will find the bombers.'

'No one's claimed responsibility. There was a protest banner in the men's lavatory—some kind of anti-travel tirade.'

'I see. You're thinking of Kay and Joan, at the Hammersmith court. There's no connection, believe me.'

'I accept that,' I said. 'All the same, there's a hint of violence in the air. It's more than talk.'

Dexter shook his head, a finger counting the tins around the primus stove. 'The video attack this evening—it wasn't in character. Violence was bred out of the middle classes years ago.'

'Does that include Richard Gould? He was involved in an arson case, setting fire to a department store his father built.'

'You found that on his website? The internet is our confession box. He was a child, a troubled teenager.' Head still lowered to avoid my eyes, the clergyman took my arm and led me into the hall. 'David, we need sleep, and time to think things over. A lot

of time. Don't talk to anyone about the video store. I'm not pushing you out, but I have to prepare a sermon.'

'I'm glad to hear it.' As we stood outside the front door I
pointed to the darkened chapel. Its doors were padlocked, and a
pile of circulars lay unattended on the steps. 'You don't hold services at Chelsea Marina?'

'We've had trouble with the roof.' He gestured vaguely. 'And
other problems. Sometimes I substitute at St James's, Piccadilly.'

'Kay Churchill thinks you've lost your faith.'

Dexter placed a strong arm around my shoulders. More comfortable in the dark, he raised his chin to stare at the quiet street.
He knew I was trying to provoke him, but he had recovered his
confidence. 'My faith? I'd say it was beaten out of me. Agnostics
give too much weight to faith. It's not what you believe—who
really knows? Far more important is the map you draw of yourself. My map was faulty, in all senses. A nasty accident derailed
me for a while . . .'

'In the Philippines?'

'Mindanao. I lost my bearings and landed on a runway controlled by local guerrillas. For two weeks I was soundly thrashed
every day. They said they were converting me to Islam.'

'You resisted?'

'Not for long.' He touched the scar on his forehead. 'I thought
of going back to schoolmastering, but my duty is here. Social
unrest always throws up a few really dangerous types. People
who use extreme violence to explore themselves, like some people use extreme sex.'

'Kay Churchill?'

'Not Kay. She's too generous with herself.'

'What about Vera Blackburn?'

'More of a problem. I'm watching her.'

'And Dr Gould?'

Dexter turned away and gazed at the black water in the

marina. 'Richard? It's hard to say. He faces enormous danger—
from himself.'

Before we parted, I said: 'A last question. Why haven't the
courts locked us up for good? Kay, Vera, you and I, all the others.
The Home Office must know what's going on.'

'They do. They're letting us run with the ball. They want
to see where this leads. Nothing frightens them more than the
thought of a real middle-class revolution . . .'

He watched me walk away, troubled face hidden from the
light, and then returned to the shelter of his unsheltering roof.

14

FROM GUILDFORD
TO TERMINAL 2

SALLY THREW her walking sticks onto the floor and strode across the lounge, shocked by how unconcerned I seemed.

'David! You could go to prison . . .'

'It's possible. Don't worry, though. I'm probably in the clear.'

'These people are completely mad. Keep away from them.'

'Dear, I intend to. All I did was spend an afternoon with them.'

'An afternoon? You set fire to Twickenham.'

'That sounds like a painting by John Martin. *Twickenham Aflame.* The stadium burning, the tennis courts scorched, swimming pools beginning to boil—that really would be the end of the world.'

'David . . .' Trying a different tack, Sally sat on the arm of my chair. She had been asleep when I reached home, but over breakfast I described my baptism as a Chelsea Marina terrorist. She said nothing, frowning hard at her toast, thought about it for an hour and then made a fierce effort to bring me to my senses. Anger, wasted on her doltish husband, gave way to cajollery. She took my face in her hands. 'David, you're far too involved. Ask yourself why. These people have got to you, for some reason. Arson, vandalism, incendiary bombs? Out in the suburbs, videos are practically sacred objects. Setting off explosions—it's all unbelievable.'

'Smoke bombs. The fire was an accident. The fuses were too powerful—why, I don't know.'

'Why? Because whoever set them was on drugs.' Sally grimaced, remembering her own addiction to hospital painkillers. 'That's Chelsea for you. Like my mother's set in the seventies. Lesbians, heroin, mad boutiques opening all the time, freaky people pretending to be pop stars. Always avoid Chelsea.'

'Fulham, actually. No hard drugs and the Protestant work ethic going full blast. Middle managers, accountants, civil servants. The promotion ladders have been kicked away and they see the bailiffs swarming.'

'They should be in Milton Keynes.' Sally smoothed my scalp, trying to conjure up the contours of respectability. The excitements of the previous day had left my hair springing like a Mohawk. 'Chelsea, Fulham ... you're north London, David. You're Hampstead.'

'Old-style socialism? Psychoanalysis and Jewish scholarship? Not really me. You'd like the people at Chelsea Marina. They have passion. They hate their lives and they're doing something about it. The French revolution was started by the middle class.'

'Revolution? Attacking a video shop?'

I took her hands and pondered the life-lines, time-routes that ran for ever, still callused by the handles of her walking sticks. 'Forget the video shop. The interesting thing is that they're protesting against themselves. There's no enemy out there. They know *they* are the enemy. Kay Churchill thinks that Chelsea Marina is a re-education labour camp, the sort of place they have in North Korea, updated with BMWs and BUPA subscriptions.'

'She sounds mad.'

'She is, a little. It's deliberate. She's winding herself up, like a child with a toy, curious to see where she'll go. Those big houses in Twickenham were an eye-opener. Civilized people, golden retrievers, but each of those homes was a stage set. All they do is inhabit the scenery. They reminded me of my grandmother's place in Guildford.'

'You were happy there.' Sally pinched my ear, trying to wake me. 'Think what the alternative was—racketing around with your mother, sleeping in strange beds in north Oxford, smoking pot when you were eight years old, drinking Scotch with R.D. Laing. You'd never have become a psychologist.'

'I wouldn't have needed to.'

'Exactly. You'd have been an architect in Chelsea Marina. Going to bijou little dinner parties and worrying about the Volvo and the school fees. At least you're doing well.'

'Thanks to your father.'

'That's not true. You've never liked him.'

'Face it, Sally. I'd hate us to have to rely on my Adler salary. His company's retainer is half our income. It's a kindly way of giving you a hefty allowance without making me lose my self-respect.'

'You do useful work for him. That problem over car parking at the Luton factory. You made the executives walk further than everyone else.'

'Common sense. The most useful work I do for your father is keeping you happy. That's what he pays me for. In his eyes I'm just a glorified counsellor and medical attendant.'

'David!' Sally was more baffled than shocked. She stared at me like a ten-year-old finding a spider in her sock drawer. 'Is that how you see our marriage? No wonder you're so keen on Chelsea Marina.'

'Sally . . .'

I tried to reach her hand but the doorbell distracted us. Swearing under her breath, Sally made for the hall. I sat in the arm-chair, staring at the house around me, a gift from Sally's mother that reminded me of the role that money played in my life, other people's money. As Sally had noticed, I felt a growing closeness to the residents of Chelsea Marina, to the feckless film lecturer and the evasive priest with the Harley and the Chinese girlfriend. I liked the way they were looking frankly at themselves and throwing their useless luggage out of the window.

Too many of the props in my own life were baggage belonging to someone else that I had offered to carry—the demeaning requests from my father-in-law's managers, the committee meetings in my year as a governor of an approved school in Hendon, my responsibilities for my ageing mother whom I liked less and less, the tiresome fundraising for the Adler, little more than touting for corporate clients.

Voices sounded from the pavement. Leaving my chair, I went to the window. Henry Kendall was standing near his car, a suitcase in hand. Beside him was a senior policeman in full uniform, looking up at the house while he spoke to Sally. Without thinking, I assumed that he had come to arrest me and had invited Henry, a close colleague, to act as the prisoner's friend. The suitcase would carry the few belongings I was allowed to take with me to the police station.

I stood behind the curtains, my heart leaping against my chest like a trapped animal throwing itself at the bars of its cage. I was tempted to run, to flee through the garden gate and make my way to the sanctuary of Chelsea Marina. Calming myself, I walked stiffly to the door.

HENRY GREETED ME AFFABLY. We lunched frequently in the Institute dining room, but I noticed how well he looked. The haggard figure outside Ashford Hospital had been replaced by a confident analyst and corporate thruster with both eyes fixed on Professor Arnold's chair. He had become more patronizing towards me, and at the same time more suspicious, convinced that my interest in Chelsea Marina concealed an agenda of my own.

The policeman had returned to the car, sitting in the front

passenger seat as he scanned a white folder with the Adler crest. Henry and I paced the pavement together.

'Superintendent Michaels,' Henry explained. 'I'm giving him a lift to the Home Office. He's working on the Heathrow case.'

'I thought he'd come to arrest me.' I smiled, a little too easily. 'Is there any progress?'

'Unofficially? No. It's almost a meaningless crime. No one's claimed responsibility, and there's no apparent motive. I'm sorry, David. We both owe it to Laura to clear the thing up.'

'What about the bomb fragments? They must say something.'

'Puzzling. British Army detonators of a highly classified type. Used by the SAS and covert ops people. No one can understand how the bomber got hold of them.'

I waved to Sally, who was standing on the step by the front door, smiling at Henry whenever he looked at her. Offhandedly, I said: 'There was a bomb in Twickenham last night.'

'You heard about that? It wasn't on the breakfast news.' Henry peered sharply at me, a pointer spotting a concealed bird. 'A rugger prank, they think. It's odd how many of these small incidents there are—most of the "fires" you read about are really bomb attacks. There are some curious targets.'

'Suburban cinemas, McDonalds, travel agents, private prep schools . . . ?'

'Good guesswork.' Henry's chin rose even higher, and he gazed at me down his nose. 'You're in touch with someone at the Yard?'

'No. It's . . . in the air we breathe.'

'You've obviously got a feel for the subversive.' Henry handed the suitcase to me. 'A few things of Laura's. I've been clearing out the house with her sister. Papers you wrote together, one or two books you gave her, conference photographs. I thought you'd like to have them.'

'Well . . .' I held the suitcase, surprised by how light it seemed, the documents of a ten-year relationship, the last deeds of mar-

riage and memory. Holding it as Henry watched me, it seemed to
grow heavier in my hand.

SALLY MADE her way down the steps, using the walking sticks
to complicate her descent, a sure sign that she was thinking her
way to an important decision. Henry and I waited for her to
join us, but she left us standing on the pavement and stepped
into the street, making a laboured circuit of the car. Superintendent Michaels noticed her in his wing mirror, and held out
his arm to halt an approaching taxi. He tried to climb from the
car, but Sally leaned against the passenger door, her elbows on
the roof.

'Sally?' Henry waited for her, our conversation forgotten, taking his keys from his pocket. 'Do you want a lift?'

She ignored him, and stared across the roof of the car, her eyes
levelled at me as I stood with the suitcase, filled with my first
wife's mementoes. I realized that she was about to report me to
Superintendent Michaels, and tell him of my involvement in the
video-store fire. She watched me without smiling, as if review-
ing our entire life together across the polished cellulose of Henry's car, a stretch wider than the Hellespont.

Puzzled by her presence at his elbow, the superintendent edged
open his door and spoke to her. Sally noticed his concerned smile,
and I heard her apologize for not inviting him in for a drink.
They waved to each other as the car pulled away.

LATER, IN THE KITCHEN, I watched Sally sip a small sherry,
nose twitching at the volatile fluid. Her face seemed sharper, and
for the first time I saw the older woman in her bones, less spoilt
and less sure of either her husband or the world.

'Sally ...' I spoke calmly. 'The superintendent—you were
going to ...'

'Yes.' She stirred the sherry with her finger. 'I thought about it.'

'Why? He would have arrested me on the spot. If it came to court there'd be a good chance of my ending up in prison.'

'Exactly.' Sally nodded sagely, as if this was the first sensible thing I had said. 'And if you go on with this Chelsea Marina nonsense you'll definitely go to prison. For a very long time, if someone gets killed. I don't want that, and maybe now's the moment to stop it.'

'It won't happen.' I stepped across the kitchen, intending to embrace her, and realized I was still carrying Laura's suitcase. 'Believe me, it's finished.'

'It isn't.' Wearily, Sally pushed away her glass. 'Just see yourself. Hair standing on end, bruised face, that old suitcase. You look like an illegal immigrant.'

'I am, in a way. An odd thought.' I left the suitcase on a chair, and turned confidently to Sally. 'I've seen all I need to. Chelsea Marina probably has no connection with the Heathrow attack. They're not in the same league.'

'Are you sure? These people are amateurs, they haven't a clue what they're doing. Anyway, the Heathrow bomb isn't why you're going back to Chelsea.'

'No? Then why am I going back?'

'You've picked up some kind of trail there. You think it leads to a new self you're searching for. Maybe you need to find it. That's why I said nothing to the superintendent.'

I moved the sherry glass and pressed her hands to the table. 'Sally, there's no trail, and there's nothing to find. I'm happy here, with myself and with you. The people at Chelsea Marina can't cope with their overdrafts. They're fed up with themselves and are taking it out on a few double yellow lines.'

'Find out why. That's the world we're living in—people will set off bombs for the sake of free parking. Or for no reason at all. We're all bored, David, desperately bored. We're like children left for too long in a playroom. After a while we have to start breaking up the toys, even the ones we like. There's nothing we believe in. Even this flying parson you met seems to have turned his back on God.'

'The Reverend Dexter? He hasn't turned his back, but he's keeping his distance. It's hard to know what exactly, but there's something on his mind.'

'And on yours.' Sally placed her sherry glass in the sink. She smiled gamely, the same confidence-boosting grin I had seen in her orthopaedic ward, willing me on as she had once willed herself to walk. 'Find out what it is, David. Follow the trail. Guildford to Terminal 2. Somewhere along the way you'll meet yourself . . .'

15

THE DEPOT OF DREAMS

THE REBELLION of the new proletariat had begun, but was I foe or friend? Surprised by myself, I helped to drag the handcuffed security guards into the manager's office, and tried to shield them from the combat boots aimed at their faces. Kay Churchill caught me when I tripped over the sprawl of legs. She steered me around the desk and sat me in the manager's chair.

'David, make up your mind.'

'I have. Kay, I'm with you.'

'Get a grip for once.' Her large eyes with their aroused pupils peered at me through the slits of her ski mask. 'Do you know what you're doing?'

'I stay by the box office until everyone leaves. I make sure the doors are locked and let no one in. Kay, I've rehearsed everything.'

'Good. Now stop rehearsing. This is the real thing.'

Vera Blackburn, cool and suspicious in her blue overalls, stood in the corridor, waiting for the assault teams to move to their demolition points. She raised a gloved hand towards me, palm upwards, and clenched it fiercely, as if crushing my testicles.

'Right . . .' Kay hesitated, and then rallied herself. She adjusted her ski mask, supplied like our snatch-squad overalls and CS gas by a former lover of Vera's in the Surrey Police. Planned in Kay's living room, argued over endless bottles of Bulgarian wine, the action against the National Film Theatre had promised to be little more than a student prank. I was unprepared for the ruthless violence of these middle-class saboteurs. Tempted to call the police, I had lagged behind when they gassed and stunned the three security guards.

Two of the guards were moonlighting film students at City University. They lay face down, coughing a gas-green phlegm onto the manager's carpet. Both were weeping, as if shocked to find themselves in a brutal drama straight from the gangster movies they so venerated.

The third guard was a security company regular, a fifty-year-old man with the heavy shoulders and close-cropped hair of a retired nightclub bouncer. He had been sitting at his console in the next-door office, watching the surveillance-camera screens, when Vera Blackburn stepped quietly behind him. He caught the CS spray straight in his face, but put up a fight, wresting the can from Vera's hands. She stepped back, surprised by this show of ingratitude, drew her truncheon and beat him to the floor. He now lay at my feet in the manager's office, blood leaking across his scalp, unfocused eyes staring at the ceiling.

'Kay . . .' I knelt beside the guard and searched for a pulse through the blood and vomit. 'This man needs help. There must be a first-aid kit.'

'Later! We have to move.'

She threw a security-company jacket over my shoulders and forced my arms into the sleeves, then propelled me into the corridor. In the camera room Joan Chang was stripping out cassettes of surveillance videotape and tossing them into a duffle bag. She was white-faced with fear, but turned and gave me a vigorous thumbs up.

Doors swung in the corridor as two team-members in overalls stepped into NFT1. Junior barristers who were near-neighbours of Kay's, they carried briefcases holding the incendiary charges and timers. They moved in step, entering the silent auditorium like bagmen for the mob.

Kay paused to focus herself when we reached the NFT lobby. The high glass doors exposed the box-office area to the concrete night of the South Bank complex. A slip road ran from the NFT to the Hayward Gallery car park below the staircases and pilotis of this cultural bunker. A security company van was stationed near the artists' entrance of the Queen Elizabeth Hall, but its crew would be by the coffee machine in the foyer upstairs, staring across the river at Big Ben and counting the long hours to the end of their shift.

'Kay . . .' I held her arm before she could leave. 'Aren't we taking a risk? Anyone can see me.'

'You're a security guard. Act like one.' She pulled the ski mask from my head. 'Vera needs time.'

'Fifty minutes? Why so long?'

'She has to switch off the fire alarms. There are dozens of them.' She pinched my cheek in a fleeting show of affection. 'Do your best, David.'

'And if someone tries to get in?'

'They won't. Salute and stroll away. You're a bored security man.'

'Bored?' I pointed to the framed film posters. 'This place holds a lot of memories.'

'Start to forget them. In an hour they'll all be ash.'

'Do we need to go that far? Burt Lancaster, Bogart, Lauren Bacall . . . they're just movie actors.'

'Just? They poisoned a whole century. They rotted your mind, David. We have to make a stand, build a saner England . . .'

SHE SLIPPED AWAY into the shadows, a faceless assassin of the most famous faces the world had known. The six of us had arrived in pairs at the South Bank, posing as film noir enthusiasts, an easy task for me but a difficult one for Kay, who considered the Hollywood motion picture her sworn enemy. We took our places in NFT2 for a late-night showing of *Out of the Past*. As we sat among the Mitchum fans it was hard to believe that the theatre where I had spent so many formative hours would soon be reduced to cinders. I was too unsettled to concentrate on a single frame, but Kay sat forward, engrossed by this brutal tale of infatuation and betrayal. At one moment of high drama, when the heroine feigned a pang of despair, I even felt the pressure of her hand on my wrist.

Thirty minutes before the end-titles we slipped from the theatre, and made our way to the disused Museum of the Moving Image, now a storeroom filled with packing cases. Here we joined the other members of the team, and changed into police overalls and ski masks. Vera Blackburn kept watch by the locked doors, whose key she had duplicated while working as a volunteer cataloguer of religious films.

Crouching in the darkness, we waited for the performances to end and the complex to empty. In the open crates around me I felt the antique cameras and dismantled lights in their moisture-proof wrappings, the costumes worn by Margaret Lockwood and Anna Neagle, the scripts of *The Sound Barrier* and *The Winslow Boy*, the unforgettable furniture of the 20th Century's greatest dream, about to exit through a furnace vent of its own making.

DREAMS DIED different deaths, taking unexpected doors out of our lives. Trying to behave like a bored security guard, I paced the carpet by the box office, thinking of the countless hours I had spent here with Laura. I had argued my case with Kay and Vera, urging that we spare the NFT and target a suburban multiplex. Kay, however, had set her mind on the NFT's destruction.

Despite her casual betrayal of me in the Twickenham video store, Kay had welcomed me back to Chelsea Marina. In the struggle for a better world, she told me without embarrassment, no one was more disposable than a friend. Unless friends were prepared to betray each other, no revolution would ever succeed.

Visiting Chelsea Marina in the week after our Twickenham expedition, I listened to the doorstep meetings, trying to catch any hint of involvement in the Heathrow bomb. I was surprised by the growing number of protest groups. Leaderless and unco-ordinated, they sprang up at dinner parties and PTA meetings. One committee planned a sit-in at the offices of the management company responsible for Chelsea Marina's abysmal services, but most of the residents were now set on a far more radical response to the social evils that transcended the local problems of the estate. They had moved on to wider targets—a Pret A Manger in the King's Road, Tate Modern, a Conran restaurant scheduled for the British Museum, the Promenade Concerts, Waterstone's bookshops, all of them exploiters of middle-class credulity. Their corrupting fantasies had deluded the entire educated caste, providing a dangerous pabulum that had poisoned a spoon-fed intelligentsia. From sandwich to summer school, they were the symbols of subservience and the enemies of freedom.

THE NFT WAS SILENT, a pale blue light filling its toneless corridors. I straightened my jacket in the mirror behind the pay desk. A smear of blood-stained vomit was drying on the iden-tity badge clipped to my breast pocket. Either I had been sick with panic, or one of the security guards was more injured than I realized.

I pulled on my ski mask and walked to the manager's office. The prisoners sprawled on the carpet beside the desk. The two students were awake and lay back to back, trying to disguise their attempt to loosen each other's handcuffs. The older guard was barely breathing, his head lolling on the vomit-stained car-pet. He seemed to be deeply unconscious, a faint breath moving through his bloodied teeth.

Smoke hung in the corridor outside the office, diffusing below the ceiling lights. I assumed that Vera had decided on a quick cigarette, once the fire alarms were disconnected. Somewhere a window had been opened onto the night, and a cooler air moved around me, the street scents of diesel fuel, rain and cooking fat from the all-night cafés near Waterloo Station.

I left the manager's office and crossed the corridor to NFT1. As I pushed back the curtain a cloud of chemical vapour was rising from the stage, an acrid fog that rolled across the empty seats like a wraith freed from a monster movie. The vapour streamed below the ceiling, found the open exit and flowed around me in looping swirls.

I tried not to gag on the plastic stench, closed the doors and ran to NFT2. I searched the aisles for Kay or Vera. The screen loomed above me, a clouded mirror drained of its memories. On its metallized skin floated the pale shadow of my own reflection, a trapped spectre. An acid vapour was filling the auditorium, and there was a flare of light from the stage. The walls glowed with the electric white of an arc furnace, and a hundred shadows flinched behind the seats.

In the entrance lobby the glass doors were open to the night. Smoke flowed over my head and vented itself into the air, rising towards the promenade deck of the Hayward Gallery. The two students stumbled through the smoke in the corridor, hands cuffed behind them.

'Get out! Run for it!' One of them stopped to raise his cuffs to me, and I seized his shoulder. 'Run!'

In the manager's office I knelt beside the older guard and tried to lift his heavy torso. His eyes were open, but he was barely conscious, blood caked on his chin and shirt. I gripped his ankles and pulled him across the carpet, his huge legs against my thighs.

As I paused by the door, trying to mask my face from the smoke, his feet slipped from my hands. I bent down to seize them, but he drew back his leather boots, arched himself off the floor and kicked me in the chest.

Winded by the blow, I fell against the door, too stunned to breathe. The guard was wide awake, his eyes fixed on my face. Wrists cuffed behind him, he edged himself across the carpet and drew his knees back, ready to kick my head.

A boot brushed my left ear, and I rolled away from him into the corridor. He propped himself against the door, turned onto his side and rose to his feet.

'Get out of here!' I shouted through the smoke that filled the office. 'Run for the lobby . . .'

He steadied himself on both feet, lowered his shoulders and charged at me, emerging from the fog like a rugby forward out of a steaming scrum. His head caught a framed film poster of Robert Taylor and Greer Garson, and knocked it to the floor. He stepped onto the glass pane, kicked the fragments out of his way and hurled himself at me through the smoke.

He followed me into the night, past the lobby doors and onto the slip road to the Hayward Gallery, hands behind his back, smoke rising from his clothes. Only twenty feet ahead of him, I ran around the parked security van, searching for the staircase to the Purcell Room. The students stood back to back, still trying to unpick their handcuffs. The guard head-charged them, throwing them aside with his powerful shoulders.

His boots rang on the concrete steps when I reached the promenade deck of the Hayward Gallery. Behind the glass doors two security men watched me run past, apparently followed by an injured colleague. Their eyes turned towards the column of smoke rising from the roof of the NFT. Both spoke into their radios, and I heard the first police siren wail along the embankment near Westminster Bridge.

I crossed the upper terrace beside the Festival Hall, gasping at the damp river air. I could barely stumble, but my pursuer had given up the chase. Bent double, he leaned exhausted against a piece of chromium sculpture, phlegm dripping from his mouth, eyes still fixed on me.

I set off towards the Millennium Wheel. Launched onto the night sky, the gondolas circled the cantilever arm, a white latticework cut from frost, the armature of a swan that sailed the dark air. A corporate party was taking place in three of the gondolas, and the guests pressed against the curved glass, watching the first fires break through the roof of the NFT.

I smoothed my security jacket, brushing away the sooty smuts, and walked past the catering vans parked below the Wheel. Waitresses were clearing away the trays of half-eaten canapés. I chewed on a chicken drumstick, and gulped from a bottle of Perrier water. Together we watched a fire engine turn into Belvedere Road, bell clanging. A police car stopped outside the Festival Hall, and its spotlight played on the Hayward Gallery. Firemen and police on foot were closing in on the NFT, and would soon find the handcuffed security guards.

An empty gondola moved past me, its doors open. The corporate party would be over in an hour, and as the guests strolled across the green to their cars I would lose myself among them.

I stepped into the gondola and leaned on the rail overlooking the river, almost too weary to breathe. While we moved along the boarding platform an off-duty waiter swung himself through the door, a tray bearing two champagne flutes in his hand. He placed the tray on the seat and sat beside it, searching his pockets for a cigarette.

As we rose above County Hall the fires lit the night air and seemed to burn on the dark water of the Thames. A huge caldera had opened beside Waterloo Bridge and was devouring the South Bank Centre. Billows of smoke leaned across the river, and I could see the flames reflected in the distant casements of the Houses of Parliament, as if the entire Palace of Westminster was about to ignite from within.

The waiter pointed to a champagne glass on the tray. Without thanking him, I tasted the warm wine. The bubbles stung my lips, cracked by the fierce heat in the auditorium. I thought of the smoke-swept corridors lined with the portraits of the film world's greatest stars. The fires set by Vera Blackburn had taken hold, burning fiercely throughout the NFT, engulfing the smiles of James Stewart and Orson Welles, Chaplin and Joan Crawford. My memories of them seemed to rise with the turning Wheel, escaping from a depot of dreams that was giving up its ghosts to the night.

I crossed the gondola, my back to the smoking waiter and the Thames, and searched the streets around County Hall. I almost expected to see Kay and Joan Chang darting from one doorway to another as the police cars sped past, sirens wailing down the night. Needless to say, they had escaped without warning me, through the riverside entrance to the theatre cafe, which they had left open to create a fire-spurring draught.

The first smoke had reached the windows of the gondola, laying itself across the curved panes. I began to cough, tasting the acrid vapour that had churned outside the manager's office. I retched onto the rail, and spilled the champagne over the floor at my feet.

Concerned, the waiter stood behind me, and nodded when I cleared my throat, smiling in an oddly complicit way. He was so close that I almost expected him to whisper some proposition, and it occurred to me that the Millennium Wheel might be a favoured place for gay pick-ups.

I tried to wave him away, but he took the empty glass from my hand. He was a slim, agile man with a strong forehead and bony, almost emaciated face, and a tubercular pallor that should have ruled him out as a waiter. I imagined him moving on the fringes of a twilight world of obscure corporate venues. Like so many waiters I had known, he was friendly but slightly aggressive, a skin-thin charm overlaying a barely concealed aloofness.

When he stepped behind me there was something evasive about him that reminded me of another shadowy figure who had concealed his face. There was the same odour of forgotten hospital wards and languishing children. But his movements were quick and decisive, and I could see him reaching between one of his small patients and a clumsy nurse, a syringe in one hand and distracting toy in the other.

'Dr Gould?' I turned to face him, trying to see behind the disarming smile. 'We've met before.'

'At Kay Churchill's, that's right.' He steadied me as the gondola rocked in the billows of smoke and overheated air. 'You did well tonight, David.'

'You remember me?'

'Of course. I wanted us to meet, at the right time and place. There's so much I need to show you.' He took my arm in a firm grip as the gondola began its final descent. 'But let's get out of here before someone else remembers you . . .'

The flame-lit buildings along the Thames threw their light into his unsettled eyes. I tried to free myself from him, but he held me with a hard hand.

A darker fire drew closer.

16

THE CHILDREN'S SANCTUARY

A CHEERFUL FRIEZE of children's drawings looked down on me when I woke, a lively patchwork of armless men, two-legged tigers and shoebox houses that peeled from the walls of the empty ward like the sketches of disassembled dreams.

I lay on the shabby mattress with its stains of ancient urine and disinfectant, glad that this amiable gallery had watched over me as I slept. A thick dust covered the Victorian panes, and trembled in the ceaseless drone of airliners landing at Heathrow. The handicapped children in their dormitory beds must have sensed that the entire world around them suffered a perpetual headache.

I sat up and steadied my feet on the floor. I had slept for four deep hours, but my thighs jumped as I remembered the violent night at the National Film Theatre. A rush of images scanned themselves across my mind like a cassette at fast forward—the spectral smoke that searched the corridors, Vera Blackburn's hard fists, the flinching shadows in the auditoriums, the desperate run to the Millennium Wheel and Richard Gould in his waiter's jacket, offering me a glass of champagne as he fired the Thames.

I stood up, swaying slightly on the unsteady floor, and waited for my bones to engage with each other. Thinking of Sally and a hot bath in St John's Wood, I walked between the worn mattresses. Few parents, I guessed, had ever visited the retarded children who had lingered here. Yet the drawings were touchingly hopeful, the optimistic echoes of a world these handicapped infants would never know. A patient and kindly teacher had steered them towards the crayons and a colourful pathway into their own minds.

Beyond the connecting doors was a stone landing that led into the next dormitory, another high-ceilinged space filled with dust. A dark-haired man in a white coat, his head lowered in thought, appeared briefly and waved to me, then hurried up a staircase to the next floor.

'Dr Gould! We need to . . .' I called to him, my voice lost in the infinite space of this disused hospital, and listened to Gould's footsteps making their way to the roof. The ancient but imposing architecture, moral judgements enshrined in every forbidding corbel, reminded me of other halls where justice was dispensed. I wanted to warn Gould, this elusive author of the Chelsea Marina rebellion, that we would soon be hunted down by the police and locked away for the next five years.

I slapped my thighs, trying to calm the jumpy nerves. I had taken part in a serious crime, against a museum of film and my memories of my first wife, but I felt curiously uninvolved. I was an actor standing in for the real self who lay asleep beside Sally in St John's Wood. A dream of violence had escaped from my head into the surrounding streets, driven on by the promise of change.

I remembered our flight across London only a few hours earlier. Gould's car had been parked outside the Marriott Hotel in the old County Hall, a Citroën estate with Hospice de Beaune stickers on its rear window. From the way Gould searched the controls I guessed that he had never driven the vehicle with its complex hydraulics, left for him by a francophile resident at Chelsea Marina. Concerned by the keening sirens and the police cars blocking Westminster Bridge, I offered to drive, but Gould waved me aside, calming me with his distant but ever-friendly smile. Hunting the dashboard and control levers for the ignition lock, he reminded me of Sally when she first sat in the adapted Saab, faced with a geometric model of her own handicaps.

We lurched away, leapfrogging along the kerb, and rarely left second gear as we accelerated through the dark streets south of the river. I could see the fear in Gould's eyes, and thought of him serving drinks to the corporate clients on the Millennium Wheel. Out of the smoke and fire I had blundered into his look-out post, but he seemed relieved to see me. When we swerved past the Lambeth Palace roundabout the window pillar struck my head, and he held my arm with surprising concern, as if I were a frightened child at a fairground.

We crossed Chelsea Bridge and turned into the darker streets that led to the King's Road. The headlights picked their way through a maze of turnings, drawing us past shop windows filled with kitchen units and bedroom suites, office furniture and bathroom fittings, tableaux of a second city ready to replace the London that burned behind us. Gould withdrew into himself, retreating behind the bones of his face. As he watched the rear-view mirror he became a tired graduate student in a threadbare suit, undernourished and self-neglected.

We crossed the stucco silences of South Kensington with its looming museums, so many warehouses of time, and headed westwards along the Cromwell Road. Inner London fell behind us when we left the Hammersmith flyover and Hogarth House, joining the motorway to Heathrow. Twenty minutes later, we entered the operational zone of the airport, a terrain of air-freight offices and car-rental depots, surrounded by arrays of landing lights like magnetic fields, the ghosts of business parks and industrial estates, a night-world haunted by security guards and attack dogs.

Somewhere near the airport we stopped by a cluster of high

Victorian buildings that stood beside a vast construction site. Gould edged the Citroën past the mud-flecked hulls of graders and tractors, and parked in a yard filled with Portakabins and bales of breeze blocks on wooden pallets.

We left the car, and Gould led the way into a disused building, through a crumbling foyer filled with signs pointing to relocated hospital departments. We climbed the iron steps to the fourth floor. Exhausted, I followed Gould into a ward of dusty and unmade beds. Too tired to resist, I let this odd man, a thoughtful fanatic with gentle hands, pick out a mattress for me. I fell deeply asleep among the drawings of deranged children.

GOULD WAS on the roof when I joined him, face raised to the sunlight, shielded from the wind by a breastwork of Victorian chimneys. He held his mobile phone to one ear, apparently listening to an update on the night's action against the NFT, but he was more interested in the builder's cranes below the parapet. Looking at his sallow face, I could see years of hurried canteen meals and nights spent dozing fitfully in hospital dayrooms. He wore a doctor's name-tag on his coat, as if he was still the paediatrician in charge of the departed children.

I watched a police helicopter flying along the motorway, and tried to work out how I could get away from this derelict hospital. I scanned the huge buildings, immense masonry piles with gables like the superstructures of battleships. This was the architecture of prisons, cotton mills and steel foundries, monuments to the endurance of brick and the Victorian certainties. Three buildings still remained, beside a neglected park where patients had once been wheeled by starch-obsessed VADs.

'David?' Gould switched off the phone in mid-message and turned to survey me, like a busy consultant faced with an unexpected patient. 'You feel a lot better. I can see it.'

'Really? Good . . .'

I guessed that to Gould I seemed exhausted and fretful, in

urgent need of coffee and definitely out of my league as a weekend revolutionary. By contrast, he was surprisingly calm, as if he had injected himself with a strong sedative before going to sleep and a strong stimulant on waking. The muscles in his face had relaxed their grip on the underlying bones, and he moved jauntily in the quiet Sunday air. He was at home in this one-time asylum, and it occurred to me that he had not been a doctor here but a patient. Released into the community when the hospital closed, he had assembled a new identity that easily convinced the residents at Chelsea Marina. The website and its story of the department-store fire would be a clever touch. He was a little too friendly, keeping a careful watch on me out of the side of his eye, but there was a frankness that was almost likeable, and a nervous authority to which everyone at Chelsea Marina had responded.

He waited until the police helicopter was safely out of view, and reached across to pat my arm.

'You're unsettled, David. Operations like last night's—they leave the heart pounding for days. You'll recover, and feel stronger for it.'

'Thank God. I'd hate to be like this for the rest of my life.'

'It won't happen. There's nothing better for us than acting out of real conviction.'

'I'm not sure if I was.' I stared at my bruised palms. 'I nearly handed myself in to the police.'

'The others didn't wait for you? No ...' Gould shook his head in a display of sympathy. 'These middle-class revolutionaries—they've been repressed for years. Now they can taste ruthlessness and betrayal, and they like the flavour.'

'Too bad. They'll be tasting cold porridge before they know it.'

'It's a risk. We're safe, as long as we keep up the element of surprise.' Gould frowned at the sun, resenting its efficient control over events, and then fingered his badge, reminding himself of his own identity. 'Don't worry about prison. At least, not yet.'

'So everyone got away. How's the NFT?'

'Completely gutted. Sadly, some reels of an early Fritz Lang were lost. Still, Vera Blackburn knows her stuff.'

'She's unbalanced. You need to watch her.'

'Vera?' Gould turned to look at me, and then nodded in full agreement. 'She's a damaged child, trying to make sense of the world. I'm doing my best to help her.'

'Drawing her out? Giving scope to her natural talents?'

'That sort of thing.' Amused by the sarcasm in my voice, Gould waved a white hand at the derelict buildings around us. 'David, who cares about the NFT? Look what they've done here. For three hundred children, this was the only home they knew.'

His bloodless fingers pointed to the isolated wings. High walls masked by rhododendrons surrounded each building. There were courtyards within courtyards, barred windows on the upper floors.

'Walls and bars,' I commented. 'It looks like a prison. Where are we?'

'Bedfont Hospital. A mile south of Heathrow. A good place for a madhouse—you can't hear anyone scream.' Gould made a mock bow. 'The last of the great Victorian asylums.'

'A mental hospital? So the children were——?'

'Brain-damaged. Encephalitis, measles cases that went wrong, inoperable tumours, hydrocephalus. All of them severely handicapped, and abandoned by their parents. Social services didn't want to cope.'

'Grim.'

'No.' Gould seemed surprised by my reflex response. 'Some of them were happy.'

'You worked here?'

'For two years.' Gould gazed across the empty roof, smiling as if he could see the children skipping around the chimneys. 'I hope we gave them a good life.'

'Why did you leave?'

'I was suspended.' Gould caught a fly in his hand, then released it to the air and watched it swerve away. 'The General Medical Council has spies everywhere. They're like the Gestapo. I used to take a few children to the theme park at Thorpe. They loved it, packed into an old minibus. No supervision, I let them run free. For a few minutes they knew wonder.'

'What happened?'

'Some of them got lost. Police tipped off the social services.'

'Too bad. Still, it doesn't sound that serious.'

'Don't believe it. In today's climate?' He tilted his head back, closing his eyes at the follies of bureaucracy. 'There was another matter. The great taboo.'

'Sexual?'

'A good guess, David. Genital molestation, they called it. You look shocked.'

'I am. It doesn't seem . . .'

'Like me? It wasn't. But I sensed it was going on.'

'Another doctor?'

'One of the nurses. A very sweet young Jamaican. She was their real mother. Some of the children had brain tumours and only weeks to live. She knew a little sexual stimulation did no harm. It was the only glimpse of happiness they would ever feel. So, a bit of mild masturbation after lights out. A few seconds of pleasure touched those damaged brains before they died.'

'You were the doctor in charge?'

'I defended her. That was too much for the governors. Six months later the health authority closed the place down. Bedfont Asylum was due for a makeover.' Gould pointed across the park. 'They sold the whole site to a property company. Look closely, and you can see the future moving towards you.'

I stared beyond a screen of poplars at the western perimeter of the park. Advancing across the grass were rows of timber-framed houses, the vanguard of a huge estate. Already the first roads were laid out, cement diagrams that led to car ports and minuscule gardens.

'Starter homes,' Gould explained. 'Rabbit hutches for aspiring marrieds. The first taste of middle-class life. A no-deposit, low-interest dream, cooked up by my father's old firm. One day they'll cover the whole of England.'

'It's quite a place to pick.'

'The old asylum?'

'Heathrow.' Shielding my eyes, I could see the tail fins of passenger jets beyond the roofs of the air-freight terminal. 'They're living in the suburb of an airport.'

'They like that. They like the alienation.' Gould took my arm, a teacher relieved to find an intelligent pupil. 'There's no past and no future. If they can, they opt for zones without meaning—airports, shopping malls, motorways, car parks. They're in flight from the real. Think about that, David, while I make some coffee. Then I'll drive you back to London.'

'Good.' Glad to get off the roof, I reached for Gould's mobile resting between us on the parapet. 'I ought to tell my wife where I am.'

'Don't worry.' Gould slipped the phone into his pocket and steered me to the staircase door. 'I called her last night. You were asleep.'

'Sally? Was she all right?'

'Absolutely. I explained you were staying at Chelsea Marina. She might have contacted the police.' Gould patted my back as I lowered myself down the narrow stairs. 'Interestingly, she asked me if you were sleeping at Kay Churchill's house.'

I paused on the steps, trying not to lose my footing. 'What did you tell her?'

'Well . . . I'm never the soul of discretion, David.'

I listened to his generous laughter echo off the stone walls, carried through the silent dormitories as if summoning the ghosts of his dead children and calling them out to play.

17

ABSOLUTE ZERO

'SALLY SOUNDS very sweet, David.'

'She is.'

'That's good. Traffic accidents often bring out the worst in people.'

'She told you she was . . . ?'

'Handicapped?' Gould slowly shook his head. 'An awful word, David. You don't think of her like that.'

'I don't. Her "handicap" isn't physical. She can walk as well as you or I can. It's her way of reproaching the world, reminding it of the evil it's capable of doing.'

'I'm impressed. She's a woman of spirit.'

We sat at the table in the fourth-floor dispensary. Without moving from his chair, Gould hunted the line of refrigerators. The electric current had been switched off for months, and each refrigerator was an Aladdin's cave of rotting cakes and lurid cordials. He found a bottle of mineral water with an intact seal, and began to warm a saucepan over a can of jellied heat.

'So . . .' After spooning instant coffee into the pan, Gould poured the dark brew into paper cups decorated with Disney characters. 'I'd like to meet her. Bring her along to Chelsea Marina.'

'Perhaps not.' I watched Gould sip thirstily at the scalding liquid, his lips almost inflamed. 'It's not her sort of place. Besides, she has a thing about . . .'

'Physicians?' Gould nodded tolerantly. Eyeing my own coffee, he wiped his mouth on the back of his hand, leaving a blood-like smear on his white skin. 'She prefers your diagnostic computers and virtual doctors. Press Button B if you're having a nervous breakdown. Right?'

'Yes and no. Curiously, people prefer talking to a video screen. They're far more frank. Face to face with a real doctor, they'll never admit they have VD. Give them a button to push and they uncross their legs.'

'Great.' Gould seemed genuinely pleased. He took the coffee cup from my hands and sipped at it encouragingly. 'You don't realize it, David, but you're the apostle of a new kind of alienation. You should move into one of those starter homes. I watched you on that TV series, whatever it was called—a kind of DIY take on the Almighty.'

'It was facile. *A Neuroscientist Looks at God*? Television at its most glib. A game show.'

'About God?' Gould smiled at the ceiling. 'That's quite a thought. But I remember one or two things you said—the idea of God as a huge imaginary void, the largest nothingness the human mind can invent. Not a vast something out there, but a vast absence. You said that only a psychopath can cope with the notion of zero to a million decimal places. The rest of us flinch from the void and have to fill it with any ballast we can find—tricks of space-time, wise old men with beards, moral universes . . .'

'You don't agree?'

'Not really.' Gould finished my coffee and pushed the empty cup back to me. 'It isn't only the psychopath who can grasp the idea of absolute nothing. Even a meaningless universe has meaning. Accept that and everything makes a new kind of sense.'

'Difficult to do, without dragging in your own obsessions.' I tossed the cup into the cluttered sink. 'We all carry baggage. The psychopath is unique in not being afraid of himself. Unconsciously, he already believes in nothing.'

'That's true.' Gould waved his hands over the table, an underbidder throwing in his cards. 'You're right, David. I'm too close to the ground. Besides, there were real voids here, unlimited space inside a small skull. Looking for God is a dirty business. You find God in a child's shit, in the stink of stale corridors, in a nurse's tired feet. Psychopaths don't manage that too easily. Places like Bedfont Hospital are the real temples, not St Paul's or . . .'

'The NFT?' Before Gould could reply, I said: 'A building on fire is quite a spectacle, especially if you're trapped inside it. As a matter of interest, did we need to burn it down?'

'No.' Gould waved the question away, consigning it to the bedpans under the sink. The coffee had brought a wintry colour to his face, but his skin was as pale as the unwashed tiles. Undernourished for years, he was held together by professional resentment and his commitment to the lost children. 'The NFT? Of course not. That was absurd—completely pointless, in fact. And dangerous.'

'Then why the firebombs?'

Gould let his limp hands circle the air. 'It's a matter of momentum. I have to keep the wheels turning. Ambition feeds on itself. Kay, Vera Blackburn and the others at Chelsea Marina, they want to change the world. Always the easy option. Near-nonentities have pulled it off. That's why I need people like you, David. You can calm the hotheads. And your motives are different.'

'I'm glad to hear it. As a matter of interest, what are my motives? It might be useful to know, if I get asked by the police.'

'Well . . .' Gould cleared the table, placing his paper cup in the sink and returning the saucepan and jellied heat to a cupboard. 'Your motives are fairly clear—your first wife's death at Heathrow. That affected you deeply.'

'Is that all?'

'Don't underestimate it. First wives are a rite of passage into adult life. In many ways it's important that first marriages go wrong. That's how we learn the truth about ourselves.'

'We were divorced.'

'Divorce from a first wife is never complete. It's a process that lasts until death. Your own, that is, not hers. The Heathrow bomb was a tragedy, but it didn't bring you to Chelsea Marina.'

'What did? I take it you know.'

'Something much more mundane.' Gould leaned back, trying to adopt a sympathetic pose, his toneless face pulled in rival directions by a series of small grimaces. 'Look closely in the mirror, David. What do you see? Someone you don't like very much. When you were twenty, you accepted yourself, flaws and all. Then disenchantment set in. By the time you were thirty your tolerance was wearing thin. You weren't entirely trustworthy, and you knew that you were prone to compromise. Already the future was receding, the bright dreams were slipping below the horizon. By now you're a stage set, one push and the whole thing could collapse at your feet. At times you feel you're living someone else's life, in a strange house you've rented by accident. The "you" you've become isn't your real self.'

'But why Chelsea Marina? A collection of club-class professionals complaining about their legroom? Kay Churchill trying to shock the bourgeoisie out of its toilet training?'

'Exactly.' Gould leaned forward, arms raised to take me into the fold. 'The entire protest is ludicrous—I knew that when I first set things going. Double yellow lines, school fees, maintenance charges . . . a rumour here, a murmur there. Everyone responded, even though they knew it was senseless to fight back. This was the last throw of the dice, and the more meaningless the better. That's what brought you to Chelsea Marina. It's a wild card, an impossible bet, a crazy gesture that signals some kind of message. Blowing up a video store, setting fire to the NFT—completely absurd. But that alone made you feel free.'

'Kay and the others have a point, though. Middle-class life at their level can be fairly tight.' I stood up, trying to avoid Gould's pale hands as they reached for my wrists. 'Cheap holidays, over-priced housing, educations that no longer buy security. Anyone earning less than £300,000 a year scarcely counts. You're just a prole in a three-button suit.'

'And we don't like ourselves for it. I don't, and you don't either, David.' Gould watched me as I tried to turn a tap on the cluttered sink. 'People don't like themselves today. We're a rentier class left over from the last century. We tolerate everything, but we know that liberal values are designed to make us passive. We think we believe in God but we're terrified by the mysteries of life and death. We're deeply self-centred but can't cope with the idea of our finite selves. We believe in progress and the power of reason, but are haunted by the darker sides of human nature. We're obsessed with sex, but fear the sexual imagination and have to be protected by huge taboos. We believe in equality but hate the underclass. We fear our bodies and, above all, we fear death. We're an accident of nature, but we think we're at the centre of the universe. We're a few steps from oblivion, but we hope we're somehow immortal . . .'

'And all this is the fault of . . . the 20th Century?'

'In part—it helped to lock the doors on us. We're living in a soft-regime prison built by earlier generations of inmates. Somehow we have to break free. The attack on the World Trade Center in 2001 was a brave attempt to free America from the 20th Century. The deaths were tragic, but otherwise it was a meaningless act. And that was its point. Like the attack on the NFT.'

'Or Heathrow?'

'Heathrow . . . yes.' Gould lowered his eyes, careful not to catch my own. He stared at his hands, lying in front of him like a pair of surgeon's white gloves, and noticed the coffee smear. He licked a thumb and tried to rub it away, so intently that he seemed not to notice me. 'Heathrow? That's difficult for you to think about. I understand, David, but your wife's death wasn't necessarily pointless.'

I watched him sit back, glancing at his watch as he decided whether it was time to leave. Had he played any part in the Heathrow bomb attack? He was so confined within his own shabby universe, this ruined hospital and his memories of the children, that I doubted it. I could almost believe that he had created the entire protest movement at Chelsea Marina as an act of defiance against the medical establishment. At the same time I found myself liking him and drawn to his wayward ideas. His threadbare suit and neglected body spoke of a certain kind of integrity that was rare in the corporate world of corridor politics taking over our lives.

He seemed aware of my feelings, and as we moved down the iron stairs he suddenly stopped and shook my hand, smiling at me in an eager and almost boyish way.

I felt his hand, and the bones waiting for their day.

18

BLACK MILLENNIUM

IT WAS NOON when I reached St John's Wood, and the late editions of the Sunday newspapers carried vivid colour photographs of the fire at the National Film Theatre. The same inferno glowed from the news-stands in Hammersmith and Knightsbridge. At the traffic lights I stared down from the taxi at the fierce orange flames, barely grasping that I had been partly responsible for them. At the same time I felt an odd pride in what I had done.

On a whim, when we reached Hyde Park Corner, I asked the driver to detour to Trafalgar Square and the Embankment. The last smoke rose from the rubble of the NFT, a moraine of ash that had given up its dream. A hose played on the charred timbers, sending a plume of vapour over the Hayward Gallery. Engineers on a trestle below Waterloo Bridge were examining the damage to the arches. The Millennium Wheel hung motionless beside County Hall, its gondolas blackened by the smoke, a swan that had shed its plumage. A silent crowd lined the Embankment and stared across the slack water, as if waiting for the Wheel to turn, a machine from a painting by Bosch, grinding out time and death.

We set off for St John's Wood, past the same images of disaster hanging from the kiosks in the Charing Cross Road. Central London was dressed for an apocalyptic day. Arson in a film library clearly touched deep layers of unease, as the unconscious fears projected by a thousand Hollywood films at last emerged into reality. I thought of Kay Churchill in her dressing gown, forking scrambled eggs into her mouth while she watched the television news. Vera Blackburn would be in her apartment, playing moodily with her fuses and timers, ready to tackle another bastion of middle-class servitude, Hatchards or Fortnums or the V&A. The Day of Judgement was being planned by neurotic young women with badly bitten nails, and put into effect by out-of-breath psychologists with guilt complexes and dying mothers.

The taxi reached our house, and pulled to a stop behind Sally's car. I decided to say nothing about my role in the NFT attack, which Sally would never understand and soon confide to her friends—when I arrived at the Institute on Monday morning Professor Arnold would be waiting for me, Superintendent Michaels at his shoulder.

I let myself into the house, picking the newspapers from the doorstep. I waited for Sally to call to me, but the undisturbed air carried no trace of her morning shower, the aroma of towels and fresh coffee, and the soft, wifely realm where I now felt like an intruder. The kitchen was untouched, the dishes of a supper for one, an omelette and a glass of wine, lying by the sink.

I climbed the stairs, realizing how exhausted I was, bruised and bludgeoned as if I had spent the night with a violent policewoman. No one had slept in our bed, but the imprint of Sally's body dappled the silk spread. The telephone sat squarely on my pillow, almost reducing my husbandly role to a series of digits and unanswered messages. I assumed that Sally had waited up for me, watched the midnight news from the NFT and never guessed that her husband had been one of the arsonists. But Richard Gould's call had probably unsettled her. Confused by this maverick doctor, she decided to spend the night with a girlfriend.

Waiting for her to ring, I lay in the bath for an hour, then watched the lunchtime bulletin. The NFT attack still led the broadcast. No credible motive had emerged, but there was talk of an Islamic group protesting against the vilification of Arab peoples in Hollywood films. Once again, thanks to luck and bungling, we had got away with it.

Picking out a clean pair of shoes, I noticed Sally's overnight bag on the cupboard floor. Her dressing gown hung next to mine, but she had taken her painkillers from the bedside table, and the foil sachet of contraceptive pills.

I sat on the bed, staring into the open drawer. I lifted the telephone receiver and pressed the redial button, jotting the number on Sally's scribble pad.

The digits were painfully familiar, a number that I had often called, a long-standing private code for feelings of loss and regret. It was the number I dialled whenever I rang Laura to discuss the solicitor's slow progress with our divorce, in the year after she moved in with Henry Kendall.

I PARKED THE SAAB by the kerb, a series of complex and exhausting manoeuvres, and lay back gratefully, hiding my face behind a newspaper propped against the steering wheel. Fifty feet away was Henry's small terraced house in Swiss Cottage, a red-brick villa I had always disliked. The short drive from St John's Wood had tested to the full the tolerances of both the north London traffic system and my own temper. But by mastering the difficult and headstrong car I was in some way maintaining my grip on its errant owner.

Crossing Maida Vale, I tried to change gear and pulled the handbrake, stalling the engine under the eyes of a nearby policeman. He walked over to me, staring gravely into my face, and then recognized the adapted controls. Assuming that I was a crippled driver, he held back the traffic until I restarted the engine, and waved me on.

By the time I parked in Swiss Cottage I almost felt that I had become a cripple—more so than Sally, who dispensed with her sticks when the mood took her, and could easily drive my Range Rover. I resembled a skilled ballroom dancer obliged to do the tango on his hands. Sitting like a haunted husband in the car of his faithless wife, controls chafing my knees and elbows, I was now a distorted version of myself, reshaped by my sweetly affectionate and promiscuous wife.

I waited for an hour, gazing at the yellow blaze of forsythia beside Henry's dustbins, while the Sunday traffic carried families towards Hampstead Heath. I assumed that Sally had spent the night with him, though her telephone call had possibly been an attempt to find me. The terrorist bombs made her nervous of sleeping alone. But she had not rung for a taxi, and someone had driven to St John's Wood to collect her.

As I knew perfectly well, Sally insisted on the freedom to have her affairs. There had been only a few during the years, none lasting more than a week, and some briefer than the parties where she would pick an unattached man and slip away into the night. Often she reached home before I did. She always apologized, smiling hopelessly over a social gaffe, as if she had dented my car or ruined a new electric razor.

She took for granted that she had earned the right to these impulsive gestures. Like Frida Kahlo, the tram accident entitled her to indulge her whims, to play her own games with chance and a tolerant husband. Giving way to these infidelities was a means of paying me back for being so kindly and understanding. In her mind she remained a perpetual convalescent, free to commit the small cruelties she had displayed at St Mary's. I knew that the affairs would go on until she found a convincing explanation for the accident that had nearly killed her.

Cramped in the driver's seat, I stretched myself against the wheel, arranging my knees and elbows between the invalid controls, a contorted world that seemed to mimic a realm of deviant sexual desires. I held the pistol grip of the accelerator, and heard the linkages click and spring, the sound of relays coupling and uncoupling.

In many ways, my life was as deformed as this car, rigged with remote controls, fitted with overriders and emergency brakes within easy reach. I had warped myself into the narrow cockpit of professional work at the Adler, with its inane rivalries and strained emotional needs.

By contrast, the firebombing of the NFT was a glimpse of a more real world. I could still taste the smoke in the doomed auditoriums, rolling above my head like a compulsive dream. I could hear the hot breath of the goatlike figure who chased me to the Festival Hall, and see the calming smile of the waiter offering me a glass of champagne in the gondola of the Wheel. My quest for Laura's murderer was a search for a more intense and driven existence. Somewhere in my mind a part of me had helped to plant the Heathrow bomb.

A TAXI PULLED to a halt twenty feet from the Saab. Henry Kendall stepped out and paid the driver. He was tired but elated, his handsome face flushed by more than a good lunch. He reached through the passenger door and helped an attractive woman with shoulder-length hair, a long-stem rose in her hand. As he guided her from the taxi he seemed to lift her onto the pavement like a husband carrying his bride over the threshold.

Sally took his arm, smiling wryly as if the two of them had pulled off a clever conjuring trick. Laughing together, they paused to stare at Henry's house, pleasantly unsure where they really were.

Sally strolled across the pavement while Henry hunted for his keys, but her eye was caught by the headlines on the front page of the newspaper shielding my face. She stopped, recognizing her car, and pointed to the handicapped person's sticker on the windscreen.

'David . . . ?' She waited as I lowered the window, and then beckoned to Henry, who was staring at me as if we had never met. 'We've just had lunch.'

'Good.' I waved to Henry, who made no movement. 'Is everything all right?'

'Why not? Thanks for bringing the car round.' She bent down and kissed me with unfeigned affection, clearly glad to see me. 'How did you know I was here?'

'I guessed. It wasn't hard to work out. I'm a psychologist.'

'So is Henry. I'd give you a lift home, but . . .'

'I'll take a cab.' I stepped from the car, extricating myself from the controls, and handed her the keys. 'I'll see you soon. There's a lot going on. The NFT . . .'

'I know.' She searched my face, and touched a small bruise on my forehead. 'You're not fighting with the police again?'

'Nothing like that. I'm still looking into the Heathrow bomb. Some new leads have come up—I think they're important. You can tell Henry.'

'I will.' She stepped back, giving me a clear run at Henry, waiting for a show of husbandly outrage. When I failed to react, she said: 'Right, I'll be home later.'

'Good. When you're ready . . .'

I watched her hurry away, head down and her eyes on the pavement. For once, she had failed to provoke me. Henry stood by his front door, the rose in one hand. He waved it at me, but I ignored him and walked past.

Heading towards St John's Wood, I lengthened my step. I had made a small payment in masculine pride, but the investment had been worthwhile. The attack on the NFT had unlocked the door of my cell. I felt free again, for the first time since I joined the Adler and was inducted into the freemasonry of the professional class. Its suffocating regalia still hung in a wardrobe of my mind, the guilt and resentments and self-doubt, demanding to be taken out and paraded in front of the nearest mirror, a reminder of civic duty and responsibility. But the regalia were heading for the dustbin. I no longer resented my mother for her offhand self-ishness, or my colleagues at the Institute for the bone-breaking boredom they inflicted on the world. And I no longer resented Sally for her little infidelities. I loved her, and it mattered noth-ing if I was her father's private nurse.

I crossed Maida Vale and saluted the constable on duty, who seemed surprised that I was now striding along with such a skip in my stride. I was thinking of Chelsea Marina and the fire on the South Bank, and the black Millennium Wheel ready to turn above the ruins. I remembered Kay Churchill and Vera and Joan Chang and, above all, Dr Richard Gould, and knew that I needed to see them again.

19

THE SIEGE OF
BROADCASTING HOUSE

UNPREDICTABLE AS EVER, the police had decided not to intervene. I stood in the crowd of demonstrators outside Broadcasting House, waiting in vain for the sirens to sound and the riot vans to swerve into our ranks. But calm reigned, by order of the Police Commissioner. Double-decker buses moved along Langham Place, tourists gazing down at us, keen to observe one of London's historic rituals, the raising of fists against the establishment.

Across the street two constables patrolled the pavement near the Chinese Embassy. A third guarded the doors of the Langham Hotel, chatting to a limousine driver. None of them took any interest in the hundred or more protesters now blocking the entrance to the BBC's flagship headquarters. But without the police and a brisk confrontation, we would never rouse ourselves to action. We needed to lose our tempers, push aside the security men and seize the building.

'They must think we're fans,' I muttered to the fifty-year-old woman standing beside me in a sheepskin jacket. A veterinary surgeon and volunteer sexton at the Chelsea Marina chapel, she was a neighbour of the Reverend Dexter. 'Mrs Templeton—why is it you can never find a policeman when you need one? They must think we're here for some pop star . . .'

'Mr Markham? You're talking to yourself again . . .'

Like most of the protesters, Mrs Templeton was listening to her portable radio, tuned to the Radio 4 channel at that moment transmitting a commentary on the demonstration. Microphone at his lips, the reporter stood behind the security guards in the foyer of Broadcasting House, and there were hoots of laughter at some absurd comment about our motives for picketing the BBC.

Looking at the attentive faces around me, ears to their radios, I realized that we were taking our orders from the organization against which we were demonstrating. During the past three days the one o'clock news programme had run an investigation into the unrest at Chelsea Marina, and into similar outbursts of middle-income disquiet in Bristol and Leeds.

As expected, the journalists had missed the point. They blamed the revolt on the deep dissatisfactions of the baby-boomer generation, a self-indulgent and over-educated class unable to hold their own against a younger age-group thrusting their way into the professions. Pundits, backbench MPs, even a Home Office junior minister offered similar pearls. Listening to them in Kay's kitchen as she sliced the salad cucumber, I knew that I would have been just as glib if I had never set foot in Chelsea Marina.

So incensed by the BBC's patronizing tone that she cut her finger, Kay set about organizing a demo. We would flood Portland Place with protesters, rush the venerable deco building and seize control of the *World Today* studio, then broadcast a true account of the rebellion gathering pace across the map of middle England.

A large charge of resentment waited to be lit. As Kay explained, using a megaphone to address the crowd outside her house, for more than sixty years the BBC had played a leading role in brainwashing the middle classes. Its regime of moderation and good sense, its commitment to the Reithian aims of education and enlightenment, had been an elaborate cover behind which it imposed an ideology of passivity and self-restraint. The

BBC had defined the national culture, a swindle in which the middle classes had colluded, assuming that moderation and civic responsibility were in their own interest.

Steadying Kay as she teetered on her kitchen chair, I nodded confidently at her tirade. She introduced two fellow residents, former BBC arts producers recently made redundant. They knew their way around Broadcasting House, and would lead the assault on the *World Today* studio. All we lacked, when we made our separate ways across London the next morning, was a determined and ruthless enemy.

BUT I WAS still gripped by the excitements of the revolution. After leaving Sally and Henry Kendall outside Henry's house, I had waylaid a passing minicab, and kept it waiting in St John's Wood while I packed a small suitcase. I had no idea how long I would stay in Chelsea Marina, or how much luggage Lenin carried from the Finland Station, but I assumed that revolutionaries travelled light.

I felt a surge of relief when we reached the King's Road, like a child returning to a happy foster home. I had taken three weeks' leave, assuring Professor Arnold that my dying mother needed me with her. He had known her in her younger days, and was understandably sceptical. I would be happy to see Sally later, once she had emasculated Henry with her complex needs. At the moment, what was happening in this west London housing estate had far more meaning, and in some way held the key to my future.

Despite all this, the Pakistani driver refused to enter the estate, and stopped by the gatehouse.

'Far too dangerous, sir—the police advise us to stay out. A Harrods van has been stoned.'

'Stoned? What's behind it?'

'It's a question of ethnic rivalries. The people here have their own little Kashmir problem. There's a dominance struggle

between the traditional *Guardian* supporters and the new middle class from the financial services field.'

'Interesting.' I noticed a copy of *The Economist* on the front
seat. 'Now which side do I belong to?'

The driver turned to peer at me. 'Non-aligned, sir. Undoubt-
edly . . .'

I PAID UP and left him to it, setting off on foot past the boarded
windows of the estate manager's office. A police car patrolled
Beaufort Avenue, trailed by two residents in a battered Mini,
which flashed its lights in warning. I expected to find Kay's
house under close surveillance, but the cul de sac was at peace,
the silence broken only by the snipping of Kay's shears as she
trimmed her hedge.

She embraced me eagerly, took my hands and pressed them
to her breasts, then seized my suitcase. We spent a happy afternoon with several bottles of wine, debriefing each other after the
attack on the NFT. Kay had already forgotten that she had abandoned me—in the hope, I now suspected, that I would be caught
and betray her. Martyrdom waited in the wings of her ambition, ready to bestow stardom. She graphically described further
planned assaults on the South Bank, an outpost of the new tyranny, enslaving those who huddled for cultural shelter against
its brutalist walls.

'Undressed concrete, David. Alcatraz revival, always beware.
Built by the sort of people who liked Anna Neagle and Rex
Harrison . . .'

I was delighted to be with Kay and her chaotic enthusiasms.
At night I slept soundly on another child's mattress in her daughter's bedroom, surrounded by cheerful pastel drawings of the
Trojan War. Troy, I noticed, had a marked resemblance to Chelsea Marina, and the wooden horse was the first I had seen furnished with a stripped-pine penis. Shortly after dawn, when she

was woken by a police helicopter, Kay slipped into bed beside me. She lay quietly in the grey London light, inhaling the scent of her daughter's pillow before she turned to me.

DURING THE NEXT fortnight the Chelsea Marina rebellion made significant strides. More than half the residents were involved in the protest actions. As the *Daily Telegraph*—now the house journal of the revolution—noted in an editorial, many of the activists were senior professionals. Doctors, architects and solicitors took a prominent part in the sit-in at Chelsea Town Hall protesting against the new parking charges. A retired barrister led the demo outside the offices of the management company, demanding the surrender of the estate's freeholds.

The first confrontation with the police came a week after I returned. Bailiffs tried to force their way into a house owned by a young accountant, his wife and four children. The couple refused to pay their outrageous utility bills and were threatened with repossession.

But the bailiffs were met by a force of articulate and indignant women, who attacked their van before they could unload the sledgehammers. Twenty minutes later, the police arrived with a French television crew in tow. A storm of missiles rained down, stones lovingly gathered from the Seychelles, Mauritius and the Yucatan. The police tactfully withdrew, persuaded by a Home Office minister whose sister lived at Chelsea Marina. But the television scenes of the accountant's terrified children, screaming from their bedroom windows, prompted uneasy memories of sectarian violence in Belfast.

Many parents withdrew their children from their fee-paying schools, rejecting the entire ethos of private education, a vast obedience-training conspiracy. Concerned for their families' safety, many residents took unpaid leave, hoping to give themselves time to think. Their wives and children turned to pilfering from the King's Road supermarkets and delicatessens. Hauled in front of the magistrates, they refused to pay their fines, and the *Daily Mail* dubbed them 'the first middle-class gypsies'.

When an Inland Revenue office in Fulham was forced to close, after a walkout by the key computer managers, the authorities at last roused themselves. A sustained middle-class boycott of the consumer society would have disastrous effects on tax revenues. Investigators from the Department of Health roamed Chelsea Marina with their questionnaires, trying to isolate the underlying grievances.

The wide scatter of chosen targets made it difficult to find a common psychology at work. The pickets who blocked the entrances to Peter Jones and the London Library, Legoland and the British Museum, travel agencies and the V&A, a Hendon shopping mall and a minor public school, had nothing in common other than a rejection of middle-class life. Two smoke bombs in Selfridge's food hall and the Dinosaur wing of the Natural History Museum seemed unrelated, but closed both institutions for a day. The 'Destroy the museums' cry of Marinetti's futurists had a surprising resonance.

During a local by-election, when Kay and Vera set out for the polling station, hoping to deface their ballots, they found that the rejection of civic cooperation had become a serious threat to the democratic system. Parliamentary elections had long been run by middle-class volunteers. The stay-at-home decision by even a few experienced tellers forced a postponement, applauded by the residents at Chelsea Marina, who regarded parliamentary democracy as a none too subtle way of neutering the middle class.

Pleased by all this, Kay sent me out to buy the broadsheet newspapers, and over her wine read out the worried editorials. *The Times* and *Guardian* were baffled why so many of their readers were seceding from society. Both quoted a deputy head teacher and Chelsea Marina resident interviewed on television:

'We're tired of being taken for granted. We're tired of being used.
We don't like the kind of people we've become . . .'

OUTSIDE BROADCASTING HOUSE the demonstrators pressed
closer to the entrance, pushing back the wooden barriers that the
BBC security men had placed in front of the doors. A crowd of
some two hundred protesters had now formed, listening on their
radios to a news programme that discussed the events unfolding
below the BBC's windows.

I scanned the familiar faces of Chelsea Marina residents, but
there was no sign of Kay, Vera Blackburn or Richard Gould. I
knew that a protest was planned at the V&A, which Kay termed
'an emporium of cultural delusions'. The target was the Cast
Room, where the copy of Michelangelo's *David* would be pulled
from its plinth, in much the way that statues of Stalin and Lenin
were toppled after the fall of the Berlin Wall. The *David*, Kay
claimed, deluded the middle classes that a developed 'cultural'
sensibility endowed them with a moral superiority denied to
football fans or garden gnome enthusiasts.

'Oh, my God . . .' Mrs Templeton rocked back on her heels.
Around us, people were laughing in disbelief.

'Mrs Templeton? Has something happened?'

'It certainly has.' She brushed a fly from the sleeve of her
sheepskin jacket. 'Chelsea Marina is "the first middle-class sink
estate". We're the "underclass" of the bourgeoisie. Dear God . . .'

I tried to think of an adequate response, but an angry confrontation had broken out between the security guards and a group
of protesters knocking over the wooden barriers. A tug of war
quickly followed, the security men insisting that the barrier was
BBC property and taunting the demonstrators for refusing to pay
their licence fees.

A thunderflash burst near the entrance, a hard explosion that
cuffed our ears. In the shocked silence a cloud of blue smoke floated
over our heads. Taking Mrs Templeton's arm, I saw a TV news car

in Portland Place forced onto the pavement. White police vans, sirens seesawing, swerved through the traffic and pulled to a halt by All Souls church in Langham Place. Officers in riot gear, shields and truncheons at the ready, leapt from the vans and pushed their way through the watching lunchtime crowds.

A smoke bomb shot a gust of black vapour into the air. A startled security guard tripped over one of the barriers and fell to the ground. The protesters seized their chance and surged past him, forcing their way through the doors. Still holding Mrs Templeton's arm, I felt myself propelled into the foyer by the police pressure.

A hundred of us packed the reception area, overwhelming the security staff trying to guard the lifts. A group of guests cowered among the armchairs, pundits at last confronted by reality. The smoke followed us into the foyer, swirling into the lift shafts as the elevators carried the advance parties of demonstrators to the upper floors. Led by one of the BBC producers who had come over to our side, they planned to invade the news studio and broadcast the manifesto of middle-class rebellion to the listening nation, mouths agape over their muesli.

The other BBC man, a slim-faced Anglo-Indian, herded us towards the stairs to the left of the foyer. One floor above, we burst through a door marked 'Council Chamber'. The high-ceilinged room, with its semi-circular south wall, was hung with portraits of the BBC's director-generals, who had presided over the Corporation's benevolent tyranny.

Like a revolutionary rabble breaking into an *ancien régime* drawing room and confronting the effigies of a corrupt aristocracy, we stared aghast at the portraits, dominated by the BBC's principal architect, Lord Reith. I noticed that the subjects' heads grew larger as the years passed and the BBC's power increased, culminating in the smiling balloon-head of a recent appointee, an immense inflated blimp of self-satisfaction.

A nervous line of junior producers and studio engineers faced

us across the chamber, barely convinced of any sacrifice they
might have to make. They surrendered limply when we pushed
past them. Mrs Templeton drew an aerosol can from her handbag. As smoke drifted into the chamber from the foyer below,
she expertly aimed her paint jet at the portraits, endowing them
with a series of Hitler moustaches and forelocks.

FIVE MINUTES LATER it was all over. As the riot police manhandled us through the lobby we learned that the assault on *The
World Today* had failed. Long before our arrival, the entire production team had moved to a secure studio in the basement. The
police snatch squads had entered Broadcasting House through
a side door in Portland Place. They were waiting for us, truncheons warm and at the ready, and made short work of any protesters lost in the mazelike corridors. We were roughly rounded
up and ejected from the building, and the Corporation resumed
its historic task of beguiling the middle classes.

Police violence, I noted, was directly proportional to police
boredom, and not to any resistance offered by protesters. We were
saved from any real brutality by our own incompetence and the
swift end to the demonstration. Helped along by kicks and baton
blows, we were bundled into the smoke-stained air of Portland
Place. In half an hour we would be bussed to West End Central, charged and bailed to appear before the magistrates. First
offenders like Mrs Templeton would be spared, but I was almost
certain to be given a thirty-day sentence.

Flung through the doors by a sweating constable, I tripped
over a wooden barrier. A woman police sergeant stepped forward
and took my arm. As she helped me to my feet I recognized the
determined face of the demonstrator at Olympia who had bandaged my injured leg.

'Angela . . . ?' I peered under the lowered brim of her hat. 'The
cat show, Olympia . . .'

'Cat show?'

'Kingston, two children . . .'

'Right.' Vaguely recognizing me, she relaxed her strong grip. 'I remember.'

'You joined the police?'

'Looks like it.' She moved me towards the church, where the prisoners were being processed. 'You're a long way from Olympia, Mr—?'

'Markham. David Markham.' I stared into her steely eyes as a police van veered past us. 'Quite a change of heart. When did you join?'

'Four years ago. Never felt better.'

'So, you were . . . undercover?'

'That sort of thing.' She led me through the throng of dog handlers and police drivers. 'You look all in. Find a different hobby.'

'Undercover?' Remembering my £100 fine for going to her aid, I said: 'I'm impressed.'

'Someone has to keep the streets safe.'

'I agree. As it happens, I was also undercover.'

'Really? Who with?'

'Hard to explain. It's connected to the Heathrow bomb. The Home Office is interested.'

'Now I'm impressed.' She pointed to the last protesters being expelled from Broadcasting House. Mrs Templeton, her jacket torn, was complaining to a weary inspector. 'What about today? Is this part of your project?'

'No. It's more serious than it looks. We have a point to make.'

'You may be serious, but it's a very small point. You're wasting police time and giving cover to people who want to do real damage.'

Already she had lost interest in me. Her eyes picked up a change of mood among the police units. Handlers were urging their dogs into the backs of vans, drivers started their engines. All but a few of the officers guarding the protesters on the church steps turned and ran to their vehicles. Leaving me without a word, Angela slipped into the front passenger seat of a police car that halted briefly beside us.

Sirens wailed down Upper Regent Street as the convoy departed. Almost the entire police presence had gone, a vacuum filled by ambling tourists who began to photograph us. The protesters corralled on the church steps were listening to their radios again, and began to disperse as the constables beckoned them away.

Mrs Templeton walked towards me, radio held to her ear. She seemed ruffled and confused, unaware of her torn jacket and the paint on her chin.

'Mrs Templeton? We'll share a taxi. I think we've got away with it.'

'What?' She stared wildly at me, her attention fixed on the radio. She had lost the heel of her right shoe, and in an odd middle-class reflex of my own I felt that she was letting the side down by appearing so dishevelled.

'We're safe, Mrs Templeton. The police—did they hurt you?'

'Listen . . .' Eyes almost crossed, she handed the radio to me. 'A bomb's gone off at Tate Modern. Three people were killed . . .'

I listened to the reporter's urgent voice, but around me all sound seemed to withdraw from the street. Tourists wandered past Broadcasting House, staring at maps that led nowhere. Rag-trade despatch riders hovered at the traffic lights, exhausts pumping, ready to race from one meaningless assignment to another. The city was a vast and stationary carousel, forever boarded by millions of would-be passengers who took their seats, waited and then dismounted. I thought of the bomb cutting through another temple of enlightenment, silencing the endless murmur of cafeteria conversations. Despite myself, I felt a surge of excitement and complicity.

20

WHITE SPACE

'IF THE MEANS are desperate enough, they justify the ends.'

Kay spoke with her hands on my shoulders, standing behind me as we watched the breakfast news in her kitchen. Despite the closeness and affection prompted by the Tate bomb, I could feel her fingers trembling as if they were trying to break free from me. I thought of the deep night we had spent together, the hours passed talking in the dark, each of us unpacking a lifetime's memories. But the destruction at the Tate rekindled nerves that had been numbed by too much talk of violence, the conspirator's blank cheque that might one day have to be cashed. Protest tapped all Kay's high ideals, but violence devalued them, making her uneasily aware that reality waited for us outside an already open door.

She squeezed my shoulders, staring through the sitting-room window at a convoy of neighbours' cars leaving to support a rent strike in north London.

'Kay?'

'I'm all right. There's so much going on.'

'The Mill Hill demo—do you want to join them?'

'I ought to.' Her worn fingers felt the spurs of bone in my neck. 'There's a lot to think over.'

'The two of us?' I tried to calm her. 'Kay?'

'Who?'

'You and I. Do we need to talk anything through?'

'Again? Slow-motion replays make me nervous. Cinema died when they invented the flashback.' Taking pity on me, she massaged my temples with her forefingers. 'It's all starting to happen. You can feel we're on the edge of something.'

'We are. Ten years in jail.'

'That's not a joke.' She held my head protectively to her breast, like a mother with her child. 'You could do some real time. I always thought you might be a police spy. You took so many chances, and came back even though we left you in the shit. Either you were very careless or you had some special friends looking after you. But that wasn't it at all—I knew that yesterday. You were so involved.'

'Good. The BBC demo?'

'No. That was a joke. Even Peggy Templeton couldn't get herself arrested. I mean the bomb at Tate Modern.'

'Kay . . . ?' I turned and held her hips, looking up at her troubled face. 'Tate Modern? That was horrific. I wasn't involved in any way at all.'

'It was horrific, but you were involved.' Kay sat down at right angles to me, looking at my face in profile, like a phrenologist trying to read my character in the angles of my forehead. 'Last night in bed—you were so wrapped up in the violence of it, the horror of those deaths. You had the best sex in your life.'

'Kay . . .'

'Be honest, you did. How many times did you come? I stopped counting.' Kay held my wrists. 'You wanted to bugger me, and beat me. For God's sake, I know when a man's balls are alight. Yours were on fire. You were thinking of that bomb, suddenly going off and tearing everything apart. The meaningless violence—it excited you.'

'Unconsciously? Maybe. Once we went to bed I didn't talk about it.'

'You didn't need to. You got up to pee and looked in the bath-room mirror. You could see it in your eyes.' Frustrated by her-self, and her too tolerant responses, Kay switched off the TV set. She pointed accusingly at the blank screen. 'Three people died. Think about it, David. Some poor warder giving his life for a Damien Hirst . . .'

THE PREVIOUS EVENING, still charged by the adrenalin rush of the BBC protest and the news of the Tate explosion, we had drunk far too much wine. The bomb, a Semtex device hidden inside a large art book, had detonated near the bookshop at 1.45 pm, killing the visitor who carried it, and blowing out a large section of the masonry above the entrance. A French tourist and a warder were also killed, and some twenty visitors injured. The police had cordoned off the surrounding area, and a forensic team was picking through the dust and rubble that covered the nearby grass and parked cars.

No one took responsibility, but the bomb gave a sharper edge to London's grey and muffled air. Boredom and volatility marked the future. The device exploded on the same day as the Broad-casting House protest, and seemed to point towards Chelsea Marina and its middle-class rebellion, but Kay strongly con-demned the Tate attack. Phone-in audiences who watched her TV interviews accepted this, if only because the bomb-maker's sinister competence clearly belonged to a different realm. Chel-sea Marina's architects and solicitors, with their smoke bombs and thunderflashes, claimed that they had never tried to kill anyone. For the first time, Kay found herself regarded as a voice of moderation.

Perhaps to offset this novel image she told me as she undressed for bed that she had slept with all her lodgers, from eighteen-year-old film students to an alcoholic cartoonist ejected from his home near the marina by his exasperated wife. 'All landladies

over forty have sex with their lodgers. It's the last surviving link
with matriarchy . . .'

TAKING A BOTTLE of wine from the refrigerator, Kay set two
glasses on the table. She sat down, hands pressed to her face, staring at me.

'Kay? A little early?'

'You're going to need this. Me, too, as it happens. I'll miss you.'

'Fire away.'

'Go back to Sally. Get in your car and drive straight to St
John's Wood. Dust off your briefcase and become a corporate psychologist again.'

'Kay . . . ?' Her calm tone surprised me. 'Why, for heaven's
sake? Because of last night?'

'Partly.' She sipped her drink, sniffing her fingers as if the scent
of my testicles still clung to her nails. 'That's not the only reason.'

'I was over-excited. The BBC demo, being kicked around by
the police. Then the Tate bomb. What if I'd been impotent?'

'I wish you had been impotent. I'd have preferred that. Impotence would have been the normal reaction. Instead of which,
you were like Columbus sighting the New World. That's why you
need to go back to Sally. You don't belong here.' She reached out
and held my hand. 'You're a domestic man, David. You feel hundreds of small affections all the time. They haunt every friendly
pillow and comfortable chair like household gods. Together they
add up to a great love, big enough to ignore this silly man who's
hanging around your wife's skirts.'

'Domestic . . . ?' I stared at my reflection trembling in the surface of my wine. 'You make me sound like some sort of ruminant,
grazing in a quiet field. I thought Chelsea Marina was trying to
change all that.'

'It is. But for us, violence is only the means to an end. For you,
it is the end. It's opened your eyes, and you think you can see a

world that's much more exciting. No more comfy cushions and friendly sofas where you and Sally watch the late-night news. It wasn't the Tate bomb that got you going last night.'

'Kay . . .' I tried to take her wrists but she pulled away from me. 'That's what I've been trying to say.'

'It was the Heathrow bomb.' Kay paused to watch me biting a childhood scar on my lip. 'That's been driving you all along. It's why you came to Chelsea Marina.'

'You brought me here. Remember—you found me outside the courthouse. I don't think I'd ever been here before.'

'But you were looking for somewhere like it. All those demos and marches. Sooner or later you would have found us. The Heathrow bomb still rang inside your head; you could hear it in St John's Wood. A call sign signalling a new world.'

'Kay . . . my wife was killed.' I waved away my repeated slip of the tongue. 'Laura. I wanted to find whoever planted the bomb.'

'But why? You're happily married, though you don't seem to know it. Laura was years ago, and you didn't even like her that much. Not the way you like Sally—or me, for that matter.'

'Liking someone has nothing to do with our real feelings for them.' I tried to smile at Kay. 'Laura provoked the world. Almost everything she did, the smallest things she said, somehow changed me a little. Oddly enough, I could never work out how. She opened doors.'

'And the Heathrow bomb was the biggest door of all. There wasn't anything to see, but there was this huge white space. It meant everything and nothing. It gripped you, David. You're like someone who's out-stared the sun. Now you want to turn everything into Heathrow.'

'Chelsea Marina? Video stores and plaster statues?'

'You're bored with all that.' Kay moved aside the wine bottle and our glasses, clearing the table so that she could think. 'You're bored the way Richard Gould is bored. You're looking for real violence, and sooner or later you'll find it. That's why you've got to get into your car and go back to Sally. You need those double yellow lines, those parking regulations and committee meetings to calm you down.'

'Sally? I'd like to go back, but not yet.' I touched my lips and pressed my fingers to Kay's fierce forehead, grateful to her. 'She has her own problems to work out. In some ways she's as involved with the Heathrow bomb as I am. She needs to make sense of it.'

'Sense? There is no sense. That's the whole point.'

'Difficult to put over, though. Only a psychopath can grasp it. Richard Gould thinks I'm wrong there.'

'Richard?' Roused, Kay looked up from her broken nails. 'Keep away from him. He's dangerous, David. You can stay here a little longer, but don't get involved with him.'

'Dangerous?' I pointed to the elderly computer on her desk, partly buried in a pile of unread student scripts. 'You used to run his website.'

'That was in the early days. He's moved on. Chelsea Marina failed him.' She tried to take the cork out of the wine bottle, but gave up. 'Richard Gould is waiting for you, David. I don't know why, but he has been all along. When I rang him from the court-house he asked me to bring you here . . .'

I THOUGHT about this as I changed into my tweed suit, which hung in the bedroom wardrobe among Kay's camouflage jackets and spangly party dresses. Kay was the disappointed fan, who had once hung on every word of the charismatic Dr Gould as he tub-thumped his way around Chelsea Marina, urging the residents to fight for their rights. But now Kay had become a politi-cal figure, arguing her case on discussion programmes, profiled in the Sunday broadsheets and backed by ambitious young law-yers with time on their hands. Gould was Peter Pan, mentally marooned on his asylum island, searching for his lost boys as reality moved towards him in the menacing form of a thousand starter homes.

As I set off for the Adler, for the first time in three weeks, Kay watched me from the door. She leaned on one foot like an usherette gazing at a film with an unconvincing plot-line.

'David? That's a very good impression of a man going to the office.'

'I am. I need to cheer up my secretary, see one or two clients.'

'And those bruises?'

'I'm not going to undress. I'll say I've been scuba-diving. I bumped into some strange fish.'

'You did.' She let me kiss her, and straightened my tie. 'You look like an imposter.'

'Kay, that's the fate of anyone who's too sincere. As long as I convince myself. When I can't do that any longer I'll know it's time to go back to St John's Wood.'

I stood in the sunlight, thinking of Sally, whom I had not seen since leaving her outside Henry Kendall's house in Swiss Cottage. I missed her, but she had begun to slip into the past, part of a life that I wanted to reject, a castle of obligations held together by the ivy of middle-class insecurity.

21

THE KINDNESS OF LIGHT

I WAVED TO KAY, a husband leaving for work, watched by several puzzled residents, who stared at me as if I were an actor rehearsing an activity like maypole dancing. Self-conscious in my well-cut tweeds, I crossed the street to the Range Rover. When I opened the door I noticed that I had a passenger. A black-suited man in an unwashed white shirt lounged on the front leather seat, dozing in the morning sun. He woke and greeted me with a generous smile, helping me behind the wheel. He seemed as neglected as ever, the bones of his face straining to expose themselves to the light.

'Dr Gould?'

'Climb aboard.' He steered a sports bag onto the rear seat. 'It's good to see you, David. You don't mind if you drive?'

'It's my car.' I hesitated before inserting the ignition key, in case the safety lock had been wired up to some practical joke. 'How did you get in?'

'It was unlocked.'

'Rubbish.'

'No. The middle classes don't steal cars. It's a tribal thing, like not wearing a brown suit.'

'I thought all that was going to change.'

'Exactly. After the revolution the middle class will be shiftless, slatternly, light-fingered, and forget to wash.' He peered into my eyes, pretending to see something. 'Speaking as a doctor, I'd say you were in surprisingly good shape.'

'Surprisingly? After Broadcasting House?'

'No. After Kay Churchill. Sex with Kay is like a resuscitation that's gone slightly wrong. You're deeply grateful, but parts of you are never going to be the same again.'

Gould talked away to himself, enjoying his own patter. He was more relaxed than the haunted paediatrician in the asylum at Bedfont. In his shabby black suit he resembled an unsuccess-ful gangster let down by intellectual tastes. He had annoyed me by breaking into the car, but knew that I was glad to see him.

'I'm heading for the office,' I told him. 'Where can I drop you? The West End?'

'Please . . . Too many police wandering around in circles. We need a day in the country.'

'Richard, I have to see my clients.'

'Your father-in-law? See him tomorrow. The place we're visit-ing is important, David. It may even shed light on the Heathrow bomb . . .'

WE SET OFF for Hammersmith, and took the flyover towards the brewery roundabout, passed Hogarth's house and drove into the west along the M4. Gould lay back, gazing at the single-storey factories, the offices of video-duplicating firms and the lighting arrays of unknown stadiums. This was his real terrain, a zone without past or future, civic duties or responsibilities, its empty car parks roamed by off-duty air hostesses and betting-shop managers, a realm that never remembered itself.

'Tell me, David—how did yesterday go? At the BBC?'

'We broke in, briefly. Everyone enjoyed themselves trying to get arrested. Moral indignation lit up the whole of Regent Street. A few people were cautioned.'

'Too bad. A mass arrest would have put Chelsea Marina on the map.'

'The police were called away. The Tate bomb stopped everything in its tracks.'

'Grim. Truly grim. Vera and I were in Dunstable, checking out a gliding school.' Gould covered his eyes with a shudder. 'Looking back at the BBC demo, how do you feel about it?'

'We all arrived on time, and knew what we were doing. Parking was difficult. When Armageddon takes place, parking is going to be a major problem.'

'But the action as a whole—what did you think of it?'

'Broadcasting House? It was childish.'

'Go on.'

'And pointless. A lot of responsible people pretending to be hooligans. A student rag for the middle-aged. The police didn't take it seriously for a second.'

'They've seen too many sit-ins. They're easily bored—we need to take that into account.'

'Put on more lavish productions? Burning down the NFT was irresponsible. And criminal. People might have been killed. If I'd known I'd never have taken part.'

'You weren't fully briefed. Breaking the law is a huge challenge for professionals like you, David. That's why the middle class will never be a true proletariat.' Gould nodded to himself, and put his feet up on the dashboard. 'As it happens, I agree with you.'

'About the NFT?'

'About everything. Fortnums, the BBC, Harrods, Legoland. Smoke bombs and pickets. A complete waste of time.' He reached out to take the wheel. 'Careful—this is not where I want to die.'

A horn sounded behind us, and headlamps flared in the rearview mirror. Surprised by Gould's comments, I had braked as we passed the Heathrow Hilton on the fast dual carriageway to Bedfont. I picked up speed again, and moved into the slow lane.

'Richard? I thought you planned the whole campaign.'

'I did. When we started. Now Kay and her chums pick the targets.'

'So the revolution has been postponed?'

'It's still on. Something significant is happening. You've sensed it, David. Chelsea Marina is only the beginning. An entire social class is peeling the velvet off the bars and tasting the steel. People are resigning from well-paid jobs, refusing to pay their taxes, taking their children out of private schools.'

'Then what's gone wrong?'

'Nothing will happen.' Gould examined his teeth in the sun-visor mirror, a grimace of infected gums that made him close his eyes. 'The storm will die down, and everything will peter out in a drizzle of television shows and op-ed pieces. We're too polite and too frivolous.'

'And if we were serious?'

'We'd kill a cabinet minister. Or sneak a bomb into the Commons chamber. Shoot a minor royal.'

'A bomb?' I kept my eyes on the traffic, conscious of the tail fins of parked airliners a few hundred yards inside the Heathrow perimeter. 'I'm not sure . . .'

'It's a large step, but it might be necessary.' Gould touched my hand with his bloodless fingers. 'Would you do that, David?'

'Kill a cabinet minister? I'm too polite.'

'Too docile? Too well brought up?'

'Absolutely. Anger was bred out of me long ago. I'm married to a rich man's daughter who's very sweet and very loving, and treats me like one of her father's tenants. If she's chasing her latest fox she gallops over my potato patch without a thought. And all I do is smile and settle her charge account at Harvey Nicks.'

'At least you know it.'

'I couldn't plant a bomb in the Commons or anywhere else. I'd be too nervous of hurting someone.'

'You can get over that, David.' Gould spoke offhandedly, like a doctor making light of a patient's trivial worry. 'If your motives are sound, anything is possible. You're waiting for a greater challenge. You haven't found it yet, but you will . . .'

GOULD SAT FORWARD, hands smoothing his toneless face, trying to massage a little colour into his cheeks. We turned off the airport road and entered East Bedfont, moving past a small business park towards the children's hospice which had taken responsibility for the infants at Bedfont Hospital.

Gould guided me up a gravel drive that led to a three-storey Georgian house. There were carefully trimmed shrubs and a wide lawn unmarked by human feet. Brightly coloured swings and slides sat on the grass, but the children were absent. Leaves and rainwater lay on the tiny seats, and I guessed that this was a playground where no child had ever played.

Gould was undismayed. As we stopped by the rear entrance to the hospice he lifted the sports bag from the seat. He opened it on his lap, revealing a selection of plastic toys. Pleasantly surprised, he began to test them, and his face came alight when one of the dolls began to talk back to him in her recorded voice.

He stepped eagerly from the car, like a devoted godparent at a birthday party, and drew a white coat from the sports bag. He pulled it over his suit, hunted the pockets and found a name-tag, which he pinned to my lapel.

'Try to look professional, David. It's surprisingly easy to impersonate a senior consultant.'

'"Dr Livingstone"?'

'It always works. You're a colleague of mine at Ashford Hospital. Now . . . you'll like the children, David.'

'Are we allowed in?'

'Of course. These are my children. The world is meaningless to them, so they need me to show them they exist. In a way, they remind me of you . . .'

———

WE ENTERED a rear hallway beside the kitchens, where lunch was being prepared for the small staff. Gould kissed the nursing sister in charge, a handsome black woman with a welcoming manner. Gould held her arm while they climbed the stairs, as if they were fellow conspirators.

The three sunny wards held thirty children, almost all bed-ridden, passive little parcels posted to death soon after they were born. But Gould greeted them like his own family. For the next hour I watched him play with the toddlers, making glove puppets out of old socks and Christmas tape, swooping around the ward with his arms raised, handing out toys from his holdall while wearing a Santa Claus jacket borrowed from the sister. She told me that he had brought Christmas forward for the children living out their last weeks.

I followed her from the ward when she left Gould to his high spirits. She accepted a cigarette and lit it for herself.

'You do a remarkable job,' I complimented her. 'The children seem very happy.'

'Thank you . . . Dr Livingstone? We do what we can. Many of the children will soon be leaving us.'

'How often does Dr Gould come here?'

'Every week. He never lets them down.' Her smile drifted across her broad face like a sunny cloud. 'He's very involved with the children. Sometimes I wonder what he'll do when the last of them goes . . .'

When I returned to the ward Gould was sitting beside the cot of a three-year-old boy with a shaved head. A wide scar ran across his scalp, crudely stitched together. His eyes had shrunk into his face, but were fixed unblinkingly on his visitor. Gould had lowered the side of the cot and sat forward, an arm under the wool blanket. He looked up at me, waiting for me to go, making it clear that I was intruding on a private moment.

LATER, WHEN GOULD appeared in the car park, I said: 'I'm impressed. No computer could have done all that. One or two almost recognized you.'

'I hope so. David, they know me. I'm one of them, really.'

He tossed the empty sports bag and the white coat into the rear seat of the Range Rover, and then stared at the lawn with its silent slides and swings. He seemed almost boyish in his edgy way, younger but more intense than the amateur terrorist I had met in the gondola above the National Film Theatre.

Trying to reassure him, I said: 'You help them, Richard. That's worth something.'

'No.' Gould's fleshless hands warmed themselves on the car roof. 'They're not really aware of me. I'm a vague retinal blur. Their brains have switched themselves off.'

'They could hear you. Some of them.'

'I doubt it. They're gone, David. Nature committed a crime against them. Besides, certain things are meaningless. After all the theorizing, all the chains of cause and effect, there's a hard core of pointlessness. That may be the only point we can find anywhere . . .'

I waited before starting the engine, while Gould stared at the windows of the wards on the first floor.

'Richard, tell me—did you touch that little boy?'

Gould turned his head to look at me, clearly disappointed. 'David? Would it matter?'

'Not really. It's arguable.'

'Talk it over with Stephen Dexter.'

Impatient to leave, he reached across me and turned the ignition key.

AFTER AN HOUR'S DRIVE, we reached a small gliding school high in the Marlborough Downs. Gould had enrolled by e-mail for a course of lessons, but the school's secretary seemed sur-

prised by the undernourished and unkempt appearance of this
odd young doctor with his white skin and shabby suit. I offered
to vouch for Gould, but he sent me back to the car. As I knew
he would, he soon convinced the secretary of his powerful need
to fly.

I sat in the clubhouse and watched Gould inspect the tandem
cockpit of a training glider. Through the open windows I listened
to the flutter of air over the grass aerodrome, the fabric of parked
gliders shivering in the cool wind. Gould nodded to the woman
instructor, eyes on the sky as if already planning to stow himself
away on the Space Shuttle.

'Right,' he told me when we walked back to the car. 'Trial
flight next week. You can come and watch.'

'I might.'

'It's a challenge, David.' He touched his ear. 'I have a small
problem with my balancing organ. Oddly enough, airline hijack-
ers tend to suffer from it. One could see the hijack as an unconscious attempt to solve the problem.'

'Far-fetched?'

'Why?' He looked back as a glider rose into the air, released
the towing cable and soared away with the icy grace of a condor.
'Besides, it's all part of the great search.'

'For what?'

'This and that. Some kind of tentative explanation. The mystery of space-time, the wisdom of trees, the kindness of light . . .'

'Gliding? More than powered flight?'

'Heaven forbid. The world turned into noise; life and death
measured by legroom.'

'And gliding?'

'You're above the sky.'

He lay back in the passenger seat as we headed for the motorway, his shirt unbuttoned to the waist, unpacking himself for
the sun.

———

I SWITCHED ON the radio, flattering myself that the Broad-casting House invasion would lead the news. The bulletins were dominated by the bomb at Tate Modern, the most popular cultural centre in London, which performed the role once assigned to the Dome. No group admitted its part in the attack, and security had been tightened at the British Museum and the National Gallery.

'From now on it's going to be a lot harder,' I commented. 'The Science Museum, the British Library . . .'

'David, they're the wrong targets.' Gould closed his eyes in the sun, lost in a reverie of wings and light. 'They're the targets people expect us to hit. They're zebra-crossing protests writ large, educated mothers demonstrating for speed humps outside schools. It's what the middle classes do.'

'Anything wrong with that?'

'They're too predictable, too sensible. We need to pick targets that don't make sense. If your target is the global money system, you don't attack a bank. You attack the Oxfam shop next door. Deface the cenotaph, spray Agent Orange on Chelsea Physic Garden, burn down London Zoo. We're in the business of creating unease.'

'And a meaningless target would be the best of all?'

'Well said. You understand me, David.' Gould touched my hand, pleased to be driven by me. 'Kay and her crowd, they're still locked into honesty and good manners. All those architects and lawyers—the most radical thing they can imagine is burning down St Paul's School for Girls. They don't realize their lives are empty.'

'Is that true? Most of them love their children.'

'DNA. Biology's first commandent. Take no more credit for loving your children than birds take credit for nest-building.'

'Civic pride?'

'The gene pool's neighbourhood-watch scheme. Look at you, David. Concerned, thoughtful, kindly, but nothing you do matters a damn.'

'You're right. Religious faith?'

'Dying. Now and then it sits up and seizes the undertaker by the wrists. A pointless act has a special meaning of its own. Calmly carried out, untouched by any emotions, a meaningless act is an empty space larger than the universe around it.'

'So we avoid motives?'

'Absolutely. Kill a politician and you're tied to the motive that made you pull the trigger. Oswald and Kennedy, Princip and the Archduke. But kill someone at random, fire a revolver into a McDonald's—the universe stands back and holds its breath. Better still, kill fifteen people at random.'

'Better?'

'Figuratively, that is. I don't want to kill anyone.' Keen to reassure me, Gould rehearsed a disarming smile in the visor's mirror, and then treated me to the full grimace. 'You see all this, David. You've grasped the point. That's why I trust you. People are nervous of violence. Excited, of course, but it unsettles them.'

'Not you?'

'You've noticed that? I suppose it's true. Violence is like a bush fire, it destroys a lot of trees but refreshes the forest, clears away the stifling undergrowth, so more trees spring up. We'll have to think of the right targets. They need to be completely pointless . . .'

'Keats House, the Bank of England, Heathrow?'

'No, not Heathrow.' Distracted by a roadside sign, Gould reached over and held the wheel. 'Slow down, David—there's something I want to see . . .'

WE WERE PASSING through a pleasant country town a few miles from our junction with the motorway. The traffic was surprisingly heavy, tourists peering through their car windows. On the outskirts of the town there were bosky lanes and high sycamores, and Gould gazed at the distant boughs like a latter-day Samuel Palmer, searching the window of the sky for a glimpse of the light beyond. His pale hand traced the overlay of branches, as if working out a route through a maze.

But the town itself was nondescript, cottages with simulated thatch roofs converted into dry-cleaners and video shops, a half-timbered Chinese takeaway, souvenir stores and coffee bars. There was a forest of signs helpfully guiding the visiting motorist to the car parks, though it was unclear why the town should have so many visitors or why they would want to park there.

Yet Gould seemed satisfied, smiling over his shoulder as we approached the motorway.

'A charming place, David. Don't you think?'

'Well . . . Watford with fields?'

'No. There's something very special. You saw all those tourists. It's almost a place of worship.'

'Hard to believe.' I followed the slip road and joined the motorway traffic. 'Where is it, exactly?'

'It's off the A4, on the way to Newbury.' Gould lay back, inhaling deeply, as if he had held his breath for minutes. 'Hungerford . . . it's where I'd like to end my days.'

HUNGERFORD? The name flitted around my mind like a trapped moth as we drove back to London. I was surprised by Gould's response to the town, and I suspected that our visit to the gliding school had been an excuse to drive through its streets. If he became a glider pilot he would be able to fly over its car parks and souvenir shops, satisfying some deep dream of rural peace.

Childhood arsonists carried their apocalyptic fantasies into adult life. Fire and flight seemed to fill Gould's mind. I watched him dozing beside me, only stirring when we approached Heathrow. The airport had as great a hold on his imagination as it did on mine, binding us together in an unusual partnership. I had wasted half a day driving him into the country, hoping that he would reveal more of himself. But in fact he had ensnared me in his bizarre world, drawing me into his fragmentary personality, almost offering himself as a kit from which I could construct a vital figure missing from my life. I admired him for his kindness to the dying children, and he had skilfully played on this, and on my own weaknesses. I was drawn to him and the way that he had sacrificed everything to his quest for truth, an exhausted captain still ready to feed his own masts into the furnace.

All these thoughts left my mind when I dropped Gould off at Chelsea Marina and went on to the Institute. Buying an evening paper that headlined the Tate bomb attack, I read the names of the three victims, a warder, a French tourist, and a young Chinese woman living in west London. Joan Chang, the Reverend Dexter's friend in the Puffa jacket . . .

22

A VISIT TO THE BUNKER

THE THAMES shouldered its way past Blackfriars Bridge, impatient with the ancient piers, no longer the passive stream that slid past Chelsea Marina, but a rush of ugly water that had scented the open sea and was ready to make a run for it. Below Westminster the Thames became a bruiser of a river, like the people of the estuary, unimpressed by the money terraces of the City of London.

The dealing rooms were a con, and only the river was real. The money was all on tick, a stream of coded voltages sluicing through concealed conduits under the foreign exchange floors. Facing them across the river were two more fakes, the replica of Shakespeare's Globe, and an old power station made over into a middle-class disco, Tate Modern. Walking past the entrance to the Globe, I listened for an echo of the bomb that had killed Joan Chang, the only meaningful event in the entire landscape.

I had parked in Sumner Street, a hundred yards from the rear of the Tate. Police vehicles surrounded the gallery, and crime-scene tapes closed the entrance to the public. I took the long route round, down Park Street to the Globe, then turned onto the embankment. I strolled through the tourists drawn across the Millennium Bridge, eager to see the damage to this bombastic structure, more bunker than museum, of which Albert Speer would have thoroughly approved.

Like all our friends, Sally and I saw every exhibition held in this massive vault. The building triumphed by a visual sleight of hand, a psychological trick that any fascist dictator would understand. Externally, its deco symmetry made it seem smaller than it was, and the vast dimensions of the turbine hall cowed both eye and brain. The entrance ramp was wide enough to take a parade of tanks. Power, of kilowatt hours or messianic gospel, glowered from the remote walls. This was the art show as Führer spectacle, an early sign, perhaps, that the educated middle classes were turning towards fascism.

I walked through the tourists to the main entrance, and stared across the grass at the bomb damage. The device had detonated at 1.45 pm, as I was being led from Broadcasting House by Sergeant Angela. Witnesses stated that a young Chinese woman was running around the bookshop. Evidently distraught, she seized a large art book from the shelves and ran into the turbine hall. The staff chased her, but gave up when they realized that she was warning people away. At the top of the entrance ramp the book exploded in her hands, its force amplified by the sloping floor. Glass and masonry lay across the grass, and covered the cars parked in Holland Street.

I thought of Joan Chang, sitting cheerfully behind Stephen Dexter on the Harley-Davidson. I guessed that after viewing an exhibition she had passed a few minutes in the bookshop, and by tragic mischance saw the terrorist plant his bomb, a lethal device intended to inflict the largest number of casualties. The police had identified the injured victims, but Stephen Dexter was not among them. The clergyman had vanished from Chelsea Marina, leaving his Harley sitting in the rain outside his chapel. Kay had telephoned a friend in the film unit at the Tate, but no one remembered seeing Dexter in the bookshop or galleries. Weeping over the Chinese girl's death, Kay

assumed that he had fled London and gone to ground at some
religious retreat.

Remembering the devastation at Heathrow, I knew that Dexter and I now had something in common. A terrorist bomb not
only killed its victims, but forced a violent rift through time and
space, and ruptured the logic that held the world together. For
a few hours gravity turned traitor, overruling Newton's laws of
motion, reversing rivers and toppling skyscrapers, stirring fears
long dormant in our minds. The horror challenged the soft
complacencies of day-to-day life, like a stranger stepping out of
a crowd and punching one's face. Sitting on the ground with a
bloodied mouth, one realized that the world was more dangerous
but, conceivably, more meaningful. As Richard Gould had said,
an inexplicable act of violence had a fierce authenticity that no
reasoned behaviour could match.

A rain squall, thrown up by the strutting river, lashed the
face of the gallery. The crowd scattered to the shelter of the side
streets, leaving the police forensic team to work on, sifting the
debris and decanting the broken glass into plastic bags.

A constable shouted to two German women who crossed the
crime-scene tapes and took refuge behind a police van. They
moved away, buttoning their raincoats as they hurried past a
small car covered with dust and fragments of masonry.

I followed them, but stopped beside the car, a Volkswagen
Beetle. Under the coating of dirt and rubble I could see the white
paintwork of a car identical to Joan Chang's. I watched the constable guarding the forecourt, stamping his feet and talking to
the forensic officers sheltering in the entrance.

Already I had decided to make a forensic examination of
my own.

I RETURNED from Sumner Street ten minutes later, wearing the white coat that Gould had bundled into the back of the
Range Rover when we left the children's hospice. The constable

was busy with the tourists brought out by the fitful sun, and the forensic team pegging out their stakes and string barely glanced at me, assuming that I was a Home Office investigator, perhaps a pathologist searching for human remains.

I approached the Beetle and gripped the door handle, ready to break the driver's window with my elbow. As I raised my arm I felt the mechanism open smoothly under my thumb. When she stepped from the car, Joan had forgotten to lock it, perhaps distracted by a passing vehicle or some acquaintance she had agreed to meet.

I eased back the door and slipped into the seat, recognizing the pale scents of jasmine and orris oil. The windows were thick with a bricky dust, streams of ochre mud that hid me from the police twenty yards away. I turned and scanned the rear seat, a clutter of tissues, discarded perfume samplers and a tourist guide to China, pages turned back to a five-day boat trip through the Yangtse gorges.

Stretching my legs, I pressed the brake and clutch pedals, barely able to reach them. The seat had been racked back, giving room to longer legs than Joan Chang's. Driving the Beetle, the petite Chinese sat with her chin touching the steering wheel.

Someone else, almost certainly Stephen Dexter, had driven Joan to the Tate. Uncomfortable with my legs extended, I felt below the seat and searched for the release handle.

There was a faint bleep of electronic protest. I was holding a mobile phone. Waiting for it to ring, I placed it against my ear, almost expecting Joan's piping voice. The phone was silent, and had been lying under the driving seat for the past two days, unnoticed by the police investigators.

Through the smeary windscreen I watched the forensic team at work, dividing the forecourt into narrow allotments, a laborious anatomy that might yield a few pieces of bomb mechanism. I rang the last number dialled, and listened to the ringing tone.

'*You are calling Tate Modern.*' A recorded voice spoke. '*The gallery is closed until further notice. You are calling . . .*'

I switched off the phone, assuming that Joan had rung the Tate before setting out, perhaps to book a restaurant table. As I sat in her car, with her mobile in my hand, I felt that I was reliving the last moments in the life of this pleasant young woman.

A hand fumbled at the driver's door, scraping the wet dust over the window. I had locked the door from the inside, pushing down the safety toggle. Fingers scrabbled at the glass, like the paws of a huge dog. I could see the blurred face and shoulders of a man in a black raincoat, perhaps one of the detectives working on the case.

I wound down the window. A faint rain was falling again, but I recognized the stressed and dishevelled face of the man who looked down at me.

He reached out and pulled me against the door pillar. 'Markham? What are you doing here?'

'Stephen . . . let me help you.' I pulled his hand from my shoulder, but hesitated before opening the door. Sweat sprang from the clergyman's forehead, beading around his enlarged eyes. He had lost his dog collar, torn away in his panic, and his unshaven cheeks were flushed and swollen, as if he had been weeping as he ran all night through profane and empty streets. When he gazed into the car, aware of its impossible void, I thought of him running along the river through the nights to come, forever following its journey into the dark.

He peered at my face, confused by my white coat, and showed me a set of ignition keys, clearly hoping that he had approached the wrong vehicle. 'Markham . . . ? I'm looking for Joan. Her car's here . . .'

Pushing back the door, I stepped into the rain. I placed my hands on Dexter's shoulders, trying to calm him.

'Stephen . . . I'm sorry about Joan. It's horrific for you.'

'For her.' Dexter forced me aside, and stared at the rubble-strewn entrance to the Tate. 'I wanted to call her.'

'What happened? Stephen?'

'Everything. Everything happened.' He stared into my face, fully recognizing me for the first time, and stepped back, flinching from me as if I were responsible for Joan Chang's death. In a rush of words, a blurted warning of approaching danger, he shouted: 'Go back to your wife. Get away from Richard Gould. Run, David . . .'

He turned from me, one hand still gripping my shoulder, and pointed across the roof of the car. Thirty feet from us, a young woman with rain-soaked hair was standing on the embankment. Her patent leather coat streamed with moisture, as if she had just emerged from the river, or stepped from a dark barge that plied the deeper tides below its surface. She watched the clergyman with the punitive gaze of a wronged parishioner set on revenge.

Dexter's grip tightened on my arm. He was clearly cowed by the young woman, who seemed to have punished him once and would soon punish him again. Staring at the inflamed scar on his forehead, I thought of the Philippine guerrillas whose whips had broken his spirit.

'You two . . . off!' A policeman shouted to us from the Tate entrance, waving us away from the impounded cars. I saluted him, and turned to steer Dexter across the crime-scene tape. But the clergyman had left me. Head down, hands sunk in the pockets of his raincoat, he moved in a half-run down Sumner Street and set off for Blackfriars Bridge.

The bare-headed young woman was hurrying towards the Globe theatre. Seeing her from behind, I recognized her quirky walk, part fussy schoolgirl, part bored tour guide. She was smart but drenched, and I guessed that she had been walking the streets around the Tate for hours, waiting for Stephen Dexter to appear.

A tugboat's siren vented itself across the river, emptying its deep lungs in a threatening blare that rebounded from the facades of the office buildings near St Paul's. Startled, Vera Blackburn tripped on her high heels. I caught her before she could fall, and led her into the entrance of the Globe, joining a small party of American tourists sheltering from the rain.

Vera made no attempt to resist. She leaned against me, smiling sweetly, self-immersed and emotionally dead, a vicious and lethal child. Watching her size me up, I saw again the chemistry prodigy in the suburban back bedroom who had graduated into a Defence Ministry pin-up, the dominatrix of every deskbound warrior's dream.

'Vera? You're out of breath.'

'"Dr Livingstone"? You're quite convincing. Who would dare presume?'

'One of Richard Gould's disguises. He left it in my car.'

'Get rid of it.' Her fingers opened the top button. 'People will think I've escaped from a mental home.'

'You have.'

'Really?' Her hand lingered over the buttons. 'Is that a compliment, David?'

'In your case, yes. Tragic about Joan Chang.'

'Appalling. She was so sweet. I had to come here.'

'You saw Stephen Dexter?'

Her face remained composed, but a raindrop winked from her left eyebrow, signalling a covert message. She was more unsettled than she realized, and a tic jumped across her upper lip. For once the real world had made a bigger bang.

'Stephen? I'm not sure. Was he by the car?'

'You're sure.' The damp tourists had entered the Globe and were gazing at the rain-swept gallery. I raised my voice. 'You were following him. Why?'

'We're worried about Stephen.' She took the white coat from me and folded it neatly, then dropped it into a litter bin. 'He's very upset.'

'That isn't the reason.'

'What else?'

'I'm trying to guess. Did he know about the bomb?'

'How could he?' She touched my chin. 'He'd never have let Joan get near it. People saw her running with the thing.'

'It's amazing how she found it. All those thousands of books, and she managed to pick one with two pounds of Semtex between the covers.' I watched the rain retreat across the river. 'I think Stephen was sitting in the car.'

'When the bomb went off? Why?'

'The seat was racked back. Joan's feet wouldn't have reached the pedals. Almost certainly he drove her to the Tate.'

'Go on. You think Stephen was the bomber?'

'It's just possible. They may have been working together. She took the bomb into the bookshop and left it on a shelf. For some reason she had a change of mind.'

Vera opened her compact and scanned her make-up. She glanced at me, unsure whether I was being naive or trying to lead her on.

'A change of mind? Hard to believe. Anyway, why would Stephen want to bomb the Tate?'

'It's a prime middle-class target. He's a priest who's lost his faith.'

'And detonating a bomb . . . ?'

'. . . restores his faith. In some lonely, deranged way.'

'How sad.' Vera lowered her bony forehead as two policemen walked along the embankment. 'At least you don't think I was behind it.'

'I'm not sure.' I held Vera's arm, and felt the pulse beating above her elbow. 'Some very dangerous people are being tempted into the violence game. You might have made the bomb, but you'd never have handed it over to a pair of amateurs. You're too professional.'

'That Ministry of Defence training. I knew it would come in useful.' Pleased, she brightened up, smiling as the sun wavered behind the clouds. 'Still, poor Stephen.'

'Why did you want to meet him here? He's frightened of you.'

'He's in a dangerous state of mind. Think how guilty he feels, even if he didn't plant the bomb. He might talk to the police and make something up.'

'That could be dangerous for you?'

'And for you, David.' She brushed a few fragments of mortar from my jacket. 'And for all of us at Chelsea Marina . . .'

I WATCHED HER walk away, chin raised as she passed the police. I admired her chilly self-control. As Richard Gould had said, the senselessness of the Tate attack separated it from other terrorist outrages. Not one of the works of art in the gallery remotely matched the limitless potency of a terrorist bomb. I tried to imagine how Vera Blackburn made love, but no lover would ever equal the allure and sensual potency of primed Semtex.

I returned to Sumner Street and sat behind the wheel of the Range Rover, watching the parking ticket flap against the windscreen. I felt closer to the truth about the Heathrow bomb than I had been since arriving at Chelsea Marina. Kay was glad that I shared her bed, but was still urging me to go back to Sally and St John's Wood. But I needed to spend more time with Kay and Vera, and above all with Richard Gould. A strange logic had emerged from the borders of Chelsea and Fulham and would spread far beyond them, even perhaps to the carousel at Terminal 2 where Laura had met her death.

I picked up the car-phone and dialled the number of the Adler Institute. When the receptionist replied I asked for Professor Arnold.

23

THE LAST STRANGER

'HENRY IS COMING OVER,' Sally told me. 'That won't worry you, David?'

She sat in my armchair, legs stretched out confidently, sticks long returned to the umbrella stand in the hall. She was at her prettiest in this pleasant room, smiling at me with unfeigned pleasure, as if I were a favourite brother home on leave from the front. Being away from me, I had to admit, had markedly improved her health.

'Henry? No problem at all. I talked to him yesterday.'

'He told me. You rang from somewhere near the Tate. Horrible, wasn't it?'

'Grim. Very nasty. Impossible to grasp.'

'The Chinese girl—did you know her?'

'Joan Chang. She was a charmer. A kind of club-class hippy—motorbike, platinum Amex, clergyman boyfriend.'

'I wish I'd met her. The bomb wasn't part of . . . ?'

'The campaign at Chelsea Marina? No. Violence isn't our thing. We're much too bourgeois.'

'So were Lenin and Che and Chou En-lai, according to Henry.' Sally sat forward, taking my hands across the coffee table. 'You're different, David. You look slightly windblown. I'm not sure it suits you. When are you coming home?'

'Soon.' Her fingers were warm, and I realized that everyone at Chelsea Marina had cold hands. 'I need to keep an eye on things. There's a lot happening.'

'I know. It sounds like a playgroup that's out of control. Accountants and solicitors giving up their jobs. In places like Guildford, for God's sake. That really means something.'

'It does. Revolution is hammering on the door.'

'Not in St John's Wood. Or not yet.' Sally shuddered, eyes drifting to the safety locks on the windows. 'Henry says you might resign from the Institute.'

'I need to take six months' leave. Arnold is unhappy with that—I'd have to give up your father's consultancy. Don't worry, he'll double your allowance.'

Sally touched her fingertips, working through more than the arithmetic involved. 'We'll get by. At least you'll feel honest for once. That's been the problem, hasn't it? Daddy pays for everything.'

'"Daddy pays . . ."' I remembered hearing the phrase at University College, and the middle-class freshers with their expensive luggage, helped out of Daddy's Jaguar. 'Anyway, it's time I stood on my own feet.'

'Nobody does, David. That's something you've never understood. Henry says—'

'Sally, please . . . it's bad enough that he sleeps with my wife. I don't want to hear his latest opinions on everything. How is he?'

'Worried about you. They all want you back at the Institute. They know this "revolution" will peter out and a lot of sensible people will have wrecked their lives.'

'That could happen. But not yet. I'm still working on the Heathrow bomb. The clues are starting to fall into place.'

'Laura . . . you've really done your best for her.' Sally waited as

I tried to avoid her eyes. 'I never actually met her. Henry told me a lot of things I didn't know.'

'About Laura? Gallant of him.'

'And about you. Husbands are the last strangers. Are you ready to visit your mother? The manager at the home called several times. She's started talking about you.'

'Has she? Too bad. It's not my favourite topic.' I stood up and walked around the settee, trying to work out the altered positions of the furniture. Everything was in the same place, but the perspectives had changed. I had tasted freedom, and grasped how unreal life in St John's Wood had become, how absurdly genteel. To Sally, I said: 'That sounds callous, but I've given up a lot of heavy baggage—guilt, bogus affection, the Adler . . .'

'Your wife?'

'I hope not.' I stopped at the mantelpiece and smiled at Sally through the mirror, warming to her Alice-like reflection in my old husbandly way. 'Wait for me, Sally.'

'I'll try.'

A CAR WAS being parked outside the house, edging into the space behind the Range Rover, shunting and reversing as the driver made a point of not touching my rear bumper. Henry Kendall stepped out, dapper but uncertain, like an estate agent in a more exclusive neighbourhood, where different social rules applied.

After speaking to Professor Arnold I had called Henry from outside the Tate, and asked him if he still had his Home Office contacts. I needed to know if the bomber had made a warning call to the Tate in the minutes before the explosion. Glad to get off the phone, Henry promised to pursue his sources.

Now we faced each other across a domestic hearth, trying to decide which of us would first invite the other to sit down. Henry was eager to yield to me, and was surprised that I seemed keen for him to assume the duties of man of the house. Already he looked at me with the sudden panic of a lover who realizes that the cuckolded husband is only too happy to leave him in full possession of his wife.

When all this was settled, Sally left us and we sat over Scotch and sodas.

'You've changed, David. Sally noticed it.'

'Good. How exactly?'

'You look stronger. Not so evasive, or calculating. The revolution's done you good.'

I raised my glass to this, deciding that I had never fully grasped how boring Henry was, and how much I resented the years I had spent in his company. 'You're right, I was a mess. As it happens, I'm not playing any real part.'

'You were at Broadcasting House.'

'Someone told you about that?'

'The Home Office takes a keen interest in everything.'

'They must be worried.'

'They are. Key people in Whitehall resigning their jobs? Seniority, pension rights, gongs and knighthoods, all thrown out of the window. It undermines morale, breaks the chains of envy and rivalry that hold everything together.'

'That's the idea. You can thank the revolution.'

'Rather silly, though?' Henry treated me to an understanding smile. 'Boycotting Peter Jones, letting off smoke bombs in school outfitters . . .'

'Middle-class pique. We sense we're being exploited. All those liberal values and humane concern for the less fortunate. Our role is to keep the lower orders in check, but in fact we're policing ourselves.'

Henry watched me tolerantly over his whisky. 'Do you believe all that?'

'Who knows? The important thing is that the people at Chelsea Marina believe it. It's amateurish and childish, but the middle classes are amateurish, and they've never left their childhoods behind. But there's something much more important going on. Something that ought to worry your friends at the Home Office.'

'And that is?'

'Decent and level-headed people are hungry for violence.'

'Grim, if true.' Henry put down his whisky. 'Directed at what?'

'It doesn't matter. In fact, the ideal act of violence isn't directed at anything.'

'Pure nihilism?'

'The exact opposite. This is where we've all been wrong—you, me, the Adler, liberal opinion. It isn't a search for nothingness. It's a search for meaning. Blow up the Stock Exchange and you're rejecting global capitalism. Bomb the Ministry of Defence and you're protesting against war. You don't even need to hand out the leaflets. But a truly pointless act of violence, shooting at random into a crowd, grips our attention for months. The absence of rational motive carries a significance of its own.'

Henry listened to Sally's footsteps in the bedroom above our heads. 'As it happens, people at the Home Office are thinking along similar lines. The revolt at Chelsea Marina is a sideshow. The really dangerous people are waiting in another corner of the park. Take this Tate bomb, clearly the work of hard-core terrorists—renegade IRA, some demented Muslim group. Be careful, David . . .'

WHEN I LET myself out, half an hour later, I could hear Sally's bath running. I thought of her emerging from a cloud of talc and scent, ready for Henry and a long and pleasant afternoon.

'Henry, say goodbye to Sally for me.'

'She misses you, David.'

'I know.'

'We both hope you'll come back.'

'I will. I'm involved in something that needs to be worked out. All these duties, they're like bricks in a rucksack.'

'There are cathedrals built of bricks.' Henry straightened his tie as two of my neighbours walked by. Forever doomed to feel the interloper, he could still not accept that he had pulled off his extramarital coup. He leaned into the driver's window when I sat behind the wheel. 'You were right, by the way. There was a warning call.'

'At the Tate?'

'A few minutes before the bomb went off. Someone rang the main desk at the gallery.'

'A few minutes?' I thought of Joan Chang, running frantically around the bookshop. 'Why didn't they clear the building?'

'The caller said the bomb was under the Millennium Bridge. The staff assumed it was a hoax, some kind of joke about the famous wobble.'

'Who made the call? They must have traced the damn thing.'

'Naturally, but keep it to yourself. It came from a mobile phone, stolen about a week ago from Lambeth Palace. A Church of England task force was meeting there, looking into social unrest among the middle classes. The phone was stolen from the Bishop of Chichester . . .'

I STARTED THE ENGINE, and watched Henry walk back to the house. Sally was at the window, towel wrapped under her arms. She waved to me, like a child watching a parent leave on a long trip, wistful despite her hopes of seeing me again, realizing that a small revolution, however misguided and amateurish, was at last touching her.

She had invited me to the house, but made no serious attempt to win me back, leaving me alone to talk to Henry. As she stood by the window I sensed that she was glad to remind herself of my inexplicable behaviour, which went against everything in my nature. That someone as straight and stuffy as her husband could act out of character helped to explain the cruel and meaningless event that had taken place in a Lisbon street. Anger and resentment were fading, pushed into the umbrella stand with her walking sticks. In a sense I was helping to free Sally from herself. The world had provoked her, and irrational acts were the only way to defuse its threat.

24

THE DEFENCE
OF GROSVENOR PLACE

CHELSEA MARINA was ready to make its last stand. Three weeks later, from the windows of Kay's living room, I watched the residents' committee organize the defence of Grosvenor Place. Fifty adults, almost every neighbour in the cul de sac, had gathered in front of number 27, all talking at the tops of their confident voices. Indignation was working itself towards critical mass, and the explosion threatened the entire civic order of Chelsea and Fulham.

The bailiffs were due to arrive in minutes, determined to evict Alan and Rosemary Turner, both entomologists at the Natural History Museum, and their three teenage children. The Turners were one of the many families who refused to pay their maintenance charges, defaulted on their mortgage and ignored all demands from the utility companies and the local council. The Turners were now a test case, and a formidable coalition of banks and building societies, council officials and property executives were determined to make an example of them.

I had met the Turners, a high-minded but pleasant couple, and sometimes helped the younger son with the algebra problems his mother set him. For a month they had been without water or electricity, but their neighbours rallied round, feeding cable and hose-pipe extensions over their garden walls. Unable to afford the children's school fees, the Turners hung a large banner—'we are the new poor'—from their bedroom balcony.

Sadly, this was all too true. Kay organized a whip-round, but a week later Mrs Turner and her daughter were caught shoplifting in the King's Road Safeway. Listening to the list of pilfered items, from breakfast cereals to orange juice, the magistrates were ready to let Mrs Turner off with a caution. On hearing that she lived in Chelsea Marina, they closed their minds to clemency and talked darkly of Fagin gangs on the prowl, flaunting their Hermès scarves and Prada handbags. The chief magistrate, the headmistress of a local comprehensive school, lectured Mrs Turner on the perils of the middle class abdicating their responsibilities, and fined her £50. I paid this, and Mrs Turner returned to a cheerful street party, the first martyr of Grosvenor Place.

As it happened, Mrs Turner was not alone. The residents of Chelsea Marina had launched a small crime wave on the surrounding neighbourhood. As executives and middle managers gave up their jobs, there was an outbreak of petty thieving from delis and off-licences. Every parking meter in Chelsea Marina was vandalized, and the council street cleaners, traditional working class to the core, refused to enter the estate, put off by the menacing middle-class air. Removed from their expensive schools, bored teenagers haunted Sloane Square and the King's Road, trying their hands at drug-dealing and car theft.

The location vans of Japanese and American television channels cruised around Chelsea Marina, waiting for blood. But the police held back, under orders from the Home Office not to provoke an outright confrontation. Cabinet ministers were now well aware that if the middle class withdrew their goodwill, society would collapse.

Meanwhile, law and order had returned, ready to make a

small push. From Kay's window I counted three police vans parked in the entrance to Grosvenor Place. The constables sat by the windows, accepting cups of tea from nearby residents. One policewoman dropped a pound coin into a biscuit tin labelled 'community poor box'. The sergeant in charge conferred with a firm of bailiffs, a thuggish group eager to evict the Turners. A local security firm stood by, ready to change the Turners' locks and board up the ground-floor windows.

A *Newsnight* TV crew waited keenly, camera trained on the Turners, who stood bravely by their front door, pale but unbowed, like a miner's family during a pithead lock-out. Their neighbours linked arms around the gate, and a second banner flew from the balcony—'free the new proletariat'.

The sergeant raised his megaphone and urged the crowd to disperse, his words lost in the jeers and shouts. Kay Churchill pushed tirelessly through the throng, urging everyone on, kissing the cheeks of husbands and wives. Her face flushed with pride, she broke off to run back to her house. I admired her, as always, for her passion and wrongheadedness. She was often lonely, writing long letters to her daughter in Australia, but nothing roused her spirits like the prospect of heroic failure.

'David? I'm glad you're here. We may need you.' She embraced me fiercely, her body trembling against me.

'Kay? What are you doing?'

'Changing my underwear. Believe me, the police can be brutal.'

'Not that brutal . . .' I followed her into the kitchen where she towelled her arms and poured herself a large gin. 'What exactly is happening?'

'Nothing, yet. It's about to start. It could be rough, David.'

'Don't sound so pleased. I take it you have a plan?'

Kay threw the towel at me, a heady bouquet of fear and sex. 'Only a few people know. Watch the news tonight.'

'A sit-down? A mass strip?'

'You'd like that.' She blew me a kiss, tugging off her thong. 'This is our first confrontation, hand to hand with the police. This is the Odessa Steps, this is Tolpuddle.'

'All these lawyers and ad-men?'

'Who cares what they do? It's what they are that matters. This is the first time we've defended our ground. They want to evict an entire community. It's time for you to be serious, David. No more observer status.'

'Kay ...' I tried to settle her chaotic hair. 'Don't expect too much of yourself. Bailiffs repossess houses every day in London.'

'But we've chosen *not* to pay the mortgage. We're forcing a showdown, so everyone in Harrow and Purley and Wimbledon can look hard at themselves. Every schoolteacher and GP and branch manager. They'll realize they're just a new kind of serf. Coolies in trainers and tracksuits.' Kay snatched the towel from me and dried her armpits. 'Stop sniffing that. The sidelines have been abolished, David. No one can stand and watch any more. Buying an olive ciabatta is a political act. We need everyone to help.'

'Right ... I'll join you when the action starts.' I tapped the mobile phone in my shirt pocket. 'I'm waiting for a call from Richard Gould. He has some project on.'

'He ought to be here. Without him it's difficult to hold things together.' Irritated by the mention of Gould's name, Kay glanced at the corners of the sitting room. 'Where is he? No one's seen him for days.'

'He still supports us, but ...'

'It's all a bit too quaint? Sit-ins, picket lines, raw emotion. He's a cold fish.'

'He's trying to track down Stephen Dexter before the police do. The Tate bomb could derail everything.'

'Joan? The world's mad.' Kay grimaced and pressed her worn

hands to her face, trying to smooth away her lines. 'Poor Stephen, I can't believe he set off the bomb.'

She raced upstairs, eager to change and return to her riot.

A MEGAPHONE was blaring when I returned to the window, its
ponderous message lost on the crowd, orotund phrases bouncing
off the the rooftops. The police dismounted from their vans and
secured the chin-straps of their helmets. They formed up behind
the bailiffs, six stocky men in leather jackets.

The residents turned to face them, arms linked. There was
a flurry of blows when the bailiffs tried to shoulder them aside,
and a balding orthodontist fell to his knees with a bloodied nose,
comforted by his outraged wife. From an upstairs window a
sound system began to play a Verdi extract, the prisoners' chorus
from *Nabucco*. At this signal, like an audience who had stood for
the national anthem, the residents sat down in the street.

Unimpressed, the police moved in, strong hands wrenching
the protesters apart and dragging them away. A fierce ululation
rose from Grosvenor Place, the outrage of professional men and
women who had never known pain and whose soft bodies had
been pummelled only by their lovers and osteopaths.

I turned towards the front door, ready to join in, and heard my
mobile ring in my shirt pocket.

'Markham?' A flat voice spoke, faint and metallic, the recording of a recording. 'David, can you hear me?'

'Who is this?'

'What's going on?'

'Richard . . . ?' Relieved that Gould had called, I closed the
front door. 'Nothing much. Kay's organized a small riot. Meanwhile, the police are evicting the Turners.'

'Right . . .' Gould seemed distracted, his voice fading and surging. 'I need you to help me. I've seen Stephen Dexter.'

'Stephen? Where? Can you talk to him?'

'He's all right. Later, if I get a chance.'

A hum of background noise drowned his voice, the sound of a busy airport concourse.

'Richard? Where are you? Heathrow?'

'These security cameras . . . I have to be careful. I'm in Hammersmith, the King Street shopping mall. Consumer hell.'

'What about Stephen?'

'He's looking at glassware, in the local Habitat. I'm trying to move closer. There's another bloody camera . . .'

I pressed the mobile to my ear, picking up a hubbub of pedestrian noise. Gould sounded aroused but curiously dreamy, as if an attractive young woman was sharing his phone booth. He had been shocked by Joan Chang's death, dismayed by the real violence that had taken place after his relaxed talk of meaningless acts. Violence, I wanted to tell him, was never meaningless. Now I thought of Stephen Dexter, this haunted clergyman prowling the shopping mall, perhaps with another bomb, hoping to drive away his grief for Joan.

'Richard? Is Dexter still there?'

'Plain as daylight.'

'You're sure? You recognize him?'

'It's . . . him. I need you over here. Can you get to the Range Rover?'

'It's parked round the corner.'

'Good man. Give me an hour. Wait for me in Rainville Road, near the River Café. Off the Fulham Palace Road.'

'Right. Be careful. He'll see you if you get too close.'

'Don't worry. The world has too many cameras . . .'

WHEN I LEFT the house a few minutes later the protest was almost over. Kay's riot, which she hoped would engulf Chelsea Marina, had become a local brawl between the police and a few of the more aggressive residents. The others sat on the ground, exchanging insults with the constables trying to clear the street.

Too reliant, as always, on argument and social stance, the Chelsea Marina rebels were no match for the heavy squad. Property rights were involved, unlike the CND marches of the 1960s or the cruise-missile protests. A seat in the great British lifeboat was sacrosanct, however cramped and whatever posterior occupied it.

The bailiffs had reached the front door of the Turners' house and were trying the locks with a set of skeleton picks. I searched for Kay, expecting to see her in the forefront of the action, berating the sergeant or dressing down some junior woman constable. The Turners had taken refuge with neighbours and their house seemed empty, but I glimpsed a swirl of ash-grey hair in the front bedroom. I assumed that Kay had returned to the house by a garden window, and was retrieving some memento of Mrs Turner's before it disappeared into the bailiffs' pockets.

As I walked towards Beaufort Avenue, ignition keys in hand, I noticed a thickset man with a brush moustache and ginger hair standing near the police vans. I had last seen him among the mourners at Laura's cremation. Major Tulloch, once of the Gibraltar police and Henry's contact at the Home Office, was keeping an eye on Chelsea Marina, on these opinionated wives and their idle husbands. His face had the bored, hard-nosed stare of an ambitious rugby coach in charge of a third-rate team. He took in the vandalized parking meters and unswept streets, the amateurish banners hanging from bedroom windows, with the weary patience of all police officers faced with pointless criminality.

Behind me, the crowd fell silent, and the sergeant's megaphone died on the air. The bailiffs stepped into the street and stared at the roof. Smoke rose from the upstairs windows of the Turners' house. The ropes of dark vapour threaded themselves through the open transoms, knotted into ever thicker coils and raced up the mock-Tudor gable. Inside the bedroom, a fierce yellow glow expanded across the ceiling.

The first house in Chelsea Marina to be torched by its owners was now on fire, a mark of true rebellion that would baffle Major Tulloch and the Home Office. I reached Beaufort Avenue and looked back for the last time, aware that a significant step had been taken. The protest movement was no longer a glorified rent strike, but a full-scale insurrection. Well aware of this, Kay Churchill stood outside her front door, shrieking at the bailiffs and police, arms raised in triumph.

I PARKED IN Rainville Road, fifty yards from the entrance to the River Café. The glass barrel vault of Richard Rogers's design office rose beside the Thames, a transparent canopy that cleverly concealed the architect's wayward plans for London's future. It was four o'clock, but the sleek patrons of the restaurant, the television chieftains and fifteen-minute celebrities of the political world, were still leaving after their lunches, an aroma of boozy fame dispersing through the stolid streets of west London.

I searched the low rooftops for any sight of the smoke from Chelsea Marina. Farce and tragedy embraced each other like long-lost friends, but the Turners had read the wind. The middle-income residents of the estate had long outstayed their welcome. The Home Office might fear this outbreak of social unease, but the property developers who dominated the economy of London would be glad to see the entire population of Chelsea Marina exiled to the duller suburbs, the grim and bricky enclaves around Heathrow and Gatwick. The ceaseless roar of aircraft would drive out any future thoughts of revolution.

Richard Gould had been right. Inexplicable and senseless protests were the only way to hold the public's attention. During the past month, inspired by Richard, action groups had attacked a number of 'absurd' targets—the Penguin pool at London Zoo, Liberty's, the Soane Museum and the Karl Marx tomb at Highgate Cemetery. Home Office ministers and newspaper columnists were baffled, and dismissed the attacks as misguided pranks. Yet the targets were important elements in maintaining the

middle class's herd mentality, from Lubetkin's too-precious penguin walkways to the over-busy prints in Liberty's airless emporium. No one was injured, and little damage was done by Vera
Blackburn's smoke and paint bombs. But the public was unsettled, aware of a deranged fifth column in its midst, motiveless
and impenetrable, Dada come to town.

I had last seen Gould on the evening of the smoke bomb attack
on the Albert Hall. He had been away for a week, helping a team
of volunteers to give a seaside holiday to a group of Down's teenagers, and asked me to collect him from the hostel in Tooting. As
the happy children tottered home with their funfair trophies and
monster masks, Gould collapsed into the Range Rover, reeking
of carbolic and exhausted after spending his nights scrubbing out
lavatories. He slept against the window, face tubercularly pale.

He revived after a shower and a change of clothes in Vera's
flat, where he was now staying, and then suggested we drive to
Kensington Gardens. Leaving Chelsea Marina, we picked up
two young residents on their way to the last night of the Proms,
dressed in Union Jack hats and Robin Hood cloaks, ready to join
in the orgy of Elgar choruses and pantomime Britishness.

We dropped them off and then strolled through the evening
park, where Gould talked over his worries for Stephen Dexter. The
clergyman had still not returned to his house near the marina,
and the coroner had released Joan Chang's body for its lonely flight
back to Singapore. Gould feared that the Tate attack would be
blamed on Chelsea Marina and used to discredit the revolution.
From now on, only meaningless targets should be chosen, each one
a conundrum that the public would struggle to solve.

As we walked near the Round Pond I heard the sound of fire
engines and saw cerise smoke rising from the roof of the Albert
Hall. By the time we reached Kensington Gore the entire street
was filled with promenaders in their end-of-season costumes,
orchestra players holding their instruments, police and firemen.
The promenaders launched into a spirited singsong, refusing to

let their patriotism be cowed, while billows of smoke rose from the upper galleries of the concert hall and a bedlam of horns sounded from the stalled traffic.

Later I learned that the two residents we had driven from Chelsea Marina were acting with Gould's blessing. They had smuggled their smoke bombs into the auditorium and left them in the lavatories, timed to go off at the opening bars of 'Land of Hope and Glory'. But Gould seemed too tired and distracted to enjoy the spectacle, however childish and absurd. He left me by the steps of the Albert Memorial, and disappeared into the crowd, cadging a lift from the driver of a catering van. I assumed he was thinking of the Down's children, bobbing cheerfully down the Bognor front, and the larger absurdity to which nature would never provide an answer.

I WAS STILL WAITING for Gould as the last of the River Café patrons eased himself into his limousine. My parking meter had expired; feeding in more coins, I almost missed my ringing mobile.

'David? What's happened?' Gould was panting, his voice high-pitched, as if he had seized himself by the throat. 'Markham . . . ?'

'I'm outside the River Café. Nothing's happened. Have you seen Dexter?'

'He . . . got away. Too many cameras.'

'You didn't catch him?'

'Stay away from cameras, David.'

'Right. Where are you?'

'Fulham Palace. Meet me there now.' He spoke breathlessly, and I could hear an ambulance siren above the traffic, and the voices of women talking in a queue. 'David? Dexter's here somewhere . . .'

I REACHED Fulham Palace within five minutes, and waited in the visitor's car park, listening to the clamour of traffic in the Fulham Palace Road. Police cars sped across Putney Bridge, sirens cutting through the air. A lane had been cleared for them, and buses stood nose to tail on the span of the bridge, passengers peering from the windows.

Had Gould tipped off the police? He was far too slight and undernourished to restrain Stephen Dexter, and I remembered how the clergyman had shaken me roughly in Joan Chang's Beetle outside Tate Modern. Seeing Gould hovering behind him like an incompetent detective, the clergyman might well have left the shopping mall and caught a bus down the Fulham Palace Road, yielding to some atavistic urge to find sanctuary in the precincts of the bishop's palace.

I stepped from the Range Rover, and approached a family picnicking around the tailgate of their Shogun. The parents confirmed that no one resembling Gould or Stephen Dexter had walked up the approach road to the car park in the past hour.

Entering Bishop's Park, which lay between the palace and the Thames, I scanned the wide lawns and the wooden benches for a distraught cleric, perhaps still carrying his carrier bag filled with Habitat tumblers. An elderly couple circled the perimeter path, buttoned up safely in the warm September weather. The only other visitor was near the embankment, a small man in a dark suit pacing between the high beeches and sycamores that grew along the river. He paused after a few steps and raised his hands to search the topmost branches. Even across the park I could see his pale hands held against the light.

I walked along the path, hiding myself behind the elderly couple. I recognized Gould when I was thirty feet from him. He stood with his back to me, head craning at the swaying branches, hands clutching at the air like a devout seminary student gazing at a rose window in a great cathedral.

Disturbed by the strolling couple, he waited until they had passed, and then turned towards me. His bony face was lit by the sun, a pale lantern swaying among the tree trunks. He stared over my head, his attention fixed on a point far beyond the focus of his eyes. All the bones in his face had come forward, their sharp ridges cutting against the transparent skin, as if his skull was desperate for the light. His threadbare suit was soaked with sweat, his shirt so damp that I could see his ribs through the shabby cotton. His expression was numbed but almost ecstatic, and his eyes followed the swirling branches in a childlike way, apparently in the throes of a warning aura before an epileptic fit.

'David . . .' He spoke softly, introducing me to the trees and to the light. Behind him, the sirens keened through the traffic, as if the streets around us were in mourning.

25

A CELEBRITY MURDER

THE SIRENS SOUNDED for many days, a melancholy toc-sin that became the aural signature of west London, eclipsing the revolution at Chelsea Marina. Every newsreel unit and press photographer in the capital converged on Woodlawn Road, the residential street in Hammersmith only a few hundred yards from where I had parked near the River Café. The cruel mur-der of the young television performer pressed hard on one of the nation's exposed nerves. The problems of the middle class, unwilling to pay their school fees and private medical bills, sank into insignificance.

A likeable blonde in her mid-thirties, the presenter was one of the most admired personalities in television. For a decade she had introduced breakfast magazine programmes, family discus-sion panels and childcare investigations, always ready with sen-sible advice and good-humoured charm. I had never seen her on screen and could never remember her name, but her death on her own doorstep prompted an outpouring of grief that reminded me of Princess Diana.

The security cameras in the King Street shopping mall showed her leaving the Habitat store soon after four o'clock. She then took the escalator and collected her Nissan Cherry from the multi-storey car park behind the mall. The supervisor at the exit failed to remember her, but the ticket she pushed into the barrier machine bore her thumbprint. She drove to Woodlawn Road, where she lived alone in a two-storey terraced house. Her neighbours were civil servants and actors, middle-class professionals like those at Chelsea Marina, almost all at work during the day.

No one observed her murder, but her next-door neighbour, a self-employed film technician, told the police that he heard the backfire of a motorcycle exhaust at or around four thirty. Minutes later, he noticed two distressed women standing by the garden gate, pointing to the front door. He went out and found the presenter lying on her doorstep. Her white linen suit was soaked with blood, but he tried to revive her. A nearby neighbour, a midwife at Charing Cross Hospital in Fulham Palace Road, joined him and applied mouth-to-mouth resuscitation, but was forced to confirm that she was dead.

She had been shot in the back of the head as she opened the front door, dying almost instantly. The key to the front door was still in its lock, and the police were puzzled why her killer had shot her in daylight, in full view of dozens of nearby houses, rather than follow her into the privacy of the hallway.

No one saw the killer arrive at the murder scene, or remembered a possible assailant loitering in Woodlawn Road and waiting for the victim to drive up in her car. How he managed to avoid everyone's attention was a mystery that would never be solved.

The presenter had several male friends and was often away for days during the location shooting of her programmes. That the killer was able to arrive just as she returned from the King Street mall suggested that the assailant was closely aware of her movements. Staff and co-workers at the BBC Television Centre in White City were carefully questioned, but no one had known of her plans for the day. The longstanding lover with whom she spent the previous night at his Notting Hill flat stated that after a morning's shopping she had booked a manicure at her favourite Knightsbridge salon.

Once the killer had carried out the murder, he walked away or was picked up by an accomplice in a car. Several witnesses agreed that a black Range Rover was circling the nearby streets an hour before the shooting. A security camera in Putney High Street caught a similar Range Rover passing the local Burger King, but computer enhancement failed to yield the licence number.

Some days later, a Webley revolver was found at low tide on the exposed riverbed below Putney Bridge. The weapon, of World War II army issue, was entangled in a fishing net wrapped around a deflated rubber dinghy. Matching the metallic traces on the barrel with the bullet fragments found in the victim's skull strongly indicated that the Webley pistol was the killer's weapon.

The callous murder of this attractive and wholesome young woman led to a huge police operation. As a successful television celebrity, she had mastered a good-natured blandness that audiences especially prized. She had millions of admirers but no enemies. Her death was inexplicable, a random killing made all the more meaningless by her celebrity.

THREE WEEKS AFTER the murder I watched the funeral service on the TV set in Kay Churchill's kitchen. Saddened like everyone else by the death, Kay held my hand across the table as the service was relayed from Brompton Oratory. She had never seen one of the victim's programmes, and failed to recognize her photograph on the front page of the *Guardian*, but fame defined its own needs.

'Who . . . ? Who could . . . ?' Kay wiped the salt from her cheeks with a damp tissue. 'Who could kill like that? Shoot down another human being . . . ?'

'A maniac . . . it's hard to imagine. At least they've arrested a man.'

'This misfit living in the next street?' Kay threw her tissue into the sink. 'I don't believe it. They had to find someone. What was his motive?'

'The police don't say. These days, there doesn't need to be a motive.' I pointed to the screen. 'There he is—behind the police van.'

The parade of famous television faces, unsure whether to smile at the crowd outside the Oratory or stare solemnly at their feet, was interrupted by a cutaway to shots of the accused being moved between police stations. A zoom lens mounted on a roof above West End Central showed him bundled from an armoured van. He was an overweight youth with lardy white arms, a blanket over his head. When he stumbled there was a glimpse of round cheeks and an unsavoury beard.

'Grim . . .' Kay shuddered in disgust. 'He's prepubescent, like a huge child. Who is he?'

'I missed his name. His flat is around the corner from Woodlawn Road. He's a gun enthusiast. The police found an arsenal of replica firearms. He liked photographing celebrities leaving the River Café.'

'Fame . . . it's too close, standing next to you in the checkout queue. He probably saw her getting out of her car. Some people can't cope with the idea of fame . . .'

Kay leaned against me, gripping the remote control, ready to hurl it at the screen. The murder had shocked her deeply. The sight of the Turners' burnt-out house across the road reminded her of the palpable presence of evil, and made her even more determined to right any injustice within her reach.

I pressed Kay's careworn hand to my cheek, feeling a surge of affection for this passionate woman, with her hopeless dreams and careless sex. Kay had many lives—lover, incendiarist, fomenter of pocket revolutions, suburban Joan of Arc—which she struggled to control like a team of unruly mares. If I were to walk out of her life she would miss me intensely, for ten minutes.

Then the next lodger would arrive and join the game of emotional snakes and ladders that led to her bedroom.

The funeral service began, a solemn ritual that played to the worst needs of television. Kay, vaguely religious but fiercely anticlerical, switched off the set. She paced into the living room, and stared at the Turners' scorched timbers. There was a death to be avenged, video stores to be bombed, middle-class housewives in Barnes and Wimbledon to be jolted out of their servitude.

I sat in the kitchen, with the silent screen for company. Already I suspected that I knew who had killed the television presenter. Richard Gould had hinted as much after I found him in the park at Fulham Palace. Somewhere in London a priest was sitting in a rented room, watching the service on another television set, trying to wring from his mind all memory of the meaningless murder he had committed. Had Stephen Dexter killed the young presenter in an attempt to erase his memories of Joan Chang's death at the Tate? And had Gould, exhausted after following him from the King Street mall, stumbled onto the murder scene as the crime took place?

I remembered the hard soil under my feet in the park at Fulham Palace. I had taken Gould's elbow and guided him away from the great trees that trapped the sky in their branches. He tripped in his cheap shoes, and I put my arm around his shoulders, feeling the damp fabric of his suit and the cold fever that burned beneath his skin. The elderly couple stopped to watch us, clearly assuming that Gould was a drug addict in the last stages of withdrawal.

Slumped in the rear seat of the Range Rover, he briefly roused himself and pointed to Putney Bridge. We left the park and turned onto Fulham Palace Road, and crossed the river in the heavy traffic. Sirens wailing, police cars sped past us towards Hammersmith. Gould slept as we drove along the Upper Richmond Road and returned to Chelsea Marina by Wandsworth Bridge. I steered him into the coffinlike elevator at the Cadogan

Circle apartments, found his keys in his sodden pockets and left him outside the door of Vera Blackburn's flat. In the empty elevator, the sweatprints of his palms glistened on the faded mirror.

Before we parted, he noticed me, his depthless eyes suddenly in focus.

'David, be careful with Stephen Dexter.' He gripped my hands, trying to wake me from a deep sleep. 'No police. He'll kill, David. He'll kill again . . .'

THIS WAS THE LAST I saw of Richard Gould. He and Vera left Chelsea Marina that evening. When I returned to Kay's house the entire population of Grosvenor Place stood silently in the street, watching as two fire engines doused the embers that remained of the Turner home. Already the first reports of a murder in Hammersmith were coming through on the firemen's radios. On hearing who the victim was, everyone drifted away, as if there was some unconscious connection between the murder and the events at Chelsea Marina.

The next day the police and bailiffs withdrew from Grosvenor Place. Outside the Cadogan Circle apartments a neighbour told me that Gould and Vera had driven away in the Citroën estate. I said nothing to Kay, but I assumed that Gould had seen Dexter shoot his victim. Too late to save the young woman, he followed the deranged clergyman to Fulham Palace, where Dexter had thrown the revolver into the Thames and disappeared into the infinite space of Greater London, a terrain beyond all maps.

I was tempted, briefly, to go to the police, using Henry Kendall to arrange a meeting with a senior officer at Scotland Yard. But my friendship with Stephen Dexter, the sightings of the Range Rover near Woodlawn Road and in Putney High Street, our meeting at the Tate, would soon turn me into the chief accomplice of this grounded priest and pilot. Given time, Dexter's conscience would rally him, and he would turn himself in, ready to face the coming decades in Broadmoor.

Soon afterwards, a flabby loner and celebrity stalker was charged with the murder of the television presenter. He said nothing to the magistrate who committed him for trial, a vacuum of a human being who seemed almost brain-dead in his passivity. His star-struck camera, his obsessive collecting of replica guns, and a personality so blank that no one would have noticed him outside the fatal doorstep, together hinted at an extreme form of Asperger's syndrome.

His arrest took days to leave the headlines. Fame and celebrity were again on trial, as if being famous was itself an incitement to anger and revenge, playing on the uneasy dreams of a submerged world, a dark iceberg of impotence and hostility.

But I was thinking of Richard Gould, shivering and exhausted under the trees in Bishop's Park. I thought of the dying children in the Bedfont hospice, and the Down's teenagers he had helped to take on holiday, and his attempt to find a desperate meaning in nature's failings. The world had retreated from Stephen Dexter, but it rushed towards Richard Gould with all the hunger of space and time.

26

A WIFE'S CONCERN

MEANWHILE, SMALLER confrontations loomed. Quietly and stealthily, the barricades were going up in Chelsea Marina. The lull in police activity after the Hammersmith murder had given the residents time to organize their defences. The bailiffs' attempt to seize the Turners' house was a threat to every property on the estate. As in the past, we all agreed, the police were doing the dirty work for a ruthless venture capitalism that perpetuated the class system in order to divide the opposition and preserve its own privileges.

Crossing Cadogan Circle on my way to Vera Blackburn's apartment, I noticed that almost every avenue was now blocked by residents' cars, leaving a narrow space for traffic that could quickly be sealed. Banners hung from dozens of balconies, sheets of best Egyptian cotton from Peter Jones, gladly sacrificed for the revolution.

'visit chelsea marina—your nearest poorhouse.'

'you can't repossess the soul.'

'welcome to london's newest sink estate.'

'freedom has no barcode.'

Vandalized parking meters lined the kerbs. I passed a metal skip into which a family had despatched their tribal totems—

school blazers and jodhpurs, Elizabeth David's cookbooks, guides to the Lot and Auvergne, a set of croquet mallets.

I was impressed by the self-sacrifice of a threatened salariat, but it belonged to the past. I was thinking only of Richard Gould as the lift carried me to Vera's third-floor flat. I called in each afternoon, hoping they had returned, pressing the doorbell long enough for Vera's temper to snap. My chief fear was that Gould, still feverish and exhausted, might confess to the Hammersmith murder in a selfless attempt to save Stephen Dexter.

As I stepped from the lift I saw that Vera's door was open. I crossed the landing and peered into the empty lounge. Someone had disturbed the air, and the sunlight caught a faint drift of motes carried by the dust.

'Richard . . . ? Dr Gould . . . ?'

I walked into the lounge, staring at the discarded suitcases and a pile of medical journals on the sofa. Then I heard a distinctive, blind man's tapping from the bedroom. The sounds were distant but familiar, echoes from a never-forgotten past.

'Sally?'

She stood by the bedroom door, blonde hair over the collar of her tweed coat, gloved hands gripping her walking sticks. She had made an effort to dress down for her visit to Chelsea Marina, as if she were a member of a delegation of civic worthies inspecting a condemned tenement. Her groomed hair, modest but expensive make-up and air of confidence made me realize how far the residents of Chelsea Marina had declined.

A diet of indignation and insecurity had turned us into more of an underclass than we realized. I was fond of Kay, but compared to Sally the former film lecturer was an intellectual fishwife, a Bloomsbury slattern. Without thinking, I turned to the mirror above the leather sofa and saw myself, shifty and shabby, with badly shaven cheeks and self-cut hair.

'David . . . ?' Surprised to find me, Sally moved across the airless room, unsure that I was her husband. 'Are you living here now?'

'It belongs to friends. I'm staying with Kay Churchill—she has one or two lodgers.'

'Kay?' Sally nodded to herself, eyes scanning my sallow cheeks with wifely concern. 'Did you take the lift?'

'Why?'

'You look tired. Absolutely exhausted.' She smiled with unfeigned warmth, the sun in her hair. 'It's good to see you, David.'

Briefly, we embraced. I was glad of the affection I felt for her. I missed her schoolgirl contrariness and her sidelong glances at the world. It seemed as if I was meeting an old and well-liked friend, someone I had first encountered on a safari holiday. We had camped together on the slopes of a rich man's hill, shared an insulated tent and forded the choppy stream of her illness. Our marriage belonged to an adventure playground where real danger and real possibility never existed. The revolution at Chelsea Marina was against more than ground rents and maintenance charges.

Unsure that we were alone, I stepped past Sally to the bedroom door. An empty suitcase lay on the black silk coverlet. In the wardrobe a rack of mannish suits hung skewed from the rail.

'There's no one there,' Sally told me. 'I had a sniff round. People's bedrooms are such a giveaway.'

'What did you find?'

'Nothing much. They're rather odd—Dr Gould and this Vera woman.' She frowned at the black curtains. 'Are they into S&M?'

'I didn't ask.' Trying to take charge, I said: 'How did you know I'd be here?'

'I wrote out a cheque for a mother with a charity box—some architect's wife with a couple of kids to feed. When she saw my name she said you used to run errands for Dr Gould.'

'Right. Did you come alone?'

'Henry drove me. He's parking the car, somewhere off the

King's Road. You people at Chelsea Marina make him nervous.'

'I bet we do. How is he?'

'Same as ever.' She dusted the sofa and sat down, glancing at one of the medical journals. 'That's the trouble with Henry—he's always the same as ever. What about you, David?'

'Busy.' I watched her stow the walking sticks. Their reappearance meant that Henry Kendall's days were numbered. 'There's a lot going on.'

'I know. It's all rather frightening. Direct action isn't really your thing.'

'Is that why you're here—to rescue me?'

'Before it's too late. We're all worried for you, David. You resigned from the Institute.'

'I wasn't spending any time there. It didn't seem fair to Professor Arnold.'

'Daddy says he'll increase your retainer, give you a chance to do research, or write a book.'

'More useless activity. Thank him for me, but it's what I was trying to get away from. I'm too involved here.'

'With this revolution? How serious is it?'

'Very serious. Wait till you need a dentist or a solicitor and they're all out on the picket line. Things are starting to go bang.'

'I know.' Sally shuddered, then opened her compact to check that the emotion had not distorted her make-up. 'We heard the explosion two nights ago. The Peter Pan statue. Anything to do with you?'

'Nothing. Sally, I hate violence.'

'You're drawn to it, though. The Heathrow bomb—it wasn't just Laura. That bomb touched something off. Is Peter Pan such a threat?'

'In a way. J.M. Barrie, A.A. Milne, brain-rotting sentimentality that saps the middle-class will. We're trying to do something about it.'

'By letting off a bomb? That's even more childish. Henry says that a lot of people here are going to prison.'

'Probably true. They're serious, though. They're ready to give up their jobs and lose their houses.'

'A shame.' She reached out to me, mustering a bleak smile. 'You've still got your house. You'll come home, David, when you've worked everything out.'

'I will.'

I sat on the sofa and took her hands, surprised by how nervous she seemed. I was glad to be with her again, but St John's Wood was a long way from Chelsea Marina. I had changed. The guinea pigs had lured the experimenter into the maze.

I said: 'I'm glad you came. Did the architect's wife give you this flat's number?'

'No. Gould told me.'

'What?' I felt a shift in the air, a cold front moving across the airless room. 'When was this?'

'Yesterday. He knocked on the front door. A strange little man. Very pale and intense. I recognized him from the picture on his website.'

'Gould? What did he want?'

'Relax.' She leaned against my shoulder. 'I can see why he has such a hold on you. He's focused on some *idée fixe*, and nothing else matters. He doesn't care about himself, and that really appeals to you. In men, anyway. You rather like selfish women.'

'Did you let him in?'

'Of course. He looked so hungry, I thought he was going to faint. He stood there swaying, eyes miles away, as if I was some kind of vision.'

'You are. And then?'

'I asked him in. I knew he was a friend of yours. He wolfed down some Stilton and a glass of wine. This girlfriend, Vera, does a pretty awful job of looking after him. The poor man was starving.'

'She prefers him like that. It keeps him on his toes. What did he talk about?'

'Nothing. He looked at me in a very odd way. I almost had the feeling that he wanted to rape me. Be careful, David. He could be dangerous.'

'He is.' I stood up and paced the living room. Gould's motives for calling on Sally were hard to read: some kind of threat, or even a suspicion that I was sheltering Stephen Dexter. The activists at Chelsea Marina were deeply possessive, and resentful of outside loyalties.

Glancing through the window, I noticed Henry Kendall walking down Beaufort Avenue from the gatehouse. Like all professional visitors to the estate, he seemed embarrassed by the protest banners and vandalized parking meters. Henry was slumming, ready to bestow his patronizing concern on a fellow professional who had fallen on unhappy times.

'David? Is there a problem?'

'Yes. Your boyfriend. I can't cope with all that kindly forbearance.' I bent down and kissed her unlined forehead. 'I'll come home in a couple of days. Watch out for Richard Gould. Don't open the door to him.'

'Why not?'

'These are passionate days. The police might think you helped to blow up Peter Pan.'

'That was silly. What's the matter with you people?'

'Nothing. But tempers are high. One or two hotheads want to blow up Hodge's statue outside Johnson's house.'

'God . . . I hope you stopped them.'

'It was a close thing. I persuaded them not to. Any nation that puts up a statue to a writer's cat can't be all bad.'

I helped Sally from the sofa, and she followed me to the door, her sticks forgotten. In her mind, the pointlessness of the Chelsea Marina protests eased her resentment, and reconciled her to a capricious world.

'David, tell me . . .' She waited as I drummed the elevator button. 'Is Dr Gould in danger?'

'No. Why?'

'He was holding something inside his jacket. He had a peculiar smell and I didn't want to get too close. But I think it was a gun . . .'

27

THE BONFIRE
OF THE VOLVOS

AT DAWN WE WERE woken by a terror-storm of noise. I was lying in bed with Kay, my hand on her breast, smelling the sweet, sleepy scent of an unwashed woman, when a police helicopter descended from the sky and hovered fifty feet above the roof. Megaphones blared at each other, a babel of threats and incomprehensible orders. The seesaw wail of sirens shook the windows, drowned by the helicopter's engines as it soared over Grosvenor Place, spotlight flashing at the startled faces between the curtains.

'Right!' Kay sat up, like a corpse on a funeral pyre. 'David, it's started.'

I tried to shake off my dream as Kay leapt from the bed, heavy foot stepping on my knee. 'Kay? Wait . . .'

'At last!' Fiercely calm, she stripped off her nightdress and stood by the window. She flung back the curtains, hungrily scratching her breasts as she bared them to the hostile sky. 'Come on, Markham. You can't sit this one out.'

Kay swerved into the bathroom and squatted across the lavatory, impatient to empty her bladder. She stepped into the shower stall and spun the taps, staring down at the dispirited drizzle that splashed her toes.

'The bastards! They've cut off the water.' She flicked the light switch. 'Can you believe it?'

'What now?'

'There's no electricity. David! Say something . . .'

I hobbled into the bathroom and held her shoulders, trying to calm her. After twiddling the taps and light switch, I sat on the bath. 'Kay, it looks like they mean business.'

'No water . . .' Kay stared at herself in the mirror. 'How do they think we'll . . .'

'They don't. It's a little crude, but good psychology. No middle-class revolutionary can defend the barricades without a shower and a large cappuccino. You might as well fight them in yesterday's underwear.'

'Get dressed! And try to look involved.'

'I am.' I held her wrists as she pummelled the mirror. 'Kay, don't expect too much. This isn't Northern Ireland. In the end, the police will . . .'

'You're too defeatist.' Kay looked me up and down as she pulled on jeans and a heavy pullover. 'This is our chance. We can move the revolution out of Chelsea Marina and into the streets of London. People will start joining us. Thousands, even millions.'

'Right, millions. But . . .'

The helicopter drifted away, an ugly beast that seemed to devour the sunlight and spit it out as noise. Somewhere a large diesel engine was accelerating above a clatter of steel tracks, followed by the tearing metal of a car being dragged across a road.

We left the house a few minutes later. Grosvenor Place was filled with unshaven men, wan-faced adolescents and uncombed women. Small children still in their pyjamas gazed down from the windows, girls clutching their teddy bears, brothers unsure of their parents and the adult world for the first time. Many of the residents carried token weapons—baseball bats, golf putters and hockey sticks. But others were more practical. A neighbour of Kay's, an elderly solicitor and archery enthusiast, held two

Molotov cocktails, burgundy bottles filled with petrol into which he had stuffed his regimental ties.

Despite the dawn ambush by the forces of law and order, and the cowardly complicity of the local utility companies, everyone around me was alert and determined. Kay and her fellow block-leaders had done their jobs well. At least half of Chelsea Marina's residents had taken to the streets. They waved their weapons at the helicopter, cheering the pilot when he descended to within fifty feet of the ground so that the police cameraman could take the clearest possible pictures of the more prominent rebels.

In Beaufort Avenue, the central concourse of the estate, almost every resident was out on the pavement and ready to defend the first of the barricades, twenty yards from the gatehouse. A large force of police in helmets and riot gear had massed inside the entrance, next to the shuttered office of the estate manager. They were backed by some thirty bailiffs, itching to secure the dozen houses whose seizure they had announced.

Confident of success, the police had alerted three television crews, and the cameras were already transmitting pictures of the action to the breakfast audiences. A Home Office minister was touring the studios, stressing the government's reluctant decision to bring this misguided demonstration to a halt.

A bulldozer was manoeuvring itself against the barricade of cars in Beaufort Avenue. Its scoop thrust clumsily at a Fiat Uno, the smallest vehicle in the barricade, but the residents clung to its doors and window pillars, distracting the hapless driver with their boos and jeers. Many of the women carried children on their shoulders. Frightened by the menacing helicopter and the bedlam of megaphones, the smaller infants were crying openly, their sobs drowned by the din of the bulldozer's engine but not lost to the television viewers watching aghast across a million breakfast tables.

Urged on by a senior social worker, a police inspector remonstrated with the parents and tried to climb the barricade. A flurry of hockey sticks drove him back with bruised knuckles. A young constable, seeing a quick way through the barricade, opened the front passenger door of a Volvo estate and climbed into the car, truncheon at the ready as he tried to open the driver's door. A dozen residents seized the car and rocked it fiercely, backed by a chant of 'Out, out, out . . . !' Within a minute the constable was shaken insensible, flung from the front seat and tipped dazed into the road at his colleagues' feet.

The police watched patiently, waiting beside their armoured vans with chain-link visors over the windscreens, making clear that the Chelsea Marina action differed in no way from the riot-control measures they used in the East End's less savoury estates. They tightened their chin-straps, rapped their clubs against their shields and moved forward when the bulldozer at last seized the Fiat Uno and lifted it into the air. Forming into a double file, they were ready to pour through the breach in the barricade and set upon the protesters.

But the inspector threw up his arms and halted them as the toylike Fiat teetered on the upraised scoop, ready to fall onto the jeering residents. Hatless in his concern, the inspector climbed the ladder to the bulldozer's cab and ordered the driver to shut down his engine.

There was a brief stand-off, while the inspector retrieved his cap and megaphone. Petrol was dripping from the Fiat's fuel tank, drops dancing around his feet. He called on the crowd to think of their children, who were now laughing happily at the car swaying over their heads. Chortling toddlers were lifted into the air to give them a better view and, more to the point, expose them to the breakfast TV audiences watching open-mouthed over their toast racks.

The inspector shook his head in despair, but he had reckoned without the long-engrained ruthlessness of the middle class towards its own children. As I knew full well, any social group that would exile its offspring to the deforming rigours of boarding-school life would think nothing of exposing them to the hazards of an exploding bonfire.

Exhausted by all the emotion surging around me, I edged through the crowd and reached the pavement. I leaned against a damaged parking meter and searched for any signs of Kay Churchill. I soon noticed that a fellow observer was keeping watch on the action.

Standing behind the television vans was the familiar figure of Major Tulloch, barrel chest and burly arms concealed inside another short tweed jacket, ginger moustache bristling at the scent of battle. As always, he seemed to be bored by the civil uprising that unfolded around him, and watched the helicopter hovering a hundred yards away, its downdraught emptying a dozen litter bins and driving their contents across the rooftops like confetti. I assumed that he was the Home Secretary's man on the ground, and was probably in charge of the entire police action.

The crowd seemed to sense that the Chelsea Marina protest was virtually over, quietening as the driver of the bulldozer reversed his vehicle, subtracting a small but significant element from the barricade. The inspector stood solemnly in front of the protesters, smiling at the small children and satisfied that he had acted as humanely as his orders allowed. Faced by the waiting phalanx of riot police and bailiffs, the protesters began to disperse, lowering their baseball bats and croquet mallets, unable at the last moment to resist an appeal to restraint and good sense.

Then a shout went up from a window overlooking the street. People stepped aside, cheering as a car approached, horn sounding an urgent call to arms. Kay Churchill's little Polo sped towards us, Kay herself at the wheel, headlamps full on and fiercely punching the horn as she forced her way through the crowd. Her grey hair flew like a battle banner, the spectral mane of a Norn rousing her defeated troops.

She reached the barricade, braked sharply and drove into the gap left by the Fiat Uno, forcing back a constable who fell across the bonnet. Shouting defiance at the police, two-finger salutes in either hand, Kay leapt from the car. Within seconds the Polo was overturned and set ablaze, the elderly solicitor igniting his regimental ties with a Garrick Club lighter and dashing his Molotov cocktails against the exposed engine.

Already a second car was burning. Flames played around its wheels and then leapt high into the air. Fanned by the nearby helicopter, the orange billows swayed across the advancing police and touched the raised scoop of the bulldozer, where the pooling petrol from the Fiat's tank exploded in a violent blaze.

Everyone stepped back, looking at the burning car held up to the sky in the bulldozer's claw. The police snatch squads retreated to the shelter of their vans, while the inspector spoke on his radio to his superiors and Major Tulloch put out his cigarette. Sirens sounded from the King's Road, and a fire engine eased itself through the watching crowds who blocked both lanes of the thoroughfare. The flames from the burning barricade glowed in the headlamps and polished brass.

Emboldened now, and determined to defend Chelsea Marina to the last Volvo and BMW, Kay ordered the residents to make a tactical retreat. Brushing away the oily smuts on her cheeks and forehead, one arm bandaged after petrol flashed back from an overturned car, Kay led the protesters to a second barricade fifty yards down Beaufort Avenue. When she stopped to wave the stragglers on, she noticed me in the tail of the retreat. I raised my fists, urging her forward, as always driven by her confused and restless spell. The street was on fire, but Chelsea Marina had begun to transcend itself, its rent arrears and credit-card debts. Already I could see London burning, a bonfire of bank statements as cleansing as the Great Fire.

An acid cloud of steam and smoke rose from the first barricade as the firemen played their hoses on the burning cars. The vehicles glowered to themselves, doors bursting open as they unfurled like gaudy flowers. Whorls of flame swirled into the downdraught of the helicopter and raced around the eaves of the nearby houses.

Visored police leapt the garden walls beside the barricade and raced down Beaufort Avenue towards us. They were met by a hail of roof-tiles, but pressed on to the second barricade, sheltering behind the burning skips that Kay had ordered to be set alight. The bulldozer clanked forward, shook the blackened shell of the Fiat from its scoop, and rammed Kay's smouldering Polo onto the pavement. It moved down the street, followed by the fire engine and the television vans, all under the watchful gaze of Major Tulloch, strolling along behind a group of uneasy press photographers.

The second barricade was hosed and breached. The police advanced through the cloud of steam and a black, almost liquid smoke that lay over Chelsea Marina, drifting across the Thames to the Battersea shore. Crouching behind the modest barricade of three family estates blocking the entrance to Grosvenor Place, a cricket bat in my hand, I knew that the Chelsea Marina uprising was almost over. The police had reached the top of Beaufort Avenue and would soon control Cadogan Circle. After picking off the side streets one by one, they would arrest the ringleaders and wait for the remaining residents to come to their senses. An occupying army of social workers, do-gooders and carpetbagging estate agents on the prowl for a quick bargain would soon move in. The kingdom of the double yellow line would be restored, and the realm of sanity and exorbitant school fees would return.

Nonetheless, something had changed. I pressed a handkerchief to my mouth, trying to protect my lungs from the dripping smoke, and watched one of Kay's neighbours, a BBC radio actress, filling a Perrier bottle with lighter fuel. I was dazed and exhausted, but still excited by the camaraderie, by the sense of a shared enemy. For the first time I fully believed that Kay was right, that we were on the edge of a social revolution with the power to seize the nation. Peering through the steam and smoke, I listened to the bulldozer and waited for the police to make their pointless seizure of a side street in Chelsea.

Then, as abruptly as they had arrived, the police began to withdraw. I leaned wearily against an overturned Toyota, cheering with Kay and her team as a sergeant listened to his radio and ordered his men to fall back. The bulldozer abandoned its victory lap around Cadogan Circle and returned to the gatehouse. Dozens of police raised their visors and lowered their batons, striding through the smoke to the marshalling point in the King's Road. They boarded their vans and set off through the morning traffic. The helicopter withdrew, and the air began to clear as the smoke dispersed. Within fifteen minutes, the entire force of police had left Chelsea Marina.

A second fire engine arrived on the scene, followed by breakdown trucks from the local council, whose workmen began clearing away the burnt-out barricades in Beaufort Avenue. Two repossessed houses had been set on fire, and I assumed that this had forced the police to call off their action. As the bailiffs had battered their way through the front doors, their owners had poured petrol over their living room rugs, tossed burning tapers through the garden windows and waved goodbye to their pleasant homes of many years.

Faced with the prospect of a general conflagration, and the spectacle on the evening news of Chelsea Marina transformed into a vast funeral pyre, the Home Office had reined in the police and called a truce. That afternoon, a residents' delegation led by Kay Churchill sat down with the police and local council in the estate manager's office. As they spoke, emergency crews put out the fires in the two Beaufort Avenue houses nearby. The police inspector agreed that no arson charges would be brought, and promised to urge the bailiffs to delay any further repossessions. Water and power were to be reconnected, and a team of Home Office conciliators promised to look into the residents' grievances.

At six o'clock that evening, when Kay returned to Grosvenor Place, she waved her bloodied bandage at us, her face flushed with victory. As she explained in the dozen TV interviews that followed, the only demand to be rejected was her insistence that all the streets in Chelsea Marina be rechristened. She had wanted to drop the bogus Mayfair and Knightsbridge names and replace them with those of Japanese film directors, but had been warned by far-seeing fellow residents that this might damage property values. So Beaufort, Cadogan, Grosvenor and Nelson remained.

What else had changed was hard to elicit. Already the first families were leaving Chelsea Marina. Unconvinced by the bailiffs' change of heart, and unsure that the truce would hold, several residents with small children packed up, locked their front doors behind them and drove off to stay with friends. They promised to return if they were needed, but their departure was a small admission of defeat.

Kay stood on her doorstep, fist raised, undismayed by their defection. The rest of us watched them go, children crammed among the suitcases in the rear seats. Responsibly, we dismantled the modest barricade in Grosvenor Place, pushed the overturned cars into the parking bays, brushed up the broken glass and did what we could to tidy the street. The single intact meter soon received its first coin.

WHEN I ENTERED the house, broom under my arm, I could hear the sound of taps running in the bathroom and kitchen. Kay lay in her armchair, grimy bandage unravelled from her arm, sleeping deeply in front of the television news that showed her breathless with victory beside the shell of the Beaufort Avenue barricade. I kissed her fondly, turned down the sound and went upstairs to switch off the taps. In the medicine cabinet, filled with enough tranquillizers to sedate Manhattan, I found a fresh roll of bandage and antiseptic cream.

Watching from the window as another resident's car took off, it occurred to me that Kay should join them, leave Chelsea Marina and stay with friends elsewhere in London, at least until the police interest died down. Plainclothes officers were almost certainly keeping an eye on the entrance to the estate, and sooner or later the Home Office would demand a scapegoat. There was only one exit from Chelsea Marina for motor vehicles, but several pedestrian alleyways led out of the estate into nearby side streets. In one of these I had parked the Range Rover, and could easily smuggle Kay and a suitcase to safety.

I returned to the living room with a bowl of warm water, ready to bathe and dress her burn. But when I tried to unwind the bandage she briefly woke and pushed me away, clinging to the blood-stained lint like a comfort blanket.

I was proud of her, and she had earned the right to her trophy. As I took a shower, I was only sorry that Joan Chang and Stephen Dexter had not been present at her triumph. Above all, I missed Richard Gould, who had inspired the Chelsea Marina rebellion and who had now lost interest in it.

28

VITAL CLUES

WISPS OF SMOKE and steam still rose from the fire-damaged houses in Beaufort Avenue, but the rescue services had done their job. Curious to visit the battlefield before it passed into folklore, I walked towards the gatehouse. Water dripped from the charred eaves, and the crazed window-glass reflected a fractured sky. In a reversion to type, their instinct for order and good housekeeping, the residents had swept the street and straightened the protest banners thrown askew by the helicopter. Many of the cars in the parking bays were overturned, but Beaufort Avenue almost resembled its usual self, a street of middle-class housing with a mild hangover.

A group of police officers patrolled the entrance to the estate, answering the queries of any passing pedestrians like tour guides at a newly opened theme park. They had made the manager's looted office into their station house, and a council employee handed out cups of tea through a broken window. Without a trace of rancour, the constables amiably saluted the residents on their way to shoplift in the King's Road. A TV crew sat by their van, eating bacon sandwiches and listening to a pop radio station, but their cameras and sound equipment were still unpacked. By this reliable measure, the revolution at Chelsea Marina was over.

Walking back to Cadogan Circle, I found it hard to believe that only a week earlier Chelsea Marina had been the site of the most violent civil clash since the Northern Ireland troubles. Already the uprising led by Kay Churchill seemed closer to a student rag. The infantilizing consumer society filled any gaps in the status quo as quickly as Kay had driven her Polo into the collapsing barricade.

At the junction with Grosvenor Place, two ten-year-old boys played with their airguns, dressed in camouflage fatigues and military webbing, part of the new guerrilla chic inspired by Chelsea Marina that had already featured in an *Evening Standard* fashion spread. A Haydn symphony floated gently through a kitchen window, below a protest banner whose damp slogan had dissolved into a Tachiste painting.

We had won, but what exactly? Gazing at the quiet streets, I was conscious of an emotional vacuum. Our victory had been a little too easy, and like Kay I had been looking forward to my day in court. I had overturned cars and helped to fill Perrier bottles with lighter fuel, but a tolerant and liberal society had smiled at me and walked away, leaving me with the two boys in their camouflage jackets, pointing their toy guns at me with menacing frowns.

I understood now why Richard Gould had despaired of Chelsea Marina and the revolution he had launched. Without his radicalizing presence the estate would revert to type. Each morning I rang Vera Blackburn's doorbell, hoping that Gould had returned, and had recovered from the horrific experience of seeing a young woman shot to death by a deranged clergyman in a quiet west London street. A fault line had opened, and swallowed sanity and pity, though Stephen Dexter's motives were as mysterious as those of the pudgy weapons fanatic due to be tried for the murder.

I rang Vera's doorbell, listened for any sounds from the empty flat, and then rode the lift down to the ground floor. Kay was out for the day, helping to make a television documentary about middle-class radicalism in the London suburbs. Confident that a new world was on the march, she hoped that the programme would trigger uprisings in Barnet and Purley, Twickenham and Wimbledon, the bastions of moderation and good sense.

I had heard no more from Sally, and assumed that she was waiting for me to return to St John's Wood. I wanted to see her, but I knew that once I crossed the doorstep I would be committing myself to the past and its endless needs, to my father-in-law, the Institute and Professor Arnold.

I strolled down Nelson Lane towards the marina and the clearer air that lifted off the river, free of the soot and smuts and kerosene tang of helicopter exhaust. A solitary yachtswoman was coiling ropes on the deck of her sloop, watched by her two-year-old son. I had seen them at the barricade in Beaufort Avenue, the boy on his mother's shoulders as she abused the police. I assumed that she was about to raise anchor and set sail for the Thames estuary, away from Chelsea Marina and its harbour of lost hopes. I waved to her, thinking that I might ship aboard as deck hand and marine psychologist, dream-rider and tide-reader . . .

Behind me a front door opened in Nelson Lane, close to the Reverend Dexter's chapel. A woman hesitated on the threshold, fumbled with the keys and set off quickly down the steps, leaving the door ajar behind her. She wore a patent leather coat and high heels that flicked in a familiar mincing step. She hurried along the pavement, pausing to hide from me behind the school minibus, a Land Cruiser donated by the soft-porn publisher who was Chelsea Marina's richest resident.

'Vera! Hold on!'

I followed her among the parked cars, and saw her turn into a pedestrian alleyway that led from the estate into the nearby side street. Head down, she scuttled towards the security gate, slipped through and closed it behind her.

When I reached the gate she had disappeared among the

tourists strolling past the antique shops and small boutiques. I caught my breath, leaning against the wrought-iron bars. Head-high, the gate was topped by a fan of metal spikes, and could be opened by a resident's swipe card.

Someone had tampered with the mechanism, using a power tool to cut cleanly through the brass pinion. The exposed metal was already dull, suggesting that the lock had been penetrated at least a week earlier.

I pulled back the gate and stepped into the street, watching the passing shoppers. Fifty feet away, three police vans were parked against the kerb. Each carried six constables, sitting upright beside the windows while the driver listened to his radio.

I closed the gate behind me and walked back to the marina. In the narrow alleyway there was a hint of Vera's perfume, a spoor I no longer wanted to follow. I was thinking about the gate, and the police waiting in their vans. At any time during the riot they had been free to enter Chelsea Marina in force and attack the residents from the rear. The entire confrontation might well have ended within minutes rather than hours, long before any cars were overturned and the tempers of the rioters rose into open violence.

I left the alleyway and returned to Dexter's house, standing on the pavement below the front door. A helicopter circled above Wandsworth Bridge, and two launches of the river police sat in midstream, crews watching the entrance to the marina. A combined air, sea and land assault on Chelsea Marina might easily have been mounted, but the police, or whoever controlled them, had held back, restricting themselves to a show of strength in Beaufort Avenue.

Had the entire confrontation, which so lifted our spirits, been staged to test the resolve of the Chelsea Marina residents? By confining their action to a single street the police had kept the revolution within acceptable limits and tested its temper. I thought of the ever-watchful Major Tulloch with his tweed sports jackets and 'links' to the Home Office, clearly bored by the petrol bombs and hysteria. For Scotland Yard the confrontation across the burning Fiats and Volvos had been a ploy to tease out the residents and their possible access to more dangerous weapons than croquet mallets and moral indignation. I guessed that Henry Kendall had known that a large police action was being mounted, and that he and Sally had visited Chelsea Marina in an attempt to warn me.

I climbed the steps and pushed back the front door, listening to the drone of the helicopter, then closed it behind me and entered the living room. The clergyman's house had been ransacked, drawers pulled from the desk, carpet rolled back, hymn books swept from the mantelpiece. The pup tent in which Dexter had camped, the primus stove and trestle bed had been flung against the fireplace. Food cans, a Harley owner's manual and his Philippine photographs lay scattered across the floor. In the kitchen Dexter's motorcycle leathers were exposed across the wooden table, seams ripped apart by a carving knife taken from a drawer, eviscerated in a fury that seemed to be aimed at their one-time wearer.

Upstairs, in the cell-like rooms, Vera had carried out the same whirlwind hunt, wrenching Dexter's cotton flying suit and academic gown from their hangers and throwing them to the floor beside the bed. Frustrated by the spartan bathroom and its meagre hiding places, Vera had smashed a jar of expensive bath salts into the washbasin, a gift from a parishioner that formed a lurid turquoise pool.

I sat on the bare mattress, the flying overall in my hands. Vera's perfume hung in the air, a sharp mineral tang of an exotic explosive. Beside me, laid out like his dark shadow, was Dexter's cassock, black sleeves at its side. I assumed that Dexter had placed the cassock there after Joan Chang's death, knowing that they would never again sleep together in this modest bed.

Almost in sympathy, I reached out and touched the coarse

fabric, in some way hoping to conjure the unhappy clergyman from its unforgiving weave, and tried to guess what valuable trophy Vera Blackburn had been hunting down in frenzy. My palm moved across the cassock to its breast pocket, and I felt a clutch of small metal objects.

I drew out a yellow silk handkerchief, tightly folded and secured with an elastic band. I opened this miniature parcel and found a set of car ignition keys. They were old and discoloured, engrained with grime, attached to a Jaguar dealer's medallion.

I reached into the pocket again and pulled out a strip of printed card. Holding it to the light, I recognized a ticket issued by a long-term car park at Heathrow. Across it Dexter had scribbled with a green ball point pen: *B 41*, and what I assumed was the number of his parking space: 1487.

Did Dexter own an old Jaguar, for some reason parked at Heathrow? I scanned the punch-holes, trying to see if the ticket had been cancelled. My eyes played over the black magnetic strip, but my mind was fixed on something far more easily read, the time-stamped issue date on the edge of the ticket: 11.20 a.m., May 17.

This was the date of the Terminal 2 bomb. The time was almost exactly two hours before the baggage carousel explosion that had killed Laura.

29

THE LONG-TERM
CAR PARK

MEMORIES OF REVOLUTION fell swiftly behind me, lost among the marker lines receding in the rear-view mirror. I reached the roundabout near Hogarth House and accelerated towards the motorway and Heathrow. For the first time I had tangible evidence linking someone at Chelsea Marina with Laura's death. A priest brain-damaged by repeated beatings had waded like a sleepwalker into the ever-deeper violence that could alone give a desperate meaning to his life.

Ignoring the gantry cameras, I sped along the overpass, a great stone dream at last waking from its sleep. The slipstream roared past my head, blowing away all doubts, though I knew there were other explanations. The parking ticket and the Jaguar in long-term bay 1487 might belong to one of the Terminal 2 victims, perhaps a senior cleric returning from Zurich on the same flight as Laura who had mailed the ticket to Dexter and asked him to pick up the car and collect him from the arrival lounge.

Or was the priest whom Chelsea Marina knew as the Reverend Stephen Dexter in fact an imposter, an illegal immigrant on the run from the customs officers? He had helped a dying clergyman in the baggage-reclaim area, then seized his chance, stealing the dead man's documents and letter of appointment to

Chelsea Marina. At any other parish, the motorcycle, Chinese girlfriend and uncertain faith would have led to his exposure, but at Chelsea Marina they were seen as normal and almost obligatory qualifications.

Whatever their source, the parking ticket and ignition keys had been lying in Dexter's cassock. As I entered the Heathrow perimeter at Hatton Cross I was thinking of Laura, whose fading presence had woken in my mind, and seemed to hover above the signposts pointing to the airport terminals. I waited as a tractor towed a 747 across the perimeter road to the British Airways maintenance hangar. Acres of car parks stretched around me, areas for airline crews, security personnel, business travellers, an almost planetary expanse of waiting vehicles. They sat patiently in the caged pens as their drivers circled the world. Days lost for ever would expire until they dismounted from the courtesy buses and reclaimed their cars.

An airliner came in to land, turbofans sighing as it eased itself onto the runway, a whisper of dreams bruised by time. Laura had emerged from this mirage for a few last minutes, and then slipped away into a mystery greater than flight.

I TOOK MY TICKET from the dispenser, and drove past the administration office towards the B section of the car park. Despite the rapacious charges, almost every space was filled, a vast congregation of cars pointing towards their Mecca, the Heathrow control tower. I turned into B 41 and drove between the lines of vehicles, scanning the numbers on the tarmac. Despite myself, I imagined the assassin still sitting in his Jaguar, waiting for me to arrive.

Bay 1487 was occupied. An imposing Mercedes saloon filled the space, its polished body like black ceremomial armour. I stopped the Range Rover and walked across to it. Through the windows I could see the white leather upholstery, and the control panel with its satellite-navigation screen. A week-old copy of the *Evening Standard* lay on the rear seat. The Mercedes had been parked here for no more than a few days.

I found the Jaguar twenty minutes later, in a small holding area on the north side of section E. Thwarted by the Mercedes, I had returned to the administration offices near the exit gate. A helpful Asian manager explained that any vehicles unclaimed after two months were towed to the holding area and left there until the company's legal department had tracked down the owners. Joyriders, criminals escaping abroad, even overdue air travellers unwilling to pay the surcharges often abandoned their cars, assuming they would remain for ever in this automotive limbo.

I showed the manager the ticket from Stephen Dexter's cassock, and said that I had found it trapped behind a seat in a Terminal 2 boarding lounge.

'There might be a reward,' I ventured. 'It's possible.'

'I'll check it for you.' Smiling at my eagerness, he tapped the ticket and parking bay numbers into his computer. 'Right— Jaguar 4-door saloon, X registration, 1981 model. We're contacting the present owner through the Vehicle Licensing Office.'

'You have his name? He'll be glad to see the ticket.'

'It's unlikely, sir. There's an outstanding charge of £870. Plus VAT.' When I winced, he spoke with pride. 'Parking is a luxury activity, factored into business and holiday price structures. If you wish to save money, there are the public highways.'

'I'll remember that. Any phone number where I can reach the owner?'

'No phone number.' He hesitated, watching my hand slide a twenty-pound note across the desk. 'His address is Chelsea Marina, King's Road, Fulham, London SW6.'

'And the name?'

'Gould. Dr Richard Gould. You're lucky, sir. Very few doctors forget their cars.'

———

I STOOD BESIDE the ancient Jaguar, parked by the perimeter fence in the line of uncollected vehicles. Many sat on flattened tyres, covered with bird droppings and speckled with oil from the aircraft flying into Heathrow.

Next to the Jaguar was a pick-up truck with a frosted windscreen and damaged bumpers, perhaps the casualty of a road accident abandoned while the driver made his getaway. The Jaguar's windows were thick with dirt but intact, and I could read the titles of the medical brochures stacked on the rear seat. Two small teddy bears sat together by the armrest, like children waiting for an overdue parent to return, button eyes hopeful but wary.

I slid one of the keys into the lock, hoping that I had found the wrong car. But the lock turned, and I pulled open the driver's door, freeing it from the seal of grime and dust. I eased myself into the seat and gripped the steering wheel. I could scent Gould's presence in the shabby interior, with its worn leather, broken cigar lighter and overflowing ashtray. The glove drawer was stuffed with pharmaceutical leaflets, sample boxes of a new child sedative and an uneaten sandwich in a plastic wrapper, mummified by the airless heat.

I turned the ignition key, and heard the faint answering click of an engine servo responding to a brief flow of current from an almost dead battery. On the passenger seat was a copy of a large-format paperback, the BBC's edition of its television series *A Neuroscientist Looks at God*. I leafed through the full-colour photographs of Egyptian temples, Hindu deities and CT scans of frontal lobes. Among the contributors' photos was a portrait of myself, taken in the White City studios only eighteen months earlier. Adjusting the rear-view mirror, I compared my drawn features and bruised forehead, my police line-up stare, with the confident and fresh-faced figure looking back at me from the glossy pages. I seemed youthful and knowing, practised patter almost visible on my lips.

I smoothed the yellowing cover, and noticed a telephone number written in green ballpoint below the title. The defensive slope of the numerals, the smudges of ink in the scrawled loops, reminded me of another set of numerals penned by the same hand, the parking-bay number scribbled on the ticket I had shown to the Asian manager.

As I stared at the book, thinking of Stephen Dexter, a shadow fell across the instrument panel. A man was strolling around the Jaguar, his face hidden by the dust and dirt on the windscreen. He tried to raise the bonnet, and then walked to the driver's door and tapped on the window.

'David, open up. Dear chap, you've locked yourself in again . . .'

30

AMATEURS AND REVOLUTIONS

'RICHARD . . . ?' Using my shoulder, I forced back the door and took his hand, glad to see him. 'Locked myself in? God knows why.'

'You'll have to work that one out. It was always you, David . . .'

Gould greeted me confidently and helped me from the Jaguar, waving to the teddy bears in the rear seat. He seemed calm and rested, glancing at the rows of parked cars like a colonel surveying his armoured cavalry. I was relieved that he looked so well. He wore the same frayed black suit, which I had last seen soaked by his sweat in the grounds of the bishop's palace at Fulham. But the suit had been cleaned and pressed, and he had put on a white shirt and tie, as if he had come to the airport in order to apply for a job as a concourse doctor.

We smiled at each other in the sunlight, waiting for the noise of a landing airliner to fade among the terminal buildings. Once again I was struck by how this restless and unsettled man could stabilize everything around him. Even as he sniffed at the kerosene-stained air I felt that he made sense of the world by sheer will, like a physician leading a one-man charity in a blighted corner of Africa, his presence alone giving hope to the natives.

He watched the airliner land, and his tolerant gaze seemed to bless an infinity of arrivals lounges.

'Richard, we need to talk. I'm glad you feel better.' I stood with my back to the sun, and tried to see past his raised hand. 'At Fulham Palace you were pretty shaky.'

'I was tired out.' Gould grimaced at the memory. 'All those trees, they're like surveillance cameras. It was a difficult day. That strange shooting.'

'The Hammersmith murder? We were nearby.'

'Right. They say she was a beautiful woman. It was good of you to help me.' Gould leaned against the Jaguar and looked me up and down. 'You're drained, David. Chelsea Marina is hard on people. I hear there was a trial of strength last week.'

'The police put on a show. I think we fell into a trap.'

'That's no bad thing. It sharpens the focus. At least everyone rallied round.'

'Absolutely. We manned the barricades together. The revolution finally started. We took on the forces of the state and fought them to a standstill. The police backed off, though why, no one knows.'

'They were testing you. It used to be the proles who were pushed around, and now they're trying the same bully-boy tactics on the middle class. Still, you won the day.' Gould beamed at me like a proud parent listening to an account of a school sports match. 'How was Boadicea?'

'Kay? She drove her chariot into the fiery furnace. You would have been proud of her. It was really your show. You dreamed of it, Richard.'

'I know . . .' Gould gestured at the air, as if conducting the sunlight. 'I have to concentrate on so many other things—the overall strategy, then Stephen Dexter. He could be dangerous.'

'He was here.' I raised my voice above the mushy drone of a Cathay Pacific jumbo sweeping in to land. 'Stephen was in your car.'

'When?' Gould glanced over my shoulder, his attention sharpening. 'Today? David—wake up.'

'Not today. I found your ignition keys in his house this morning. There was a parking ticket date-stamped May 17. He must have taken your car and driven here a couple of hours before the Terminal 2 bomb. I think he—'

'That's right.' Gould spoke matter-of-factly. 'He drove the Jag to Heathrow. We need to warn him, before he goes to the police.'

'Warn him? He left the bomb on the baggage carousel. He killed my wife. Why?'

'It's hard to imagine.' Gould studied me, eyes moving around the abrasions on my face. He was less sure of me, as if the battle at Chelsea Marina had separated us. 'How did Stephen get through security?'

'He wore the cassock. The police would let a priest through if he said a passenger was dying. I saw the cassock at his house this morning, laid out on the bed like something from a black mass.'

'Weird. I thought he'd lost his faith.'

'He's found another—sudden death. Vera was there, ransacking the place. She and Stephen may be in this together.' I tried to rouse Gould. 'Richard, you could be in danger. Stephen killed my wife, and then the television woman. You saw it happen . . .'

'Yes. I saw her die.' Gould's voice had faded. Like a child trying to distract itself, he drew a stick-man in the windscreen dust. 'Still, we can't go to the police.'

'Why not?'

'We're too close to everything.' He pointed to my Range Rover, parked outside the entrance to the pound. 'A security camera in Putney High Street caught us going by. It's lucky they couldn't read the licence number. We're accomplices, David.'

I tried to remonstrate with him, surprised for once by his passivity. A car was approaching along the perimeter road, a grey Citroën estate, moving slowly as if on patrol. It paused by the pound, a woman driver at the wheel. As she stared at us I recognized the vivid eye make-up and bony forehead, the faintly smirking mouth with its violet lipstick.

'Vera Blackburn?'

'Right.' Gould waved to her and she moved on, resuming her patrol. 'Lady Macbeth off to Wal-Mart.'

'Richard, for God's sake . . .' Impatient with his offhand humour, I asked: 'How did you get here?'

'Today? Vera drove me. She enjoys the Heathrow run.'

'You were sure I'd find the Jaguar? I take it our meeting isn't a coincidence?'

'Hardly.' Gould held my arm to calm me. 'I'm sorry, David. I hate tricking you. You've always been so straight—with everyone except yourself. I thought it was time to bring things to a head. All this police activity, the security people closing in. There's a lot to talk over.'

'I can guess.' I caught a last glimpse of the Citroën. 'So Vera was waiting for me at Stephen's house? She knows I walk down to the marina every day.'

'Something like that. You're surprisingly punctual. It's all that bourgeois conditioning, years of seeing that the trains run on time.'

'She pretended to ransack the house, and planted the keys and ticket in the cassock. You assumed I'd find them.'

'We hoped you would. Vera gave you a little help. The cassock was her idea.'

'A nice touch. Women are shrewd at these things.'

'Did you try it on?'

'The cassock? I was tempted. Let's say I'm in the wrong priesthood.' I watched Gould smile to himself, like a schoolboy relieved that the truth had come out. 'Is Stephen Dexter still alive?'

'David . . . ?' Gould turned to me in surprise. 'He's gone to ground somewhere. He won't kill himself. Believe me, he feels much too guilty. What happened in Terminal 2 nearly restored his faith.'

'What did happen? You know, Richard.'

'Yes, I do.' Gould hung his head, staring at his scuffed shoes. 'I wanted to tell you, because you understand, you can see what we're doing . . .'

'I don't understand the Heathrow deaths. Killing people? For heaven's sake . . .'

'That's a problem. It's a deep river to cross. But there's a bridge, David. We're trapped by categories, by walls that stop us from seeing around corners.' Gould pointed to the wrecked pick-up truck. 'We accept deaths when we feel they're justified—wars, climbing Everest, putting up a skyscraper, building a bridge.'

'True . . .' I pointed towards Terminal 2. 'But I can't see a bridge there.'

'There are bridges in the mind.' Gould raised a white hand, gesturing me towards the runway. 'They carry us to a more real world, a richer sense of who we are. Once those bridges are there, it's our duty to cross them.'

'By blowing apart a young Chinese woman? Was Dexter involved in the Heathrow bomb?'

Gould seemed to slump inside his shabby suit. 'Yes, David. He was involved.'

'He planted the bomb?'

'No. Definitely not.'

'Then who did?'

'David . . .' Gould bared his uneven teeth. 'I'm not being evasive. You have to see the Heathrow attack as part of a larger picture.'

'Richard! My wife died in Terminal 2.'

'I know. That was a tragedy. First, though . . .' He turned his back, staring at the rusting cars, then swung to face me. 'What do you think has been going on at Chelsea Marina?'

'A middle-class revolution. The one you worked for. No?'

'Not really. The middle-class protest is just a symptom. It's part of a much larger movement, a current running through all our lives, though most people don't realize it. There's a deep need for meaningless action, the more violent the better. People know their lives are pointless, and they realize there's nothing they can do about it. Or almost nothing.'

'Not true.' Impatient with this familiar argument, I said: 'Your life isn't pointless. Once you're cleared by the GMC you'll be walking the children's wards again, designing an even better shunt . . .'

'Feel-good caring. I get more out of it than they do.'

'Gliding? You booked a course of lessons.'

'I cancelled them. Too close to occupational therapy.' Gould shielded his eyes, watching an airliner lift itself from the runway. It braced its wings against the sky, a titanic effort of steel and will. As it rose over Bedfont and turned towards the west Gould waved admiringly. 'Heroic, but . . .'

'Not pointless enough?'

'Exactly. Think of all those passengers, every one of them buzzing like a hive with plans and projects. Holidays, business conferences, weddings—so much purpose and energy, so many small ambitions that no one will ever remember.'

'It would be better if the plane crashed?'

'Yes! That would mean something. An empty space we could stare into with real awe. Senseless, inexplicable, as mysterious as the Grand Canyon. We can't see the road for all the signposts. Let's clear them away, so we can gaze at the mystery of an empty road. We need more demolition jobs . . .'

'Even if people are killed?'

'Yes, sadly.'

'Like Heathrow? And the Hammersmith murder? As a matter of interest, did Dexter shoot her?'

'No. He was nowhere near.'

'And Terminal 2?' I took the parking ticket from my wallet

and held it in front of Gould's face. 'He arrived in your car two hours before the bomb exploded. What was he doing when it went off?'

'He was sitting in the Jag.' Gould peered at me, curious why I was so slow to grasp the truth. 'He might even have been thinking about you.'

'Richard!' Angrily, I punched his shoulder. 'I need to know!'

'Calm down ...' Gould rubbed his arm, then reached into the Jaguar and retrieved the copy of *A Neuroscientist Looks at God*. He thumbed through the pages and found my photograph, smiling at my confident expression. 'Stephen drove me to Heathrow that morning. I had some ... business to deal with.'

'Medical?'

'In a sense. His job was to wait here.'

'Job? What exactly? Taking communion in a car park?'

'He had a phone call to make.' Gould pointed to the scrawled digits in green ballpoint. 'Call the number, David. You've got your mobile. It should explain a lot.'

I took out the mobile and waited until the airport was silent. Gould leaned against the car, picking at his nails, a mentor already bored with a once promising pupil. I stared at the numerals on the BBC paperback and dialled.

A voice spoke promptly. 'Heathrow Security ... Terminal 2. Hello, caller?'

'Hello? Sorry?'

'Terminal 2 Security. Can I help you, caller?'

I rang off and gripped the phone like a grenade. The air around me was clearer. The lines of parked cars, the chain-link fencing and the tail fins of taxiing aircraft had drawn closer, part of a conspiracy to attack the sky. Heathrow was a huge illusion, the centre of a world of signs that pointed to nothing.

'David?' Gould looked up from his nails. 'Any answer?'

'Terminal 2 Security.' I thought back to the Bishop of Chichester's mobile that I had found in Joan Chang's car outside Tate Modern. 'Why would Stephen ring them?'

'Go on. Think about it.'

'His job was to make the warning call. While someone else planted the bomb. There had to be enough time for the security people to clear everyone out of Terminal 2.'

'But there was no warning call. The police were certain about that.' Gould nodded encouragingly. 'Stephen never rang security. Why not?'

'Because the bomber was supposed to call Stephen once he'd set the device. But the bomber didn't call.'

'Exactly. So . . . ?'

'Stephen assumed there was some kind of delay.' I noticed the paperback in my hand and tossed it into the car. 'He sat here, reading about God and the neurosciences. Then he heard the explosion. He guessed the device had gone off before the bomber could reach him. He switched on the car radio and learned about the casualties. He must have been appalled.'

'He was.' Gould pushed himself away from the car and made a half-circle around me. 'He was deeply shocked. In fact, he never got over it.'

'So that's when he lost his faith. He left the car here and some-how went back to Chelsea Marina. Poor man—but how did he justify being involved in a bomb attack?'

'It was part of Kay Churchill's anti-tourism campaign. It was supposed to close Heathrow for days and make people think about the Third World. They'd cancel their holidays and send the money to Oxfam and Médecins Sans Frontières.' Gould raised his pale hands to the sun. 'A tragic mistake. There was meant to be a warning. We didn't intend to kill anyone.'

'Who was the bomber? Vera Blackburn?'

'Far too nervy.'

'Kay? I can't see her doing it.'

'Never. Stephen and I drove here alone.'

'You and Stephen arrived together? So you were the bomber?' I turned to stare at Gould, as if seeing him for the first time, this shabby little doctor with his strange obsessions. 'You killed those people . . . and my wife.'

'It was an accident.' Gould's eyeballs tilted upwards under their lids, as they had done in the park at Fulham Palace. 'No one was meant to die. You were at the NFT, David, you've left fire bombs in video stores. I didn't know your wife was on the plane.'

'You planted the bomb . . .' I turned away, my fingers touching the dust on the Jaguar's windscreen, as if this film of dirt and aviation grease could shield me from what I had learned about Laura's death. With an effort, I controlled my anger. I needed Gould to speak freely, even at the cost of telling the truth. I was shocked and depressed by myself. For months I had been the dupe of a small coterie at Chelsea Marina. I knew now why Kay had always been uneasy over my growing involvement with Gould. Surprisingly, I still felt concerned for him.

'David?' Gould looked into my face. 'You're shaking. Sit in the car.'

'No thanks. That Jaguar—I know how Dexter must have felt.' I pushed him away, and then caught his sleeve. 'One question. How did you get in? Security in the baggage area is tight.'

'Not so tight on the arrivals side. An architect at Chelsea Marina works for a firm carrying out airport maintenance. He supplied me with an identity pass. I put on my white coat and doctor's badge. The bomb was in my medical case. A low-yield device, I thought. But Vera gets carried away—it's all that anger.'

'Then you left it on the carousel? Why that one?'

'A baggage handler told me there were illegal stowaways on the Zurich flight. The passengers were held on the plane and wouldn't be through immigration for at least half an hour.' Gould spoke softly, voice barely audible above the traffic on the perimeter road. 'I set the fuse for fifteen minutes and slipped the valise onto the carousel as the Zurich baggage came out of the chute.'

'Next to Laura's suitcase. A complete coincidence.'

'No. It wasn't a coincidence. I'm sorry, David.' Before I could speak, Gould went on: 'There was a baggage tag on the handle. I noticed the surname. I thought it belonged to someone else.'

'Who, exactly?'

'You, David.' Gould managed a flicker of sympathy, trying to mask his smile. 'I'd been reading *A Neuroscientist Looks at God*. A hotel sticker on the suitcase mentioned a psychiatric conference two years ago. I assumed it was you.'

'Me? So I was . . . ?'

'The real target.' Gould touched my shoulder, like a doctor telling me that an earlier, unfavourable diagnosis had proved correct after all. 'I've always felt that the bomb brought us together. In a sense, our friendship was fused in that terrible tragedy.'

'I don't think so. But why me?'

'I'd seen you on television, talking about elective disease: self-inflicted paralysis, imaginary handicaps, states of voluntary madness—I think you put religions into that category. Fear of the void, which only the genuinely insane can contemplate without flinching. I thought I'd jolt you out of your complacency. A useful lesson, not the sort of thing you learn at Swiss conferences.'

'What went wrong?'

'Everything. Now I know why professionals always leave revolution to the amateurs. Customs were checking the suitcases of a pregnant Jamaican woman working as a drug mule. She went into an hysterical fit and started to give birth. They asked me to help, and I ended up in an ambulance on the way to Ashford. I tried to ring Dexter and then Heathrow Security but we were stuck in the tunnel. It turned out the baggage handler had been talking about the wrong plane. The Zurich passengers reached the carousel as the bomb went off. I was shocked, David. I heard your name on the news and assumed you were dead.'

'And then I turned up at Kay's house.'

'Risen from the grave. In a sense I'd already killed you, for the most idealistic reasons. I liked you, David. You were serious but flexible, and searching for some kind of truth. Laura was the door into your real self, and I'd opened it.'

'You stayed out of sight for a long time.'

'I was watching you. The middle-class revolution was up and running, and Kay was our Joan of Arc. She'd switched off the voices in her head, all those idiotic Hollywood films. Fifty years ago she'd have been married to some strapping young curate, arranging whist drives and spicing up his sex life. She couldn't understand why I lost interest in smoke-bombing video stores and travel agencies.'

'But after Heathrow everything changed.' Still controlling myself, I kept my hands at my sides, avoiding eye contact with Gould and encouraging him to talk on. 'You'd glimpsed something important there, even though people had died.'

'Well put, David. Very well put.' Gould patted my shoulder, and then searched his pockets as if looking for some little token to give me. 'Remember, I was working with these desperate children. I was their delegate, and I wanted an answer. If you're faced with a two-year-old dying from brain cancer, what do you say? It's not enough to talk about the grand design of nature. Either the world is at fault, or we're looking for meaning in the wrong places.'

'And you started looking back to Heathrow?'

'Right—the deaths there were pointless and inexplicable, but maybe that *was* the point. A motiveless act stops the universe in its tracks. If I'd set out to kill you, that would have been just another squalid crime. But if I killed you by accident, or for no reason at all, your death would have a unique significance. To keep the world sane we depend on motive, we rely on cause and effect. Kick those props away and we see that the meaningless act is the only one that has any meaning. It took me a while to grasp, but your "death" was the green light I'd been waiting for.'

'Then I rose from the grave, and you needed another victim.'

'Not victim.' Gould raised his hand to correct me. He seemed finally to have relaxed, convinced again that I understood him and was on his side. Standing in his threadbare suit beside his rusting car, he was a kind of mendicant physician, haunting airport car parks with his cure-all nostrum. Putting me straight, he said: '"Victim" implies some sort of malign intention. Whatever else, David, I'm not malign. I needed a partner, a collaborator who could join me in the search for absolute truth.'

'Someone you didn't know, and had never met?'

'Absolutely. If possible, someone famous of whom I'd never even heard. Famous, but utterly unimportant.' Gould stared at the child's stick-man he had drawn on the Jaguar's windscreen. 'Someone like a minor television presenter . . .'

31

THE SENTIMENTAL TERRORIST

WAS GOULD fantasizing to himself? I watched him stroll away from the Jaguar, eyes fixed on the rows of polished executive cars, as if the dusty saloon reminded him of shabbier days before he recognized his real vocation. He had recast himself as a messenger of the truth, dry-cleaned his suit and put on a clean shirt and tie. He stopped when he reached my Range Rover and glanced at his reflection in the black doors, the pale nimbus of a head floating behind the cellulose as it had haunted the trees in Bishop's Park, Munch's *Scream* resited to some long-term car park of the soul.

Gould took a small handkerchief from his pocket and polished a toecap, then walked back to the Jaguar, ready to give me his time. Had he placed the bomb on the carousel in Terminal 2, or was the entire account a fabrication? Desperate for violence, had he seized on a terrorist act committed by some unknown group and claimed it as his own? Had he deluded himself into believing that he was the bomber, and now had moved on to the Hammersmith murder, annexing unexplained crimes in an attempt to make sense of the inexplicable?

Yet the man who approached me was smiling with a kind of shy confidence, a concerned gaze that had nothing of the fanatic about it. He was the caring physician on the ward of the world, encouraging and explaining, always ready to sit beside an anxious patient and set out a complex diagnosis in layman's terms.

'David . . . ?' He patted my arm with his bloodless hand. 'I don't want you to be upset. These things are hard to take in. You expect everything to come to a stop—why aren't the roads silent, why aren't all the planes grounded? Earth-shaking events take place, and people are still making cups of tea . . .'

'That's all right. I'm ready to listen.'

'It's not a confession.' He smoothed his threadbare lapels in the sun. 'You have to understand—walking behind that young woman to her front door, I felt no malice.'

'I know you, Richard. I take that for granted.'

'Good. It was a sudden insight, almost a revelation. I saw her in the King Street shopping mall, and thought . . .'

'Was Stephen Dexter following her?'

'No. He was following me. He knew what was up, we'd talked it through a lot of times. After Heathrow and the Tate, she was the next logical target. He wanted to stop me before I could go through with it. When he heard that I'd seen her coming out of the River Café a couple of days earlier he started to get worried. He trailed me to the King Street mall, and all the clocks started chiming. It was difficult to shake him off. So many cameras watching us.'

'You'd met her before?'

'Never. I knew she was famous, and Vera told me who she was. In every way, she was the perfect target. It let me off the hook— no residual guilts, no toilet-training hangovers . . .'

'You were a pure, disinterested assassin?'

'David?' Gould shook his head, puzzled by me. 'That's putting it a little harshly. I was her facilitator; we were collaborating in a unique project. If we meet in the next world, I'm sure she'll understand. Remember, I never knew her.'

'You knew where she lived.'

'Vera had her address on a petition about Third-World tourism. It was somewhere near the River Café, so I asked you to wait for me in a side street.'

'How did you get to her house? She went straight home.'

'There's a car park behind the mall. I followed her there. Introduced myself and said I was a doctor involved in the campaign. She said she'd give me a lift back to Charing Cross Hospital and pick up Vera's petition on the way.'

'Then you stepped out of the car and followed her up the path? You were armed?'

'Of course. I'd been doing some weapons training, knowing the day was going to come.' Without thinking, Gould unbuttoned the jacket of his suit, revealing the muzzle of a small leather holster under his arm. 'She had her back to me, sliding her key into the lock. It was the right moment.'

'Why on the doorstep?' With an effort I controlled my breath, trying not to distract Gould. 'She lived alone. No one would have found her for days.'

'I didn't want to see inside the house. How she furnished her sitting room, the framed prints, the invitation cards on the mantelpiece. That would be getting to know her. Her death wouldn't be meaningless any more.'

'So you shot her.' I stared at Gould, thinking of Laura among the debris of Terminal 2. 'The street was empty, and you walked away. You caught a bus to Fulham Palace, and waited in the park. You were . . .'

'Unhinged. Temporarily insane. It shattered me.' Gould spoke in an almost offhand way, as if he and I were colleagues who understood each other. 'It was worth it, David.'

'That's hard to accept.'

'You will. I'm grateful to you. I needed to see those trees.'

'And you threw the gun into the river. If the police had quizzed that old couple in the park they might have identified you.'

'Me? And you.' Gould nodded to himself. 'The getaway car—you drove it. We were collaborators.'

'Not true. I'd never go along with murder.'

'Not then. But you're edging towards it. Even now.'

'Never.' Unable to cope with Gould's intense and friendly gaze, I turned towards the Jaguar. The sunlight caught the green numerals on the paperback cover. 'And the Tate bomb? That was you?'

'Another cock-up. No one was supposed to be hurt. Dexter was keen to work with me, and I told him I'd leave the bomb on the Millennium Bridge, along with an easel and artist's bric-a-brac. It was part of our campaign against everything Tate Modern stood for. Anything to make it wobble again.'

'And Stephen's job was to phone in a warning, so they could clear the bridge?'

'Exactly. But a security man wouldn't let me paint there—too bad for any budding Monet or Pissarro. The bomb was inside one of Vera's art books, so I left it in the Tate bookshop. When I went out I saw Joan Chang had appeared on the scene. Another loyal disciple keeping an eye on me.'

'She didn't trust you?'

'Not after Heathrow. She knew what I really wanted. Stephen was very edgy, he'd taken on all the guilt for those deaths.'

'You're surprised?'

'Yes and no.' Gould began to touch up the stick-man he had drawn on the windscreen, as if clarifying the image for the children in the Bedfont hospice. 'Stephen was having it both ways. After the Heathrow attack he told me he could feel God again, like a phantom limb coming back to life. He needed more and more guilt. That's why he came along on the Tate job. Unconsciously, he hoped someone would die.'

'But not Joan Chang. He saw her running around in a panic and guessed she'd found the bomb. At least he called security.'

'A little late in the day. That's the trouble with all religions—

they're too late on the scene.' Gould took the handkerchief from my breast pocket and cleaned his forefinger. 'I'm sorry about Joan. I liked her, and that spoiled the experiment.'

'And Dexter? Sooner or later he'll tell the police.'

'Not yet. He needs more guilt, if his God is going to return and save him. Besides, he understands me. You do, too, David.'

'I don't.' I slammed the driver's door of the Jaguar, trying to rally myself. 'Richard . . . it's insane. All of it—pointless violence, random murders, bomb attacks. They're vicious crimes. Life is worth more.'

'Sadly, life is worth nothing. Or next to nothing.' Undismayed by my anger, Gould took my arm. 'The gods have died, and we distrust our dreams. We emerge from the void, stare back at it for a short while, and then rejoin the void. A young woman lies dead on her doorstep. A pointless crime, but the world pauses. We listen, and the universe has nothing to say. There's only silence, so we have to speak.'

'We?'

'You and I.' Gould was almost whispering, as if talking to one of his dying children. He held my arms, steadying me. 'There's a lot to do, other actions to plan. I know you won't let me down.'

'Let you down? Richard, you killed my wife.'

'You'll understand. I won't ask you to do anything violent; it's not in your nature. Or not yet . . .'

He spoke in a silky, reassuring voice, but his hand was moving to the holster under his arm. He leaned across me, his head only eighteen inches from mine. His pupils floated upwards, retreating under the eyelids, the warning aura I had seen in Bishop's Park. I realized that he was deciding if I was too dangerous to leave behind in this car park. If I were found dead inside the Jaguar, the parking ticket in my hand, the police would quickly assume that I was the perpetrator of the Terminal 2 explosion, the killer of my former wife.

'David, I need to know . . .'

'I'm with you.' I picked my words carefully. 'I can see what you're doing.'

'Good. We have to remain friends.'

'We are friends. All this is something of a shock.'

'Naturally. You can't take it in.' Gould patted my cheek. 'Don't worry, we'll talk over the next action.'

'You've chosen the . . . target?'

'Not yet. It's going to be big, believe me.'

He turned from me and raised both hands into the air. There was an answering pulse of headlamps from a car parked a hundred yards away. The Citroën estate pulled out of its bay and rolled towards us, Vera Blackburn at the wheel. Gould set off for the perimeter road, three strides ahead of me, checking the shine on his shoes. Reaching the kerb, he stopped to fill his lungs.

'We'll be in touch, David. You're still staying with Kay?'

'Absolutely. She's in the thick of the fight. How does Chelsea Marina fit in? Or doesn't it?'

'Not really.' Gould stared at his hands, trying to flex a little colour into his palms. 'It's all rather futile—a PTA meeting that got out of hand. The parents have wrecked the staff common room and locked the head teacher in the lavatory.'

'That's unfair. There's a serious point being made.'

'You're right. The middle classes are very serious people.' Gould waved to Vera as the Citroën approached. 'That's why they've had to invent so many games. Almost every game you can think of was invented by the middle classes.'

He settled himself into the front passenger seat, reaching out to press Vera's hand to the wheel. She gave him a quick smile but ignored me, impatient to leave the car park before the Citroën's number could be logged into the computer.

Gould returned my handkerchief to me. 'By the way, I saw Sally last week.'

'She told me.'

'She's very nice. I'd say she wants you back.'

'She always does. It's one of those middle-class games. Why were you there, Richard?'

'I'm not sure. I was looking for you.'

'You were carrying a gun.'

'I have to. These are dangerous days.'

'You've made them dangerous. Were you planning to shoot her?'

'To be honest . . .'

He was still framing his answer when Vera lifted her foot from the brake and the Citroën surged away.

I WATCHED THE CAR move down the aisle, cut sharply in front of a courtesy bus and set off for the exit. Behind me the Jaguar settled into its cloak of dust. Taking out my mobile, I debated whether to call the police. The briefest pressure on a button would give me Terminal 2 Security, and the police would swiftly hunt down the Citroën.

My thumb hesitated, as I expected. Richard Gould was more deranged than any patient who had passed through the Adler, but as always I felt better for seeing him. Despite his admission that he had tried to kill me, I felt calmer and more confident. The long search for Laura's murderer had come to an end and, by claiming to have killed her, this demented paediatrician had set me free.

32

A DECLINE IN
PROPERTY VALUES

CHELSEA MARINA was burning when I returned to London. From the Hammersmith flyover I could see the clouds of smoke and steam rising from the river, and hear the wailing ambulances that ferried the injured to Charing Cross Hospital. Crowds of onlookers filled the King's Road, penned behind the steel barriers as they watched the flames lift from a dozen houses in the estate. Fire engines and police vans blocked the street, their lights sweeping the lapdancing clubs and bucket-shop agencies.

I parked in the Fulham Road, half a mile from the estate, and followed a crowd of excited schoolchildren heading towards this early Guy Fawkes display. Scraps of charred paper were falling from the air, and I picked an ashy fragment of a credit-card slip from my sleeve. Wine-store receipts, medical bills and share certificates drifted down from the sky, inventories of a middle-class life that had come to an end.

As I feared, the armistice had been brief. Soon after I had left for Heathrow a large force of police entered Chelsea Marina and swiftly seized control of the estate. Teams of uniformed officers raced through the sabotaged pedestrian gates, and an amphibious snatch squad took advantage of the high tide to make a riverborne landing at the marina.

Three hours later the police action was over. In a defiant gesture some dozen houses were set alight by their owners, but the fire engines waiting in the King's Road moved in promptly. The few residents who had burned themselves or been roughly manhandled by the snatch squads were carried to the ambulances before the TV cameras could get too close. A small barricade in Beaufort Avenue was brushed aside in seconds. Chelsea Marina was now an anomalous enclave ruled jointly by the police and the local council.

When I arrived in the King's Road the snatch squads were drinking their tea outside the manager's office, and the TV units had packed away their cameras. Jeers filled the air around me, and I assumed that the police were being abused.

But the boos were aimed at a family BMW leaving the estate. The parents and their three children sat crammed among the suitcases, a cowed labrador at the tailgate window. In the glare of arc lights I recognized a bank manager and his wife from Grosvenor Place. Heads lowered, they turned into the King's Road. The crowd jeered at them, threw coins and rattled the steel barriers. Beside me, a middle-aged usherette from a King's Road cinema shook her head in disgust.

'Where is everyone?' I asked her. 'The estate looks empty.'

'They've gone. The whole lot of them. Hundreds of cars, they just took off and left.'

'Where to?'

'Who cares?' She brushed the charred fragment of a cheque stub from her braided uniform. 'Shoplifting, buying petrol with dodgy credit cards. There's more than a touch of the gypsy in them. Good riddance.'

'You don't know where they've gone?'

'I don't want to know. Look at the state they've left the place in. Done up nicely, those houses could be a treat . . .'

Another family was leaving, wife grimly clutching the steering wheel, husband fumbling with a map, two teenage daugh-

ters sheltering a terrified Persian cat. They looked away as the
jeers followed them, and disappeared into the traffic now moving
down the King's Road.

A fire engine emerged from the entrance, its crew doffing their
helmets to the crowd. Behind it was a police car, a handcuffed
prisoner in the rear seat beside a woman officer with a bandaged
wrist. I recognized Sergeant Angela, whom I had last seen outside
Broadcasting House. She stared severely at the cheering specta-
tors, and something had clearly unsettled her. Then I realized that
the prisoner was Kay Churchill, hair held back by a camouflage
bandeau, cheeks smeared with commando blacking. She raised a
middle finger to the onlookers shaking their fists at her, exhausted
but spirited as ever, still manning the barricades inside her head.

I pushed past the jeering usherette and eased myself between
two sections of steel barrier. I crossed the King's Road, hoping to
reach Kay before the police car moved on, but a constable seized
my arm and walked me briskly to the gatehouse.

Two men in plainclothes stood by the manager's office, con-
ferring among the debris of plastic teacups. One was the sandy-
haired Major Tulloch, bored but all-seeing, his eyes on the huge
cloud of steam that rose from the gutted houses in Beaufort Avenue. Beside him was Henry Kendall, who wore a yellow police
jacket over his lounge suit. The reflected light gave his confident
face a seasick pallor, and he seemed eager to get back to the security of St John's Wood and the Institute.

When he saw me he spoke to Major Tulloch, who signalled to
the constable and then strode away through the crowd of police
and firemen.

'Henry, I'm impressed.' I accepted a plastic cup of air-raid victim's tea passed through the broken window of the manager's
office. 'You've joined Scotland Yard?'

'Professional back-up.' Henry coughed on the smut-filled air.
His tie was neatly knotted, but he looked dishevelled by the day's
violence. 'I'm putting everything into context for them.'

'Good for you. What is the context?'

'This wasn't just a riot. It's important the police grasp that.' He seemed to notice me for the first time. 'David? What are you doing at Chelsea Marina?'

'I live here. Remember?'

'Right.' Still puzzled, he said: 'Everyone's gone. They've arrested your landlady for biting a policewoman. Were you . . . ?'

'Taking part in the siege? I've just come from Heathrow. I missed the whole thing.'

'It was over in half an hour. A few die-hards set fire to their houses. The others packed up and left.'

'Why?'

'Self-embarrassment. I think they were ashamed.' He listened to two constables nearby who were discussing a weekend car auction in Acton. 'You look worn out, David. Have you talked to Sally?'

'Where? Isn't she with you?'

'No. We're seeing less of each other. I've called her a few times, but she must be away with friends. What were you doing at Heathrow?'

'Following up the Terminal 2 bomb. I might be on to something.'

'Let's hope so. The Yard are still interested in Laura. For what it's worth, they don't think she was a target.'

'I'm sure she wasn't.'

'In fact, there may not have been a target at all. There's a new kind of terrorist in the making. The old targets aren't working, so they hit out at random. It's hard to grasp.'

'I think that's the point.' Concerned for him, as he gazed uncomfortably at the steaming houses, I said: 'There are some very odd people around, Henry.'

'Especially here. Chelsea Marina was incubating them by the hour. This maverick doctor, the paediatrician . . . ?'

'Richard Gould? Sally met him once—she thought he was very attractive.'

'Really?' Henry gave a small shudder. 'He was the ringleader here. The smoke bombs and nuisance attacks. They were all his idea. The two of you were seen together.'

'Why didn't the police arrest us?'

'They were going to.' Henry nodded briskly, his eye on me. 'Sally made me step in. I talked to senior people at the Home Office, and convinced them you could be valuable to us. What happened in Chelsea Marina might be the start of something much bigger. It's bad enough when working people torch their council estates, but if the middle classes take to the streets it spells real trouble.'

'You're right, Henry. The effect on property values . . .'

'Unthinkable.' Henry pressed on smoothly. 'I explained your background, and how you were working undercover for me. They agreed to leave you in place, unless things got completely out of hand.'

'I'm grateful. So, all along I've been a police spy? Without realizing it?'

'In effect.' Henry patted my shoulder, as if awarding me a modest field decoration. 'You could have some very useful input, David. First-hand testimony, insight into how resentment fuels itself. We're planning a visit by the Home Secretary in a week or so. I'll see if I can fit you into the official party. Sally thinks it's time we began your rehabilitation . . .'

As we left Chelsea Marina the police were waving on the traffic. Disappointed by the lack of action, the crowd cheered and then booed us when we crossed the road.

ST JOHN'S WOOD was unchanged, an enduring stage set constructed in calmer times. The tourists and Beatles fans haunted the Abbey Road, and drivers hunted for parking spaces. Unable to find a vacant bay, I left the Range Rover on a double yellow line, a breach of etiquette that rendered a young warden momentarily speechless. She approached me, assuming that I was a visitor from another world, unfamiliar with the social niceties that preserved civilized life and kept the pavements clear of wolves and footpads.

When she was five paces from me she stopped and raised her booking pad, as if to defend herself. She had seen something in my manner, a feral edge hinting at an ease with violence. My bruised forehead and the smuts on my cheeks reminded her of other social outcasts, the road-ragers, Porsche-owning currency traders, and drivers with out-of-date tax discs who haunted her dreams,

I waited for her to scurry away, and then walked towards the house. I hoped that Sally would be lolling on the sofa with a favourite Kahlo volume, a signal that she needed attention from me. But a pile of newspapers lay on the doorstep, sodden after the night's rain, and I assumed that she was still away with friends.

I picked up the evening paper, delivered only a few minutes before I arrived, and studied the headlines.

'Luxury Rent Rebels Surrender.'
'Posh People's Scorched Earth Policy.'
'Win a House in Chelsea Marina.'

But we had not surrendered. The exodus had been a tactical retreat, a principled refusal to accept the rule of police and bailiffs. Rather than submit to the patronizing do-goodery of social workers and psychologists like Henry and myself, the residents had decided to leave with their heads high and integrity intact. The revolution would continue on a date to be agreed, seeding itself in a hundred other middle-class estates across the land, in Tudorbethan semis and mock-Georgian villas. Wherever there was a private school or a snow-white lavatory bowl, a Gilbert and

Sullivan performance or a well-loved old Bentley, the spectre of Kay Churchill would lighten the darkness, hope springing from her raised middle finger.

I needed to find where Kay was held, visit her as soon as possible with a change of clothes, a list of lawyers and enough money to buy a steady supply of joints during her weeks on remand. Throwing the evening paper onto the pile of damp broadsheets, I waved to the parking warden and opened the front door.

I stood in the hall, listening to the empty house. A deep entropic quiet enveloped the rooms, the peace of spent affections, of emotions run down like the batteries of talking toys that mimicked the voices around them. I assumed that Sally had given the housekeeper a week's leave. The dust hanging in the sunlight seemed to come alive, and flowed around me like an affectionate wraith.

Upstairs in our bedroom a medley of perfumes greeted me when I opened the wardrobes, memories of restaurants and dinner parties. In the bathroom I caught the scent of Sally's body, the sweet, killing spoor of her scalp and skin on the towels. The same bric-a-brac lay across her dressing table, a miniaturized city of bottles and jars. I missed her, and hoped that one day I could take her with me to live at Chelsea Marina.

I switched on the answerphone and listened to Sally's recorded message. She was away for a fortnight, touring Brittany with friends. Her voice seemed distant and almost halting, as if she were unsure of her own motives for going away.

I was concerned for her, but as I sat on her bed, feeling the faint imprint of her body under my hand, I knew that I was waiting for Richard Gould to call me.

THE NOISE OF THE AIRCRAFT at Heathrow still drummed inside my head, almost drowning Richard's voice as he set out his credo of meaningless violence. Thinking of his pressed suit and polished shoes, his pale but fleshier face with its hints of health like the first shoots of spring, I knew that he was waking from a long dream. He had been moving through an unlit world, refusing to believe in anything but his band of brain-damaged children, Peter Pan to his lost boys. In Bishop's Park he had at last seen the sun in the high trees. I liked Richard, and felt concerned for him, but was still not sure whether to believe him. Had he really detonated the Heathrow bomb, and killed the young woman on her Hammersmith doorstep? Or was he a new kind of fanatic, who needed the fantasy of absolute violence, and only seemed fully alive when he could imagine himself as the perpetrator of appalling crimes?

I sat alone by the dining-room table, drinking my warm whisky and watching the dust reconfigure itself around me. I knew that I should go to the police, but I could sense the force of Gould's logic. This ruthless and desperate man was pointing the way to a frightening truth. A legion of nonentities were multiplying the tables of a new mathematics based on the power of zero, generating a virtual psychopathology from their shadows.

GOULD NEVER TELEPHONED, but the next day Henry Kendall's assistant rang and told me that the Home Secretary would shortly visit Chelsea Marina, leading a delegation of social scientists, civil servants and psychologists. Details of the visit, and the necessary security pass, would be on their way.

I lowered the receiver into its cradle, surprised by how light it seemed. A brighter air filled the stuffy room. I knew that I would soon be returning to my real home.

33

GIVING HIMSELF TO
THE SUN

'DAVID? COME IN. We've all been waiting for you.'

Richard Gould stood near the window of the top-floor flat above Cadogan Circle, head raised to the sky, lifting his hands as if he were giving himself to the sun. Around him on the walls of the living room were the optician's charts, circular maps of the retina that resembled annotated targets. He seemed calm but light-headed, his mind moving among the high trees in Bishop's Park. Aware of my presence, he withdrew from his reverie like an actor stepping from a spotlight, and beckoned me towards him.

'David . . . I'm glad you came. I thought you'd need more time.' He frowned at my smart suit and tie. 'Is anyone with you?'

'I'm alone. I wanted to see the place before it's torn down.' Glad to be with him, I reached out to take his hand, but he stepped away. 'Richard, I need to talk to you.'

'Naturally. We'll talk later . . .' He carried on with his inventory of my appearance, shaking his head at my expensive haircut. 'You've changed, David. A few days of respectability, that's all it takes for part of the soul to die. You're sure no one's with you?'

'Richard, I came here alone.'

'No one called you? Kay Churchill? What about Sally?'

'She's in France with some friends. I haven't heard from her.' Trying to distract him from the sun, I said: 'There's a special visit this morning, very high-level—the Home Secretary, and a party from the Ministry. Various experts who think they know what happened at Chelsea Marina.'

'What did happen?' Gould turned to stare at the silent streets of the estate, at the smoke still drifting from the fire-gutted houses in Beaufort Avenue. 'It looks awfully like an experiment that didn't come off.'

'Maybe not. At least we tried to build something positive, break down the old categories.'

'You sound like an expert.' Relieved, Gould brightened up. He beamed at me, as if I had again become an old friend, and patted me on the back, ready to share a reminiscence. 'I get it now—you're with the Home Office tour. That's why you're wearing your best suit. Camouflage . . . and I thought you'd changed.'

'I have changed.' Deciding to be honest with him, I said: 'You changed me.'

'Good. You wanted to change, David. You were desperate for change.'

'I was.' Hoping to hold his attention, I stood between Gould and the sun. 'I've thought about what you were saying. These dreams you've had—the Heathrow bomb, the Hammersmith shooting. They're deep-set needs. In a way, I feel them too. I can help you, Richard.'

'Really? You can help me?'

'We'll talk through everything. Perhaps go back to Bedfont asylum.'

'Asylum? It hasn't been an asylum for fifty years . . .' Disappointed by my slip of the tongue, Gould dropped his hand from my shoulder. He watched me in a distracted way, like a tired casualty doctor faced with a potentially dangerous patient. He was wearing the same threadbare suit, which he had ironed himself, and I could count the parallel creases in the trousers. For all his

friendly welcome, he was already bored by me, his eyes turning
to the optical diagrams on the living-room walls.

'Richard . . .' I tried to skirt around an apology. 'I meant the
hospital. The children's wing.'

'Bedfont? You think that's where everything started? I wish
it were true . . .' Noticing the bloodied hand I had cut at Kay
Churchill's house, he said: 'You need to clean that up. There are
so many new infections around today, not all of them courtesy of
Air India. I'll see if the bathroom is clear.'

He stepped into the bedroom, and closed the door behind him.
I paced around the living room, which had been briefly searched
by the police. The optician's textbooks and catalogues lay askew
on the shelves, and the sofa's heavy square cushions were tumbled like boulders. I touched the blue canvas bag with its Metropolitan Police emblem, and felt the sections of what seemed to be
a dismantled fishing rod.

I guessed that Gould had been lying low at a sympathizer's
house on the south coast, and imagined him fishing off a shingle
beach, his mind empty enough to contain the sea. He seemed
physically stronger, no longer the pale and evasive man who
had hovered behind me in Kay's house. Dreams of violence had
calmed him.

'David?' Gould slipped through the bedroom door. 'Clean up
that hand and I'll look at it. There are some towels and perox-
ide in the bathroom. All these police around, they might get the
wrong idea.'

I stepped into the darkened bedroom. Heavy velvet curtains
covered the windows, blackout drapes that allowed the optician
to use part of the room as a projection booth. When the light
began to clear I saw that two women were sitting on either side
of the double bed, their backs to each other, like figures in a Hop-
per painting.

I drew the curtain, and the nearer of the women stood up.
When the light struck the bones of her face I recognized Vera

Blackburn. Her eyes and mouth were without make-up, as if she had decided to strip her face down to a minimum of features, erasing all possible emotion. Her hair was in a tight knot behind her head, stretching the skin of her forehead against her skull and exposing the sharp bones around her eyes. For the first time I saw the abused and sullen teenager she had once been, ready to terrorize any bank guard or cashier who tried to stand in her way.

'Vera? I need the bathroom . . .'

She brushed past me without a word, but I caught an odd scent from her body, a tang of tension and fear. She closed the door behind her with a strong wrist, and I could see the doorknob trembling under the nervous force of her hand.

I drew a second curtain, and turned to the woman watching me from the bed, like a prostitute hired for a corporate client.

'SALLY? WHAT ARE you doing here? Dear . . . ?'

'Hello, David. We didn't think you'd come.'

Sally sat beside the pillow, hands folded across her lap, eyes lowered against the light. She had brushed her hair, but there was a hint of sleep about her when I held her shoulders and kissed her cheek. She leaned passively against me, as if she had been roused from her bed and was not fully awake. I felt a rush of concern for her, the same affection that touched me whenever I entered the ward at St Mary's. Despite everything, I was glad to see her again, and sure we would soon be together.

'Sally, are you . . . ?'

'I'm all right. It's you we need to worry about.' She noticed my injured hand and held it up to the light, reading this new blood-line into my future. 'You're hurt, poor chap. I'm sorry, David. Your revolution failed.'

'Chelsea Marina was only the start.' I sat beside her on the bed, but she held herself stiffly, unsure of a man's body too close to her own. 'Sally, I tried to find you. On the answerphone you said you were—'

'Touring with friends? I do that a lot, don't I?' She grimaced at herself. 'Richard invited me to his cottage near the gliding school.'

'Richard Gould? And you went?'

'Why not? He's a friend of yours.'

'Just about. Was everything . . . ?'

'He's sweet, and very, very strange.' She stared at her hands, marked with my blood. 'We went to the gliding school every afternoon. Yesterday he flew solo.'

'I'm impressed.'

'So was Richard. Last night he explained his ideas about God. They're rather frightening.'

'They would be.'

'Death, violence—is that how you see God?'

'I'm not sure. He may be right. Was Vera Blackburn with you?'

'She came at weekends. Do you know her? I like Richard, but she's weird.'

'She made our smoke bombs. That's her world. Tell me, why did the police let you into Chelsea Marina?'

'I drove my car. Richard wore his white coat and said he was my doctor. A beautiful, crippled woman—they can't resist.'

'Sally . . .' I gripped her hands. 'You're beautiful but you're not crippled. I'll get you out of here and take you home.'

'Home? Yes, I think we still have one. I was careless, David. I was careless with everyone, but especially with you. That accident in Lisbon—it seemed to tear up all the rules and I felt I could do anything. Then I met Richard and saw what happens when you really tear up the rules. You have to invent zero. That's what Richard does. He invents zero, so he won't be afraid of the world. He's very afraid.' She managed a bleak smile, and noticed my suit. 'You're all dressed up, David. Like the old days. You must be with the official party.'

'The Home Secretary's? You know about the visit?'

'It's why we're here. Vera Blackburn knows everything. All

those Home Office experts—they ought to meet Richard, he'd shut them up for good.' A drop of blood fell from my hand onto her knee. She licked it, then thought over the flavour. 'Salty, David—you're turning into a fish.'

IN THE BATHROOM I rinsed my palm, watching my blood wash away into the handbasin. Beside me was a glass cabinet filled with ophthalmic supplies, part of the huge stock of pharmaceuticals that might have turned Chelsea Marina into the central drug exchange of west London. The middle-class residents could have defended a narcotic Stalingrad, pooling their expertise and resources, street by street. Instead, they had thrown in the towel and left for their dachas in the Cotswolds and Cairngorms.

But at least I now had Sally. I was impressed by how quickly she had freed herself from Richard's spell, but perhaps she had taken what she needed from him and decided to leave. Gould had persuaded her that the Lisbon accident was senseless and inexplicable—her injuries and suffering were meaningful for just that reason. Free at last from her self-obsessions, she had thought first of her husband, and I was touched that she had come to Chelsea Marina in an attempt to rescue me.

'RIGHT, LET'S GO. We'll say goodbye to Richard. Sally?'

I waited for Sally to stand up, but she leaned against the pillow and stroked the bedspread, studying the moiré patterns.

'I don't think so.' She pointed to the door. A strong hand was turning the knob, testing the mortice bolt. 'We're locked in. We need to be careful, David.'

I glanced at my watch, surprised by how much time had passed. At the entrance to Chelsea Marina the police were moving the barricades. 'Sally, the Minister will be here soon. There'll be an army of police. Richard and Vera Blackburn won't stay.'

'They will stay. Dear, you don't realize what's happening.' She looked at me in the kindly way of a wife waiting for a naive husband to get the point. 'Richard is dangerous.'

'Not any more. That phase is over. All those fantasies . . .'

'It isn't over. And they aren't fantasies. Richard's just starting. You know he left the bomb at Heathrow?'

'He told you that? It must have frightened you.' I tried to take her hand, but she moved it away from me across the bedspread. 'It's a nonsense. Like this television presenter in Hammersmith. He claims he murdered her. For God's sake, I was parked in the next street. I saw him five minutes later. He would have been covered in blood.'

'No.' Sally was watching the door. 'He did shoot her.'

'It never happened. He needs to think about violence, the more pointless the better. I've tried to help him.'

'You have. He's going to kill more people. Yesterday we went to a rifle range near Hungerford. I sat in the car with Vera. She told me he's a very good shot.'

'That must make her proud. Hard to believe, though.' I left Sally and walked to the door, then pressed my head against the wooden panel. The living room seemed empty, the silence broken by the chiming of the mantelpiece clock. 'Sally . . . you mentioned Hungerford?'

'It's off the M4. Richard rented the cottage there. A pretty little place. It's where he wants to end his days.'

I stared at the door as police sirens sounded in the King's Road, a wake-up call to more than the sleeping. I remembered that someone else had ended his days at Hungerford.

'David? What is it?'

Feet moved across the roof, almost directly above my head, the sounds of a sunbather settling himself on a mat. Or a marksman adjusting his sights. Hungerford? A young misfit named Michael Ryan had shot his mother dead, then strolled through the town shooting at passers-by. He had killed sixteen people, picking them off at random, set fire to the family home and shot himself.

The murders were motiveless, and sent a tremor of deep unease across the country, redefining the word 'neighbour'. No one, not even a family member, could be trusted. A new kind of violence had been born, springing from nothing. After the last shots at Hungerford, the void from which Michael Ryan emerged had closed around him, enfolding him for ever.

'SALLY . . .' TWO POLICE motorcyclists were driving down Beaufort Avenue. They stopped by the roundabout, their radios crackling. Uniformed constables walked along the pavement, scanning the empty houses. 'That blue canvas bag—what was in it?'

'Richard kept his gliding kit there.' Sally stood up and walked around the bed, eyes on my footprints in the carpet. 'Do you think—?'

'What about a weapon? A shotgun or . . . ?'

Sally said nothing, listening to the sounds from the roof above our heads. I lifted the shade from the standard lamp behind the door. Gripping the chromium shaft, I snapped the plug from its wall socket.

'No . . .' Sally held my arm before I could drive the shaft into the door. 'David, there's going to be a shooting.'

'You're right. A meaningless target, like a liberal Home Secretary . . .'

'Or you!' Sally tried to wrest the lamp-shaft from my hands. 'Richard knew you were coming.'

'He won't kill me. I like him. What would be the point?'

The question died on my lips. A line of official vehicles was entering Chelsea Marina, black saloons from the government car pool. The motorcade moved down Beaufort Avenue at walking pace, the passengers gazing at the silent windows and torn banners. Within a minute the procession would reach Cadogan Circle, then turn left below the windows from which I was watching.

'Sally . . .' I tried to push her away from the door. 'If they find us here—'

'They'll think we're prisoners. We'll be safe, David.'

'No.' I wrenched at the door handle. 'I owe it to Richard.'

Sally released the lamp-shaft and stepped back, watching me with weary patience as I stabbed at the door panels. She reached into the breast pocket of her shirt. On her open palm lay a door key.

'Sally?' I took the key from her. 'Who locked the door?'

'I did.' She stared into my face, unembarrassed by her ruse. 'I'm trying to protect you. That's why I went to Hungerford with Richard. I'm your wife, David.'

'I remember.' I pushed the key into the lock. 'I have to warn Richard. If the protection unit see him with a rifle they'll shoot him dead. This may be another fantasy, some Hungerford obsession inside his head . . .'

Giving up on me, Sally rubbed her skinned knuckles and turned to the window. 'David, look . . .'

The motorcade had stopped in Beaufort Avenue. The Home Secretary and two senior officials emerged from his limousine. Joined by experts from the other cars, they stood on the pavement and peered at the first of the gutted houses, as if the charred gables would reveal the inner truth of the rebellion. Solemn words were exchanged, and heads nodded sagely. A television crew filmed the occasion, and an interviewer waited, microphone in hand, to question the Minister.

'David? What's happening?' Sally took my arm, her lips fretting. 'What are they doing?'

'Grappling with the inconceivable. They should have come three months ago.'

'Those cars driving in—they look strange . . .'

Headlamps flashed behind the stationary motorcade. The police motorcyclists patrolling Beaufort Avenue stopped in the centre of the road, and blocked the approach of a dusty Volvo

labouring under the luggage tied to its roof rack. The woman
driver pressed on, forced to stop alongside the Minister's limo.
Behind the Volvo three more cars, equally battered, pushed
through the entrance gate, and I noticed a sandy-haired man in
a check sports jacket ordering away the police who tried to halt
them. Major Tulloch, as always, had seized his opportunity.

'David, who are they? The people in the old cars?'

'I think we know . . .'

'Squatters? They look like hippies.'

'They aren't squatters. Or hippies.'

The Home Secretary had also noticed the newcomers. Officials and experts turned their backs on the burnt-out house. An
alert police inspector relayed a message from the Volvo's woman
driver, and the Home Secretary visibly lightened, for a moment
standing on tiptoe. After a glance at the TV camera, he beckoned
the motorcyclists aside. Raising his arms, as if on traffic duty, he
waved the Volvo forward.

'David? Who are these people? Homeless families?'

'In a way. They're residents.'

'Of where?'

'This estate. They live here. The people of Chelsea Marina are
coming home.'

I WATCHED THE VOLVO set off down Beaufort Avenue. The
convoy of returning cars followed, dust-caked and loaded with
dogs and children, broken wing-mirrors taped to windscreen pillars, bodywork dented by miles of highland driving. I guessed
that a group touring Scotland or the West Country had held a
campfire conclave and decided to return home, perhaps suspect-
ing that the Home Secretary's visit was a signal that the demolition bulldozers would arrive soon afterwards.

Smiling cheerfully, the Home Secretary stepped into the rear
seat of his limousine. He waved to the returnees, who hooted their
horns in reply, while a Great Dane barked from an open tailgate.

As the echoes reverberated around Cadogan Circle I almost missed the sound of a rifle shot from the roof above my head. The Home Secretary's car stopped sharply, its windscreen starred by a snowflake of frosted glass. There was a moment's silence, and then police and experts scattered behind the cars, crouching against the walls of the empty houses.

A helicopter appeared in the sky over the Thames, spotlight playing across the roofs of Chelsea Marina. I waited for a second shot, but the returning families had confused the sniper, almost certainly saving the Home Secretary. Shielding him with their bodies, his bodyguards pulled him from the limousine and bundled him across the pavement towards the front door of a nearby house.

'Sally . . .' I held her against me, feeling her heart beating against my breastbone, for once in time with my own. Feet ran across the roof, and a loudspeaker blared from the helicopter, a warning drowned by sirens and motorcycle engines.

'David, wait!' Sally gripped my arm, the wife of a foolish husband coming slowly to his senses. 'Let the police catch him.'

'You're right. I'll be careful. I need to be . . .'

She watched me as I unlocked the bedroom door. The living room was empty. My laptop lay on the sofa, but the blue canvas bag had vanished with Richard Gould. Raising my hands in an attempt to reassure Sally, I left the flat and crossed the hall. I ran down the staircase, past the deserted landings and open doors, and reached the entrance lobby as the helicopter hovered above the Circle.

Through the whirlwind of noise I heard two brief bursts of gunfire from the basement garage.

34

A TASK COMPLETED

SHADOWS RACED across the basement walls, kinetic murals in a deranged art gallery. I pushed back the fire door and stepped onto the cement floor. The helicopter was landing in the service area behind the apartment building, and I could see its tail rotor through the open doors of the access ramp. Only one car was parked in the garage, Sally's adapted Saab, hidden behind a row of wheeled bins near the rubbish chute.

I walked across the floor as the shadows of the helicopter blades fled past, swerved away and then returned to overtake me. Almost deafened by the vibrating concrete, I approached the Saab, which was lit by the helicopter's spotlight shining through the transom windows.

In the white glare I saw that a man was crouched over the Saab's steering wheel, his left arm and shoulder supported by the brake and gear levers. His right arm hung through the window, as if signalling a sudden turn. Behind him a woman lay across the rear seat, bony forehead on the arm rest.

Gould and Vera Blackburn had died together in the car. Vera was sprawled face-down over the tartan rug, her tight skirt exposing her thin, schoolgirl legs. She had been shot in the back, and her blood had pooled inside a fold of her patent leather jacket, dripping onto the floor carpet. In her last moments she had clawed at the rug with both hands, tearing the nails from her fingers.

Richard Gould sat in the front seat, a single bullet wound in his white shirt. The damp puncture mark, almost colourless in the glare of the landing helicopter, seemed like a rosette pinned to the chest of a brave but impoverished civilian wearing his only suit. I touched his outstretched arm and felt his skin, warmer now than it had been in life. I noticed his frayed collar and the crude stitching of his repair work unravelling against his neck.

Clasping his hand for the last time, I steered it into the car. The blood had drained from his face, and he seemed years younger than the troubled physician I had known. But his chipped teeth were like an exposed confidence trick, cheap dentistry bared in the frankest of grimaces. To the end, Richard Gould had concealed his thoughts but displayed his wounds.

He sat among the Saab's invalid controls, small hips twisted as he tried to avoid the bullet fired at him. His left hand fumbled at the brake lever, and his knees were trapped by the metal couplings below the steering wheel. As he died, his body had contorted itself, trying to assume a desperate geometry that would mirror his mind, returning him to the handicapped children and Down's teenagers who were his true companions.

Trying to meet his eyes, I stared into his chalk-white face, now as toneless and untouched by the world as an autistic child's. His eyes were fixed on the trembling needle of the revolution counter, and I realized that the Saab's engine was on, its exhaust drowned by the helicopter. I drew Gould's hand from the ignition and turned the key, as if switching off the respirator in an intensive-care unit.

The heavy clatter of the helicopter's fans filled the garage. Deafened by the din, I looked up to find a tall man in motorcyclist's leathers standing between the Saab and the refuse bins. His face was hidden by the visor of his helmet, a window crossed by the rotating shadows, which moved more slowly now that the helicopter had landed. He wore a clergyman's dog collar, and without thinking I assumed that he had arrived on his Harley in order to pronounce the last rites on the dead couple.

In his hand he carried a heavy crucifix carved from a black and polished stone, and offered it to me as some kind of explanation for the deaths. Then the helicopter's spotlight left the garage to search the first-floor windows, and I saw that the crucifix was an automatic pistol.

'Dexter!' I stepped away from Gould and walked around the car. 'You found the gun? I think they shot themselves. Or . . .'

Dexter's face emerged from the confused light, as blanched as pain, so expressionless that I was sure he had spent the past months draining all emotion from himself, his mind set on the one task that lay in front of him. He stared at me calmly, scarcely aware of Gould and Vera Blackburn, and his gaze turned to the helicopter we could see through the transom windows. Pointing the pistol at me, he watched the light in the same way that Gould had followed the sun through the high branches at Bishop's Park.

'Stephen.' I tried to avoid the pistol. 'Get away from here. The police are armed . . .'

The clergyman stopped, testing the cement floor with his metal-tipped boots as he listened to the helicopter's fading engine and the shouts of security men. He raised his visor and moved around the car, the pistol in his hand. I knew that he had always seen me as Richard Gould's chief collaborator. Aware that he was about to shoot me, I stepped back to the Saab and opened the front passenger door, ready to join Gould at the controls.

But Dexter pressed the pistol into my hand. I caught the harsh scent on his clothes, the same reek of fear I could smell on my own skin after the burning of the NFT. I gripped the pistol, surprised by the warm metal that seemed to beat like a heart. When I looked up, Dexter had withdrawn into the shadows behind the rubbish bins. He stepped through the steel service door that led to the boiler room and the caretaker's flat. He pointed to me, like a target-master encouraging a novice at a rifle range, closed the door behind him and slipped away, vanishing into another time and space. The task he had set himself so many months earlier at Heathrow had at last been fulfilled.

I WAITED BY the car, pistol in hand, watching Gould's face empty itself, shedding all memories of the young doctor who had once gazed so fiercely at an inexplicable world. But I was think-ing of Stephen Dexter in the few moments when he raised his visor. Watching him, I had seen the temper and conviction that he had brought to his first ministry, lost under his captors' whips, and then searched for in this west London estate, encouraged by a disbarred consultant with a punitive vision of his own.

The first police were entering the garage. An inspector sig-nalled to two armed officers who trained their weapons at my chest. He shouted to me, his voice lost in the horns sounded by the residents impatient to return to their homes.

Then a thickset man in a police forage jacket stepped forward and strode over to the Saab, his sandy air ruffled by the helicop-ter's downdraught.

'Mr Markham? I'll take that . . .' Major Tulloch gripped my arm with a tobacco-stained hand and pushed me against the car. 'You're a better shot than I thought . . .'

I gave him the pistol and pointed to Richard Gould, sprawled among the controls like a crashed aviator. 'He was going to kill my wife. And the Home Secretary.'

'We understand.' Major Tulloch looked me up and down, as unimpressed and detached as ever. He leant into the Saab and checked the bodies, feeling for any weapons, and then searched perfunctorily for a pulse.

Police now filled the basement, and a forensic team was already laying out its gear, the cameras, crime-scene tapes and white overalls. Sally waited by the fire door, face tense and her hair in a swirl, but determined to stand on her own legs. Henry Kendall hovered beside her, nodding to a silent police sergeant, almost light-headed among the armed constables. He took Sally's arm, trying to calm himself, but she eased him away and walked towards me. With a brave effort, she managed to smile at me through the noise, and gestured with the damp laptop she had carried from the flat. Watching her proudly, I knew that everything would be well.

Major Tulloch spoke tersely into his radio, the identification over. Handing me into the custody of an inspector, he said: 'Mr Markham, you've been taking too many chances. Just for once, try a quiet life . . .'

Outside, louder than the engine of the helicopter, a noisy carnival filled the air, the braying horns of the middle-class returning to Chelsea Marina.